J.D. Barrett is an Australian television writer and script editor. She has worked on the writing teams for *Love My Way*, *Bed of Roses*, *Wonderland*, *Love Child* and *The Secret Daughter*. J.D. lives between Sydney, Byron Bay and Los Angeles. *The Secret Recipe for Second Chances* was her debut novel, her second book is *The Song of Us* and she is currently working on her third.

J.D. BARRETT

THE SONG OF US

hachette
AUSTRALIA

The quote on p. 42 is from the poem 'Human Family' by Maya Angelou, published in
I Shall Not Be Moved, Random House, 1990.

Published in Australia and New Zealand in 2017
by Hachette Australia
(an imprint of Hachette Australia Pty Limited)
Level 17, 207 Kent Street, Sydney NSW 2000
www.hachette.com.au

National Library of Australia
Cataloguing-in-Publication data:

Barrett, J.D., author.
The song of us/J.D. Barrett.

978 0 7336 3789 6 (paperback)

Australian fiction.
Music thanatology – fiction.

Cover design by Christabella Designs
Author photograph courtesy of Craig Peihopa
Text design by Bookhouse, Sydney
Typeset in 11.5/18.3pt Sabon LT Pro by Bookhouse, Sydney
Printed and bound in Australia by McPherson's Printing Group

The paper this book is printed on is certified against the
Forest Stewardship Council® Standards. McPherson's Printing
Group holds FSC® chain of custody certification SA-COC-005379.
FSC® promotes environmentally responsible, socially beneficial
and economically viable management of the world's forests.

To Grania, Caroline, Rob and Natasha.

For your courage.

ONE

IN THIS MOMENT, SOMEONE IS FALLING IN LOVE, SOMEONE IS receiving their first kiss, someone is having their last fight, someone is cooking spaghetti bolognaise, someone is having the best orgasm of their life, someone is getting married, someone is dying, someone is listening to what will become their favourite song, someone is crying, someone is being born. We are all so embedded in our own tales that, we forget, we are all at different times experiencing the majority of the same things – I call it my version of the hatches, matches and dispatches theory.

We all wake up wondering where the next year will take us. Perhaps that's why calendars and New Year's Day were invented: to help us try to map out the unknowable terrain of our future.

A girlfriend of mine, who is a life coach, is always quoting a Harvard study – I think it's from a few decades ago – that showed that out of a very small, stupidly intelligent and privileged group of Harvard grads, it was an even smaller group who succeeded (by whatever criteria they deemed success to be) and this group were the ones who had set 'goals'. Even more successful were the ones who not only set goals but managed to stick to them.

And then there's the rest of us. Flailing through life. Waking up on New Year's morning to what the previous night had seemed like an exciting resolution, but now in the hot unrelenting Sydney sunniness of 1 January seems more like a hassle – another thing to add to the to-do list of life.

I don't make resolutions. I subscribe more to the adage of 'Man plans and God (or whoever she is) laughs'. What's the difference between a dream and a goal and a plan anyway? Aside from a lot of red tape.

It's the first of January 2017, and unlike the majority of people who share my postcode – 2026: I live in Ben Buckler, that tiny peninsula at the top of North Bondi beach – I have woken up without a hangover. My New Year's Eve was subdued; in the same way the past four New Year's Eves have been for me . . . because I have become the age-old cliché of a woman in love with an unavailable man.

You can begin tutting, headshaking or lecturing any time you like. I doubt it will do any good. Nothing else has.

And, wait, it gets worse. He's living with his long-term partner and mother of his child. I know, I know, *I know*. But wait, there's more. She has a chronic illness with a tricky title. He's the head of emergency with a saviour complex.

And I meant for none of this to happen. So, has it happened and continued because I didn't plan? Because 'I will meet and fall in love and marry a single man' was not on my to-do list? My best friend, Lexie, would say yes. She likes plans, she likes lists, and she loves ticking things off . . . particularly the conversion of sexually ambiguous straight women to flag-flying lesbians. Lexie is a TV producer and is adept at getting what she wants. She believes a great deal of that stems from asking specifically for what you want, such as her recent Facebook post requesting one-legged jockeys for a new upcoming reality series she is working on. Lexie is specific. I am not, which she believes goes a long way to explaining my lack of splendid New Year's Eves for the past while. When did it, and by 'it' I mean Ross and I – I'm hesitant to call us a 'we' – go from one month to five years? When did I go from being twenty-nine to thirty-four? During the 'I fell in love like a schmuck' phase, I guess, and the 'I'm pretending I'm not waiting but I am *still* waiting' phase.

It's not easy when you meet the guy you believe is your One and find there's a major obstacle to being with him. Harvard grads would know to do a quick formula of the probability of it working out, and run . . . as would most people, especially other women who have inhabited the space that I currently fill, and got out of it unscathed or otherwise. What makes someone – me – hang on for so long? Falling in love has a lot to answer for. As does my stubborn heart, that persists, whispering to me to wait, hold on . . . and teasing me with the haunting words: it will work out. Days roll into weeks, weeks blur into months and silently multiply to years. Hope is what I clutch to in the face of reality. But the cold hard facts are that another year has begun and we didn't begin it together. True, he was working. But still

. . . each year he takes *that* shift so he doesn't have to deal with the great divide between the life he has and the life he wants. Or the life he tells me he wants.

And, yet, it hasn't worked out. My promise for this year is to not let another year, month, week or day slip by without knowing if Ross is going to truly be with me, or not.

On the upside, one good reason for my deafeningly quiet New Year is because I have work today. I load the Mini with my harp and head out down Military Road, past all the recovering revellers who are beginning their new year, or washing away the old one, with a refreshing dip in the Bondi waves.

I have already been for my morning swim, early before the crowds. Every morning, I head down to the old boat ramp that's just a minute's walk from home and wave to the early fishermen, and the guy who parks his tent under the rocks most nights and has one of the best views on the planet as a result.

There's a place called Flat Rock that school kids love to jump off. As the name indicates, it's a huge flat rock that's rhythmically coated with incoming waves, beckoning you to dive in and join the depths of the Bondi sea. It's a quick swim from there back to the boat ramp, or if there's time, into North Bondi beach. I cannot imagine living away from the ocean, ever. You're either a sea person or not. I practically have webbed feet.

Work is quiet. Not many people visit palliative care wards on New Year's Day. Somehow it jars against the notion of a new year; the old tide, the soon to be not here. And yet, from my experience, these are the people who know more about living than the towel-flickers down at Bondi beach.

Nothing increases your powers of perception, makes you clearer or more honest than an existential deadline.

I'm what's called a musical thanatologist (try saying that quickly after three espresso martinis). Thanatology is a Greek word meaning 'the study of dying'. So, a musical thanatologist is one who plays music to soothe and smooth the journey to death. In lay terms, I'm a bedside musician. Yes, it's a weird gig. But a good one.

I began my career as a concert harpist; I went through the Sydney Conservatorium for high school and my degree. I played with the Chicago Symphony Orchestra when I was twenty-one, then Melbourne and Sydney. I had just started a gig with the London Symphony six years ago when it happened.

I was midway through Saint-Saëns's *Fantaisie*. I'd broken up with the oboist a few days earlier, but that wasn't it. It was a woman in the audience who was a doppelganger for my mother. Well, she would have been had Mum still been alive. She died when I was five. But this woman looked exactly as I imagined Mum would have. Her hair, the tilt of her head, her semi smile – I didn't feel upset, or I didn't think I did, but I couldn't breathe, I lost where I was, and then the entire auditorium began closing in on me.

I collapsed and was taken to hospital. A huge number of tests were run. The prognosis – a massive anxiety attack. And that was the beginning. Since then, despite several therapists and numerous miracle cures, I cannot bring myself to perform or to play in front of more than a few people. I have recorded, but it's not the same . . . so, when I read an article about musical thanatology, I was drawn to it for selfish purposes. I could play for a small group and I was there as therapy, as a sideline, to help, not to be pulled apart.

My job is to sit beside the patient and play. And yes, I take requests. Everything from Bach to Bon Jovi. And some pieces I make up.

Today, I unload the harp from the Mini – it's on wheels which makes schlepping easier, though I still present an odd sight. I also have long curly blonde hair, which insists on falling into ringlets, and if I'm wearing white it can throw people. When new patients see me coming down the hallway for the first time, they sometimes cry out, 'Oh god, we're not there yet, are we?' Though others, particularly those in immense pain call out, 'Are we there yet?'

'Why would you come in today?' Waverley on reception is not a fan of the harp, or of me. She is twenty-three and her world exists in a galaxy far, far away from the gravitational pull of age, frailty, illness, mortality and classical music.

I shrug. 'I thought June might enjoy a song. It's their new year too.'

'Not for long,' Waverley mumbles and pulls out her iPhone, no doubt to survey the damage from last night's dalliances and provide the world with a much-needed selfie of 'Waverley at work with a hangover'.

I press the lift button and head up to level three.

As I manoeuvre my harp out of the lift, I think of how it is one of the oldest instruments on the planet. Its origins lie in the

Hunter's bow. Like the arrow that the bow shoots forward, the harp can pierce your heart.

At some stage most of us (often as high school students), have probably considered what song we'd want played at our funeral. But few of us think of what songs we'd want to prepare us for the end of life. Not that I just play at the final moment. Palliative care is not always about checking in for your last three days of life. People can go in and out, particularly patients with chronic terminal illnesses, and the hospice I work at also has a rehab wing where just about everyone leaves to go and live their next chapter.

But there have been many times I have played in people's final moments, and consequently I have come to realise that deaths are as varied as births and musical styles. Each one is unique. Some have been silent, some a joyous relief, some have been fraught and I still hear the echoes of their battle with their final breath. Some are unbearably sad, while others are nothing short of transcendent.

June lies with her eyes closed.

'You shouldn't be here today. Go out and have a cocktail.' She always knows it's me.

'I will later, June. "Clair de Lune"?' I say as I sit, uncover my harp and pluck a few notes.

'With your beau? Where will you go? Tell me details.'

June is ninety-five, a survivor of World War II, during which she worked as a nurse. Before that she'd been a ballerina and had performed at the Royal Opera House in London. She has a grace akin to Audrey Hepburn. Her delicate skin is almost translucent now, marked intermittently with purple roses of bruises, a consequence of her medication. She wears her silky white hair in a French roll and sports an antique lace silk gown. She is surrounded by photos of her family and one of her performing in the ballet.

'To the open-air cinema down at Lady Macquarie's Chair. The screen comes out of the water.'

'Splendid. And it's such a lovely day. A new year.'

'Happy New Year, June.'

June chuckles gently. 'Wasn't sure I'd make it, but here I am.'

'I'm glad.' I truly am. There's something so special about June, a purity of vision. I felt it when I first met her, almost a year ago now. She's become a friend and a highlight of my day is hearing about her life and watching her smile as she listens to the music.

'Me too. The kids have gone to Perth and my granddaughter is still in the States, so I can't go anywhere yet. You know how expensive holiday travel is; a funeral would be most inconvenient.' She speaks with a girlish innocence that has a fabulous edge of irony.

I laugh.

'Tell me about your suitor. I bet he's thanking his lucky stars, beautiful young lady like you. All those curls.'

Oh, how I wish. The sordid details of my non above board relationship with Ross seem not only inappropriate but also deeply inadequate.

'He makes me laugh.'

'That's good, darling.' She opens her eyes and studies my face closely. 'As long as he doesn't make you cry too much, too. Sometimes the ones who make you laugh the most do that.'

I smile in response and she pats my hand. 'It's later than you think, Zoe.'

That's the bitter pill I have been needing to swallow. It is later than I think, and now another whole year has passed. I can't do another loop around the calendar of this waiting. I have to say something to Ross . . . Today.

'I had better get playing. You rest now.'

'That's all I do . . . rest, rest, rest. Play me some Rodrigo – the *Concierto de Aranjuez* . . . you can do that on harp?'

Fortunately, I have played this for her, or tried to, before. And it was a mess, so I went home and transcribed my own version. It's Spanish composer Rodrigo's best-known work – it calls to nature and courtly dances and the exuberance of his own honeymoon . . . as well as the loss of a miscarriage. But even through its pain, it is a triumphant piece of music. And it is perfect for a new year.

I play, and June smiles and moves her hands with their balletic grace.

'Yes.' She smiles broadly when I finish though keeps her eyes shut. 'That's how true love is. Always.'

'Is that what it was like for you and your husband?' I ask.

June considers for a while, her face beckoning a memory. 'Before my husband, I had a love. A big love. My husband was a very good man. A fine husband and a great father, and we had a strong marriage, but he was more Vaughan Williams than Rodrigo. Strong and steadfast. Beautiful but less fire.'

The expression on June's face, the smile on her lips, leads me to wonder what this other love, this fire, was. I can see from her look it was big. My fingers hover over the strings, but before I begin, I hear myself ask:

'Are you still friends, with the big love?' I realise how unlikely it is; the woman is ninety-five.

'Oh my dear, I haven't seen him in over seventy-five years. But I remember him so clearly. Especially when you play.'

'What was his name?'

I can see June reaching back for him in her mind, travelling to a place beyond all my experiences.

'I think I need to sleep.'

She pats my hand. I feel guilty for asking too many questions, but then she squeezes my hand and her lips turn to a smile of secrets yet to be shared. I reply to her look with a hopeful grin. Some people can see with their eyes closed.

I stand to wheel my harp to my next visit.

'Clem. His name was Clemency Lang. Goodbye, darling. Enjoy the stars.'

I head out, thinking of Clemency Lang . . . Does he think of June too? Seventy-five years is a long time.

I play for Reg next, which is quite a change in pace. Reg sits up in bed, nimbly pressing keys on his laptop. His nose and cheeks have the ruby glow of someone who's enjoyed a lot of red wine and a lot of life. I asked him his age once and he replied that he's in the 'afternoon delight of life'. I think he's in his seventies, he likes wearing workmen's shorts and shirts with checks. Reg is rehabilitating from a triple bypass and a hip replacement. He is cheeky and warned me the first time we met that his main connection to music is that he can burp the Australian national anthem. I played it for him. He was correct, he doesn't miss a bar. Now I play it every visit as a warm-up tune.

'I can sing "Waltzing Matilda" out my other end,' he tells me. 'Wanna try?'

'Not today. Any other non-burping or farting pieces?'

He waves his hand. 'Rather be at a poker game. Can you play?'

I play him a Hungarian polka that's cheeky like him and hard not to tap along to.

'Not what I had in mind, but it'll do. You don't have a harmonica on you, do you? Prefer that to all this fancy string gumph.'

I promise to bring him in a deck of cards tomorrow. As far as I know, I'm his only visitor, though he tells me he spends a lot of time skyping various 'friends'.

I have a few other patients to see: Clara, who sleeps through my entire visit; Pedro, who loves 'La Cucaracha' and insists I play it three times before I go. He sings along. His wife and the nursing staff have told me it's the only time he speaks. Finally, I visit Kip, who is surrounded by a squabbling family. They stop when I enter. I play Mozart in the hope it will calm them all.

Death brings out the best and worst of any family dynamic. Whether it's arguing about whose turn it is to wash the pyjamas, visit at a certain time, or inherit the most money . . . I have seen families who are picture-card perfect shake and splinter in the face of a member's mortality.

One of Kip's grandchildren is outside the hospital entrance near the lift as I'm leaving. Billy: he's eleven, all elbows and teeth. He holds a skateboard, sobbing.

'The nurse wouldn't let me show Grandad how I ride it. Then Mum started yelling at me. Then Uncle Dave started yelling at her . . . then everyone was yelling.'

'He would love to see you skate, I bet.' I attempt to soothe him.

'This thing with Grandad. It's irrefixable isn't it?' Billy studies the concrete.

Irrefixable, it's the perfect word.

'It is a bit.' I can see by the pale lightness of Kip's skin these days that there's not long for him to go.

'I'm sorry,' I add. 'He talks about you all the time. Show me what you want to show Grandad.'

Billy hesitates, keeping his eyes fixed to the pavement, then places his skateboard down and performs some tic-tacs and other manoeuvres I don't know the names of. He's good. I can see by the board's colourful gleam that it's new. A Christmas present probably.

'I wish he could come and see,' he says, gaining confidence.

'Me too. I'm going to tell him how great you are.' I marvel at his balance and his bounce.

As Billy keeps skating, I take the cover off my harp and strum a few bars from Coldplay's 'Clocks' that he recognises and moves along to on his board. I can imagine him down at the ramp at Bondi, cutting it up – or whatever it is you do on a skateboard.

'Grandad's my FPITW,' he confides.

'FPITW?' I echo, attempting to decipher the acronym.

'Favourite Person in the World,' he informs me. 'Everyone knows that. Who's yours?'

I hover on the harp. 'Oh, this friend of mine. I'm going to see him now actually, so I'd better go.' I feel a bolt of adrenaline that makes my palms tingle as I think of Ross. Ross and my New Year's resolution.

Billy grins mischievously. 'Is he, like, a boyfriend or friend?'

How is it that kids nail it every time?

'Not sure.' I attempt to dodge the answer . . . for both of us.

'Sounds stupid.' Billy shrugs, scrunching his sweet face before grinning his toothy smile at me. He's nailed it again.

'Yeah . . . it is a bit.'

'Let's disqualify him. Who do you vote next?'

'Probably a tie between my bestie, Lexie, and my brother, Tom. He surfs.' I know this will give Tom an advantage in Billy's eyes.

'Cool.' He continues his skateboard moves. There must be something I can do to help him and Kip.

'Billy, can you come here really early one morning next week? Like, at five-thirty?' I ask hopefully.

'Am I in trouble?'

'Course not. I have an idea. I'll call your mum to see if she can drop you off here then, just the once. For a few hours?'

'What's it for?'

'Secret. You'll have to trust me.'

I get Billy's mother's number from him. They live in Surry Hills, so it's not too much of a big ask, not if it helps. He waves and performs a tricky turn as I leave.

TWO

LATE AFTERNOON GLOWS OVER THE BOTANIC GARDENS AS I FIND a park and walk through the ancient figs and ferns down to the cool of the water where I will meet him. A glass of bubbles. Sunset. A classic film in one of the world's most majestic settings. An evening with the man I love. Holding hands in the dark. The perfect kick-off to the new year.

My phone sounds. It's him.

'Are you here?' I look around as I speak. There's a pause.

'Work was mad last night. They must have had an end-of-year sale on ice up at the Cross.' I can hear the beeps and pings of the hospital in the background.

'You're still at work,' I say. 'You sound exhausted.'

'I'm shattered,' he replies.

'Sooner you get here the better, are you close?' I can already feel the hollow echo in my hope.

There's another pause.

'Jeanie looks like she's going to have to come in for another transfusion.'

'Tonight?' I ask, already knowing the answer.

'Yeah, she's been holding out, but she's not good.' His voice goes quiet.

'Shit.' I hear the news and the tone.

'I'm sorry, angel. I'm going to have to bail.'

And there it is, the no-win situation. Who am I to say he shouldn't be by his partner's side as she receives a blood transfusion? The horrible thing is I have become shockingly suspicious of Jeanie's timing. I'm sure that whenever she senses Ross withdrawing, preparing to leave, she's suddenly back on death's door needing a full-time carer, which has to be him.

I want Jeanie to be well and empowered so she and Ross can wish each other well, co-parent their lovely son and each move on with their life. Separately.

But here we are again. Another year beginning with Jeanie ruling my life.

'Can you ask someone else?' He gently reasons.

'Sure.' My voice is numb. New Year's night. Who will come?

'I know you're never short on options. I want to be there with you. You know that, don't you?' He asks this as a rhetorical question.

I nod to the phone and say, 'Let me know how you go.'

'I'll find you at work tomorrow. Happy New Year, baby.' He hangs up.

I watch the passing parade of cheery groups making their way down to the water and the film screen tucked away above it.

Alone again . . . naturally.

•

Lexie sits beside me, tight jeans, designer sleeveless t-shirt, peep-toe boots and black toe-polish. She sports clothes that are both expensive and edgy. Always jeans. She's like the style section from the Sunday papers that exudes cool. I'm in white from work, wearing an antique cotton dress I found at the Bondi markets and have been saving for tonight. Together we look like a chessboard. A bottle of wine is nestled between us as the screen makes the most fabulous of entrances, emerging from the sapphire water with the Opera House and the Bridge perched perfectly on top. Sydney certainly knows how to provide the most spectacular backdrop. An enthusiastic new year of applause erupts. Lexie keeps her sunglasses on, even though the sun has set sail. Unlike me, she remained at a friend's New Year's party until 5 am and has spent the day recovering via multiple swims and coconut water. She sips her wine gingerly.

'Thanks for coming.' I toast her.

'I'm glad you're starting your new year with me not Mr Limp Dick,' she says as we clink.

Lexie pretty much considers all men to be limp dicks. Though Ross is top of the heap.

'It must have been serious for him to cancel,' I counter.

'Or just inconvenient?' Lexie muses.

I finish off my glass and pour another to settle in and watch the film.

'What's your New Year's resolution?' Lexie whispers.

'Still deciding,' I say as a delay tactic. 'I'm giving myself till Chinese New Year to settle on one. You?'

She nods and looks directly and unflinchingly at me as she replies. 'I'm gonna find me a nice girl and settle down, have a kid and plant a herb garden.'

She holds her serious face for a moment before we both crack up. Lexie loves sleeping with women, a lot of women. She hates being tied down to anyone.

'You know it'll break Tom's heart when you do,' I add.

My brother, Tom, has been devoted to Lexie for decades – pretty much since the day I brought her home to play after school when I was eight. Lexie was an absolute tomboy even back then, but she made me laugh more than anyone I'd ever met. She still does. Tom was ten and immediately began teasing her, a true sign of his admiration. She threw something at him, her school shoe I think, it landed on his head and he was love-struck. Tom has made various passes at her over the years, and a few times they've fallen for the same girl. Once, Lexie turned a young woman Tom had started dating. He forgave her; I think the fantasy of the threesome she told him that they had considered offering him by way of a consolation ensured that. The threesome never happened of course, but the possibility of it lives vividly in my brother's head; a thought I find equal parts disturbing and unappealing. Or, in little-sister speak, just plain gross.

'He can be a bridesmaid,' Lexie decides.

'But I'm your chief one, right?'

'As long as you don't bring Limpy as your date, yep.'

'He may be my other half by then,' I offer meekly.

'Doubt it.' Lexie doesn't do meek.

'But if he is?' I push gently . . . hopefully.

Lexie lowers her head, raises her eyebrows and throws a look above her sunglasses.

'Babes, if he is, then he can come but he's not going to be part of the bridal party,' Lexie responds conclusively.

'Deal. Let's see if your future bride is here.'

We perform a quick scan. As we have done at various parks, blue light discos, bus stops, theatre foyers, pubs, pools, beaches, yoga schools, art galleries, football fields, cinemas, hospital foyers, restaurants, airport terminals, dental surgeries and supermarkets over the many years of our friendship. Lexie stops.

'Her, over there. Three rows up, the ginger.'

Lexie loves redheads. Her own hair is a black shiny bob with fringe, her skin a luxuriant coffee thanks to her Sri Lankan heritage. Men go mad for her, but she's too busy falling for the girliest girl in the room. I am girly too but we are like sisters. Once, in our early twenties after a big party in North Bondi, we decided to kiss. It was horrendous. I fled and hid from her for the next three days till she turned up and sat on the end of my bed and informed me it felt like incest for her too, and that I have a sub-zero gay vibe. Then she hit me over the head with a pillow and we were back to normal, and have remained pretty much inseparable ever since.

I view the potential bride. 'She has a wedding ring and she is tongue-tangoing with a guy.'

'For now,' Lexie muses . . . Like I said, Lexie loves a challenge. Considering I am in love with Mr Unavailable and my brother is in love with Lexie, I'm guessing it's something we're all attracted to.

'Know what I think your New Year's resolution is?' Lexie lands me with a producer look that says, *You need to meet the budget or I will sack you*, then continues. 'Get back on the horse. You are too good not to perform onstage. It's way past time.'

'It's too late, I'm too old,' I reply. But I do miss playing with an orchestra, being part of something that big, that amazing and, at times, that transcendent.

'Nope, you're just too scared.'

'I'll think about it,' is my reply, which has the tone of *Enough said*. Lexie calls it 'the clamp down'. I do it when I feel confronted or awkward or overwhelmed. I wish I didn't.

The feature begins.

The film is *Roman Holiday* – a gorgeous romantic comedy about another two people who don't get who they want but learn a great deal in the process. The script was penned by a writer who was blacklisted at the time so he made his mate take the credit ... and his mate then won an Oscar. I'm not sure what that tells us about life, but watching Gregory Peck and Audrey Hepburn scoot around Rome is a pleasure. It makes me long for Rome ... and Ross.

The film ends to applause and sighs of longing. The screen is a blank canvas hovering over the water, a giant sail of sorts. Lexie and I are in the crowd shuffling our way through the exit gates when I spy him.

'Zoe!' He waves us down.

It's Ross looking slightly crumpled, smiling his smile and holding a hamper.

Lexie moans as we make our way over to him.

Ross is tall so he stands out in a crowd. He's one of those men who is handsome to begin with and becomes increasingly gorgeous with each minute you spend in their presence. Magnetic to the point of hypnotic. He smells citrusy with a hint of chilli, his skin is unfairly olive, his eyes are sapphire blue and invite you to confide all ailments and concerns in him. But maybe that's a doctor thing? Ross has managed to maintain the frame of a man decades younger than his almost fifty years. He is blessed with great genes and high metabolism. He doesn't like keeping still. He waves the basket teasingly, tightens his grip around the handle with his perfect hands in a way that has me instantly wishing he was placing them on various parts of my body.

'Would you two like a nightcap?' He asks as though he's the concierge of a five-star hotel and we are his favourite guests.

'I'm out,' Lexie states in her best flat tone. 'Still recovering from the recovery. Have fun, kids. Don't do . . . oh wait you already have . . . Night!'

She kisses me and shoots me a *Be careful* look before making a swift exit to her motorbike, which is illegally parked nearby.

Ross takes my hand. 'Is this okay?' he asks.

It is . . . but seeing the film with me and being my official partner would have been better. I settle on a nod. We walk down to a quiet place near the water's edge. The reflections of the lights on the Harbour Bridge float on the water. All is quiet and calm following the buzz and excitement of last night's fireworks – it feels like even the Bridge needs an early night. Ross gently pulls me down to sit.

'Jeanie okay?' I ask, instantly berating myself for bringing her up.

He provides a half nod half headshake that makes him look like an Indian guru. He pulls out a bottle of Bollinger and two glasses. They're crystal tumblers from his rooms at the hospital.

'This is how I want to start my new year.' He pops the cork in that silent way people who host swish, subdued dinner parties do.

We clink glasses and sip.

'How did you get away?'

'Jeanie didn't need the transfusion, she's sleeping. Work sent me home, so here I am. How was the film?'

'Lonely.'

He nods. We sip more. The last of the cinema-goers pass in the distance and the still night reclines before us, bar the odd Christmas beetle and the soft lapping of the harbour water whispering to the botanical park's edges. I inhale the scent exuding from his shirt. Mandarins and ginger.

'Lose any?' he asks.

'Nup, you?'

'A few.' He tops up our glasses.

Our ongoing black joke places me immediately back in the universe of us. I met Ross at a conference on care for the dying. He was a guest speaker on unexpected death and coping with the stress of the emergency room. And he was nothing shy of brilliant. His humour and wit ensured we all left uplifted by a shockingly difficult subject. And that's the paradox of Ross: he uplifts you while he breaks your heart. Quite the party trick.

Most of the time when we see each other we chat for hours. Together we canvass subjects that travel from silly to sutures to sublime. Not tonight, though. Tonight I need to know if this year is going to be any different. For him, for me, for Jeanie.

He eases himself down, placing his head in my lap. I study him by moonlight. The perfect lips. The unflinching eyes. The clever head. He holds his arm up and gently pulls my hair, beckoning me down, and we kiss.

'Happy New Year,' he whispers.

'Happy New Year,' I echo.

And that's how I want to spend it. In the gentle, engaging ease of each other.

'What's your New Year's resolution?' I ask him.

'You,' he replies simply.

We kiss again and reshuffle our limbs till we're lying beside each other.

'How do we make that happen?' I tread carefully and speak lightly but I've promised myself to do this.

'I don't know, babe. Jeanie's so . . . she's not a bad person.'

'I never said she was.'

'She really loves me.' He sounds pained.

'Join the club,' I reply gently.

'I want to say I'm leaving, I'm getting a flat . . .' He hesitates. 'But there's Josh to think about.'

If only he knew just how much I do think about Josh, and Jeanie and him . . . rotating across the merry-go-round of my mind.

'Does he think that it's okay his parents don't share a bedroom?' I ask straight out.

'We get on, on a domestic level . . . You and I have something else,' is his crab-like, sideways reply.

Maybe New Year's resolutions are the things you daydream about but in reality know you will never do. Maybe I'm his Mount Everest.

'What are you going to do?' I ask, my mouth burning with the heat of each of the words.

I wait. A fig leaf falls beside me. He says nothing. I blurt.

'If you want to stay, stay. But I'm not ending another year the way I began it.'

I am a frigging walking cliché. As the words sound from my mouth I recognise them from daytime television soap operas. But sadly, knowing you're a cliché doesn't lessen the pain of being one . . . of being rejected. Repeatedly. In some parallel universe this is the moment I stand and pour the rest of the bottle of bubbles over his head. Or slap him and take the bottle with me off into the night. Why am I not that woman?

He is saved by the phone – mine.

'Clara is asking for you,' Waverley says by way of greeting. 'She thinks she's going. Can you come in now? Anthea says she's really unsettled.' Waverley will be imagining I am home alone, possibly stroking a cat and watching some kind of prime-suspects criminal drama . . . or trolling the net for a Valentine's date.

Clara has ovarian cancer and has been growing lighter and lighter. I knew it wouldn't be long, but . . .

'On my way.' I tell Waverley what she already knows.

'I was going to stay over,' Ross laments as I hang up.

Staying over for Ross means 3 or 5 am. Although it's fun and sexy as, I'm always left feeling slightly used. I want to wake up in his arms and walk up the street loved-up and crinkly to get the papers and coffees then head back to bed. Or, heaven forbid, spend an entire day with him.

'I think you should work on your New Year's resolution before you stay over again,' I say slowly as I rise from our ideal picnic setting.

Ross's face receives the sting of a non-sexing new year. He jumps to his feet.

'I'm just trying to keep everyone happy . . . and failing miserably on all fronts,' he mumbles.

'Pretty much.'

'Shit. I'm sorry. I'm a mess.'

'You're exhausted.'

He holds me. I hold him. We hold on, like Hansel and Gretel in the oven.

'I have to go,' I say, stepping back.

'Want me to come?' he offers, taking my head in his hands, leaning in to kiss me.

'How's your flute?' I query.

He laughs. He is a master of medicine but not of music.

He walks me to my car, waits as I get in the driver's seat.

'Don't lose me,' I whisper but he doesn't respond as he closes the door.

He takes a few steps and says something, which I don't hear because the window is up. I wind it down.

'I'm an idiot, and I love you,' he repeats.

I nod and head back to the hospital.

THREE

CLARA IS HIGH ON MORPHINE TO FIGHT OFF THE PAIN.

'Take a "Walk on the Wild Side",' she strains her request as I come into her squinted line of vision.

I give it a whirl; I'm not sure I do Lou Reed proud but Clara enjoys it. After the nurse has taken her vitals Clara motions for me to come closer to her. I take a breath, exhale slowly and move in. I've had to say farewell often in this job, and in my life, but nothing really prepares you for it.

'Favour. Are you in or are you out?' her now raspy voice utters.

I'm not sure if I am part of some trippy hallucination, but . . .

'In,' I respond. 'What can I do for you?'

'You have a car?'

'I do.'

'Go to my house . . . Watsons Bay, Cove Street. There's a key hidden in the beak of the third seagull hung on the wall.'

It's sounding trippy again but I nod.

'No one else lives there?' I ask. Often in palliative care, patients lose touch with the outside world. Time is blurred, anything can happen at any given hour; it seems like our final defiance, rebelling against what we have measured our lives by and been slave to, though of course when we run out of it, it is time who has the last laugh. Clara would have no idea of where the hands were on the clock.

'My daughter was there but now she's with her partner, and Phil, my husband, is with Debbie,' Clara answers.

'Oh.' How do I respond to that?

She watches my hesitancy and laughs. 'It's okay, I set them up; the man's useless, needs to be with someone.' She pauses to catch her breath and nods off momentarily.

'You still there?' she blurts suddenly.

'Still here – so are you,' I reply.

'Not for too much longer, I hope. The code is one-nine-seven-one. Then hash. Go up to my room.'

'Okay.'

'In the walk-in closet there's a shelf with shoes. Behind it is a drawer. Open it.' She pauses and smiles, like she's recalling a best friend or a favourite tune. 'It has a heap of journals. About ten. Make sure you get them all.'

This is still sounding on the outer edges of real, but I agree.

'I will.'

'On your way out go via the fridge and grab whatever good champagne is there. Promise me. Okay?' She sounds determined.

Why is everyone wanting me to drink champagne tonight? I have no problem with it but it's shaping up to be a strange start to the year.

'Got it,' I answer.

'Wait. I forgot. The clothes.'

'You mean the journals?'

'No. The clothes, all my lovely clothes.'

'You want me to bring you something to wear?'

'We're the same size. Or used to be till I shrunk. I want you to pick out some outfits you like. For you.'

'That's okay, Clara.'

'It'll all just go to some overpriced recycled designer shop in Paddington, I've already told my family I was offering them to you. Katie's built like a tank, she doesn't want any of it. I have a hell of a wardrobe. Fabulous.'

When she wasn't so ill, Clara was an interior designer and as fashion forward as they come. Her outfits simultaneously impressed and overwhelmed me. She was like a living work of art, self-curated from her spiky blonde Bowiesque hair through to her frill-necked lizard necklines, Issey Miyake skirts and Italian heels with laces and buckles. She always wore muted tones or black, which increased her powers of intimidation until I got to know her.

'Now listen, this is what I need you to do.' Clara has my complete attention.

•

It's close to 1 am by the time I get to Watsons Bay, Clara's instructions at front of mind.

The house is a small, old weatherboard fisherman's cottage, beautifully refurbished. A perfectly manicured miniature garden hidden behind tall bamboo ushers me to the front door. And three wooden seagulls hang, just as Clara described. I'm not sure about the seagulls, perhaps they're ironic. Or a Clara quirk.

I open the front door, turn off the alarm and switch on the lights. The house is stunning. A Zen sanctuary. Polished cement floors, light woollen rugs, a kitchen with an integrated fridge like the one I daydream about having, when I 'grow up'. A baby grand piano with a collection of elegantly framed photos sitting on top of it. I'm beginning to worry the house has been staged for an upcoming sale. Or Clara was a serial killer on the side. It's immaculate. But the photos show snapshots of family life. Clara and Phil on holidays in hammocks, Katie as a child in a white smock blowing a dandelion, Clara cuddling Katie in matching bathrobes. Perhaps some families really are perfect.

I head upstairs to Clara's 'retreat', a bedroom with its own balcony with views that extend to Watsons Bay. Everything is white with a high thread count. Then there's the wardrobe, a walk-in the size of a normal bedroom. Again, it's immaculate. She must have obsessive compulsive disorder. No one really lives this neatly, do they? Rows of exquisite designer clothes are hung – divided by size, shape and colour. Clara has colour in her wardrobe!

I reach into the secret drawer and there, also perfectly laid out, are the hidden journals. I am curious as to what the deep dark secrets are that she's confessed in them. Part of her request requires me finding out.

I take another look at her beautiful clothes, her creative expression was perfectly channelled into her wardrobe choices. How could this world, all that she had created, have been abandoned while she lies in a simple cotton robe up at the hospital? I don't consider myself overly materialistic, but Clara's home is a manifestation and an expression of her journey in life, of her role in the world, and now it all sits empty, never to be returned to.

My eyes travel across her perfectly laundered, folded and hanging garments again. I'm tired and there is still much to do. I take a pastel pink Chanel lightweight leather jacket that is as soft as butter to the touch. Clara is right: we are the same size. Two pairs of jeans, and a dress that deserves its own event – Oscar de la Renta, circa mid-80s, a black-and-white strapless cross between a sundress and a ball gown. The fabric is a thick raw silk. The bodice is horizontal stripes and the skirt is huge and billowing with the lines going in all directions. It's a scene stealer, all right. For what event did Clara wear it? It looks brand new.

I head downstairs to find a bag to put everything in, grab a bottle of Dom Perignon as instructed and head to my next destination.

•

I don't have to go far. Just the short walk to the Gap. I sit on the empty bench overlooking the wide-mouthed Gap. I open the champagne. Take a mouthful of stars – apparently that's how a Benedictine monk described drinking this champagne, though there's a fair bit of contention as to whether or not that's true. In any case, it's stellar. Next I put my phone onto torch, take one of the journals and commence reading.

I'm not sure why Clara chose me to be the one to read her innermost thoughts. She said it had to be someone who wouldn't judge her. Sometimes family is too hard. And so I begin.

The journals start in the early 1990s; the first thing that strikes me is the haphazard, scattered, messiness of them. Filled with ink spots, doodles, random dates – they seem to be the one place in Clara's life she let a bit of chaos reign.

So, what do I find? Lovers? A transsexual husband? A hidden cocaine addiction or details of where bodies are buried?

None of that.

What I do find is a woman who married before she was ready, who got swept up in her duties of pleasing people she no longer regards. A woman with such a strong desire to travel who settled on security instead, a woman who so loves her daughter but struggles with motherhood, who knew she was hiding behind her career as a way of avoiding her husband. Who stopped wanting to have sex with said husband a long time ago. All her passion, according to her written impressions, has gone into her work. There are stories of different people she's designed for, difficult clients, pivotal moments of conflict as builders fall short and jobs are lost. The terror of failure, all the while feeling a fraud in her own marriage. A few crushes, one on an architect, nothing seems to have happened beyond an infatuation and a glass of wine after a meeting. But the turmoil it gives rise to becomes consuming. So much self-criticism. So much doubt. So much pain over things that, from what I read, didn't happen.

Sometimes there's over a year between entries. Then a one-liner about Katie losing a tooth or winning an award.

I'm interrupted in early 2003. Just after Clara has been crowned Interior Designer of the Year and her picture was taken for a salubrious lifestyle magazine. But she's miserable. She and Phillip live like brother and sister. She's still planning the solo overseas getaway she never seems to let herself take for fear her jobs will collapse around her. She keeps buying clothes to wear on vacations she never takes. So she refuses to wear all the colour of her closet offerings. Why is she so hard on herself?

'Good book?' I look up at the unexpected view of a man in jeans and a t-shirt standing with a golden retriever.

He nods at me, grins and looks back out to sea.

My stomach lurches with concern. It's 4.30 am at the Gap, Australia's most notorious suicide destination. A variety of precautions have been placed here over the years, a fence to hopefully deter people from springing to their death in the steep rock face of the South Head cliffs and the ravaging waves of the Tasman Sea far beneath. There are phones from which people can call Lifeline and speak to counsellors, and a constant video camera; I hope someone close by watches it and darts down to the rescue when necessary. Though Clara says the number of police rescue trucks and helicopters down here far exceed what is officially reported.

I find the place more exhilarating than suicidal. The steady breeze of salt air, the sound of crashing waves, the knowledge this was home to the Birrabirragal clan long before it was a signal station to warn of incoming ships. I wish people came here for comfort and inspiration instead of to farewell this world. Is that this man's plan . . . and he's taking his dog with him? I grapple with what to say that won't make matters worse. He beats me to it.

'Zoe, isn't it? Interesting reading spot?'

He's vaguely familiar; I meet so many people through work, but they're usually at the coalface of life and people look very different when they're going through the process of losing someone. And it's dark. I don't want to be rude and shine the light in his face. Perhaps he's one of Tom's friends? Or a mate of Ross? At least he isn't making a running dive for the Gap. Actually, he seems incredibly calm, a bit concerned but not what I imagine suicidal looks like. Who is he?

'You probably don't remember me,' he offers.

'Right now I can barely even see you,' I reply.

He laughs. A deep lovely laugh that has the warmth of open fires and old friends.

'Sam,' he offers.

I squint . . . still nothing.

'Max's dad.'

Now I remember.

'Sam. I am – so sorry . . . Hi.' Sam – oh god what's his surname – Taylor, I think. He and his wife and their beautiful boy, who was only sixteen when he sustained terrible injuries in a motor accident. Massive brain injuries and a torturously slow death. It was gruesome. It was four years ago. I feared for Max's parents after he went, how could they possibly endure the pain of life without their son and recover from the trauma with which he departed?

'May I?' he asks. I make room for him on the seat beside me and pat his gorgeous dog.

'This is Harry the wonder dog,' he says encouragingly. He's still looking concerned.

'He's divine.' I love dogs.

'He's a vacuum cleaner when it comes to food.'

'How's Lisa?'

Sam's smile becomes wistful.

'She's on her honeymoon,' he replies.

'Sorry?'

He takes a calm breath. 'We barely survived Max's death individually; surviving it as a couple was impossible.'

He looks out to sea. A bereaved dad whose ex-wife just remarried. My stomach churns and knots some more. I was right. This is bad.

'I'm sorry.'

Sam nods. What else can be said?

'So, she's remarried?' I ask.

'Last weekend. I didn't go. I was invited, surprisingly.' His wry smile has returned. I figure smiling is a good sign, unless it's a gallows humour smile, in which case he's about to say 'Geronimo.'

'Are you friends?'

'Our divorce was pretty . . . well . . . there was a lot of grief.'

'Sure.'

'We remind each other of him. That's comforting and excruciating . . .' He drifts off but seems comfortable with the quiet.

'I can imagine.'

'We weren't good before the accident; we'd had a trial
separation.'

'I didn't know. You seemed so solid, with Max,' I say, remembering Sam rubbing Lisa's back as they sat by Max's bed day
and night.

'Good in a crisis, bad at the quotidian,' he replies.

There's a silence. It's filled with my hope Sam has gone off
the jumping idea.

'How's your harp? Still at the hospital?' He brings his focus
back to me.

'Still there.'

'Amazing, what you do.' He pauses. 'Must be a lot of pressure.'

I nod, so does he. He waits for me to reply. It's only in this
moment that I realise he's wondering if I've come to the Gap to
throw myself off. Harp player loses shit due to death overload . . .
that kind of thing. Or is he giving me a covert *I need help* look?

'It's okay,' I venture. 'I'm okay. Are *you* okay?'

He takes a beat then seems to realise I'm checking his suicide
status as much as he's checking mine. His face relaxes and he
laughs again, and in the first light of the dawn I see shades of
his handsomeness glow.

'Harry woke me up, wanting a walk. I live just over at Gibson's
Beach. And I've started . . . keeping an eye on things here.'

The Gap lost its angel some years ago. A hugely compassionate
man named Don Ritchie who brought hundreds of people back

from the edge through his kindness and comforting words. He said he never counselled. Just tried to stop them from making the decision to suicide then and there. He used to take them back to his nearby home where his wife would make them a cup of tea.

'Like Don?' I ask.

He closes his eyes for a moment. 'I wish. What a gift he had. I can't see them from my place. It's more Harry than me, to be honest. He has a bit of a nose for it. He's woken me up a few times growling and we've headed up and someone's been here.'

There was another dog, in the sixties, a German shepherd named Rexie who performed similar feats. There's a plaque in her honour at the site of the old Gap Tavern.

'Was Harry growling tonight . . . this morning?'

'No. But he kept licking my hand to wake me up. He wanted to come out. I guess he wanted us to catch up.'

'Huh.' I laugh.

'Either that or he wanted to pinch your bubbles.' Sam winks at the bottle sitting next to me.

I'd forgotten all about the Dom. I'd had one or two swigs but then became so engrossed by Clara's tales that it had been abandoned for hours. A day on no sleep is hard enough, a day of no sleep with a hangover would be unbearable.

'I'd offer it to you but it's warm and flat now.'

'Nice angle,' he jests.

I smile.

'Must be a good read to have kept you from the Dom.'

'It's a favour for one of my patients. A request.' My mind turns back to Clara.

Sam nods with an understanding gained from experience and loss. We sit in silence for a while.

'*O Mio Babbino Caro*,' I say quietly.

Sam pauses before his reply. 'Yes, that's it. Who'd a thunk Max was an opera fan.'

'Oh, My Beloved Father' is what I played most for Max, it was the tune that seemed to calm him and his parents more than others. It was also what I played as he died.

We watch the light of a new day rise, sitting silently side by side. I know Sam's mind will be revisiting his son and their farewell. Harry sits patiently at my feet, lapping up the patting I'm providing.

We continue to sit until the sun has well and truly made its grand entrance and the chorus of birds – the wrens, the rosellas, the galahs and the cockatoos – who have sung it in begin getting on with their day. We sit still, watching. There's something comfortable about Sam.

'What you do for people. What you did for Maxie and Lisa and me . . . it's really special,' Sam says quietly.

I'm touched by his words.

'Thanks, Sam.'

'It helped us get through what no one should have to go through. I think of that a lot . . . how you helped us. How you helped me. Thank you.'

His words, their sincerity, heat my chest and a lump clumps in my throat, but I want to keep the moment light; the last thing Sam needs is an existential crisis before breakfast.

'I love doing it,' is my honest reply.

'Be great to hear you play again. Do you perform with some kind of ensemble or orchestra?' he asks.

That question always makes me stumble.

'Only with my brother in my backyard.'

He absorbs this then nods. 'That's a shame. You have such a gift. And you made me start listening to opera. I'm a subscriber now.' He nods his head at his own surprise and enjoyment of his choice.

I whistle my approval.

'Would you like to come with me sometime?' he asks, looking back out at the sea.

That takes me aback. I love opera. Ross and I have been together a few times and I went once on my own last year, when Ross had to bail last minute due to some drama. Wait . . . is Sam asking me out on a date?

'I'm seeing someone,' escapes from my lips.

'I didn't mean . . . or maybe I did actually.' Sam smiles to himself then provides me with a grin that almost out-dazzles the sun in front of us. 'Good thing about grief, it makes you cut through the crap.'

I couldn't agree more. If you allow it, grief makes you fast-track to authenticity. I'm flattered with his invitation, and flustered by it. I respond with a nod and bite my lip.

We both turn our gaze to watch the new day emerge.

'I'd better let you finish your reading,' he says.

'Thanks. Sam, I'm really glad to have seen you.'

'Me too. Well, you know where to find me if you feel like a sunrise or an opera.'

He waves and heads off. Harry stays with me. Sam whistles to him and the golden retriever provides me with a blink that carries its own invitation for runs, bones and frisbee matches as he heads after his master.

I watch them make their way down through the park to Watsons Bay. Sam is tall and broad-shouldered, strong. His hair is the colour of a latte. He smiles to himself, or Harry. He looks like someone who has a perfect life. And yet he's had to overcome the direst of tragedies. He carries that with him wherever he goes. There's a humility in him that wasn't there before.

It's a riddle, isn't it – the greatest losses often provide people with the deepest connection to humanity. Maybe it's an awareness of the fragility of life that gets people to honour it?

I seldom see the families of the people I play for after the death of their loved one. There's the funeral, and then usually nothing. Perhaps to them I represent the death. Occasionally there are flowers or a card, sometimes months, years after the departure. When the loss of the loved one has been lived into a bit more.

They all live on for me in my music.

I finish reading the last of Clara's journals at 6.45 am. She stopped writing it the day she came into palliative care and stayed. Her writing scrawled and thin, she wrote beseeching the freedom her health had provided her before it left, how intensely she longed for it, how she longed to feel life, how she wanted to be brave for her family with what was ahead.

As instructed, I throw each of her journals over the cliff and into the thrashing sea, who devours them ravenously. Clara's secrets, her hopes, are all free now.

FOUR

AFTER A QUICK STOP AT HOME TO SHOWER AND CHANGE, I HEAD to work. I know she's waiting for me.

'Well?' Clara whispers. Her skin is now incandescent.

I place a beautiful muted green and lavender raw silk robe of hers over her. Her husband and daughter have gone down to the coffee shop for a break. They've been told Clara will leave us within the next day or two.

'Well, it was a bit like that Sesame Street tale, *The Monster at the End of This Book*,' I say.

She laughs weakly and coughs. 'I'm not familiar with it. Illuminate me.'

'It's Grover, I think ... the blue fuzzy one. Each page he begs you not to turn another page because he just *knows* there's a monster lurking there, one who will destroy us all. But each page there's nothing, just Grover, begging you again not to turn the next page because the next page is surely, is *definitely* the one with the monster.'

'I see.'

'Your journals, they're beautiful. They're full of wonderful insights and hopes and dreams and concerns. No monsters.'

Clara looks relieved. Perhaps all she needed was this, someone not too close to be her benevolent witness. Someone whom she feels safe enough to allow to venture into what she imagined is the awful hideous truth of her and see that nothing, in fact, is unlovable. Not in Clara's case anyway.

'But there *is* a monster. I didn't live any of those dreams or plans, Zoe. That's the monster and I think it's slowly gobbled me up.' She speaks with the tone of confession and regret through her crackling whisper.

'Most people have a secret life, Clara. An interior world they go to as a refuge where no one can hurt them.'

'That's what your music is for you.' She coughs more. She's going. This is it, she is leaving this world this morning, now, and quickly.

'That's what your work and your journals were for you, and there's nothing wrong with that,' I offer.

'Dear girl.' She reaches out her hand and continues in a whisper. 'I want that to be true but, Zoe . . . I wish I had done so many of those things, those plans, and those dreams. Even if I'd failed. I wish I'd had my adventures.'

I don't know what to say, I squeeze her hand.

'You made a beautiful sanctuary in your home. It's exquisite.'

She shakes her head. 'You know, no one has ever played that piano. Not once. No one has read the books in the library. No one has broken a glass.'

'But your fridge . . . it's awesome.' Oh, why did I say that? I was helping her and now I have to go and share my appliance daydream.

Clara laughs. 'Yes, it *is* pretty good. Did you find some nice dresses?'

'One: the Oscar de la Renta, the black and white one.'

'I bought that for another holiday I never took.' She considers for a moment. 'You take it on holiday for me. Wear it somewhere special. All of them . . . all those colours, you know from my diary what events and holidays I bought a lot of those outfits for. That's my wish: I wish you to take them and wear them where I was too scared.'

If you have been asked a favour by a dying person you will understand that saying no isn't a desirable option. And, besides, Clara's is such a beautiful and generous request.

'Yes. Thank you,' I reply to the faint thin strands of a life force that remains in her.

Clara murmurs something I don't catch . . . then repeats herself. '*We are more alike, my friends, than we are unalike.*' It's a quote from a poem by Maya Angelou, one of my favourite poets and Clara's too; she copied excerpts from it in her journal.

'Yes,' I answer – because we are.

'What else?' she queries from her wheezing depths.

'A pink leather jacket.'

'The Chanel. It will look beautiful on you. You should really wear that in London when you go.'

I laugh. 'Should I now?'

'Don't tell me that's all you took?'

'And two pairs of jeans.'

She shakes her head and wheezes again.

'Go back and take it all. Every last dress, every overpriced tank top, every over-the-top coat, every silly hat. I don't need them now, I want you to—'

She stops, out of breath.

'Please. Go back and take them and wear them, for me. Take those outfits to the places I bought them for but didn't have the courage to go. You need to live. That's your name. Zoe means life, did you know? I loved you being here, but stop treading water, stop waiting, stop hiding. Don't be me. Go – and take me with you.'

She weeps freely.

'Besides.' She is gasping now. 'I can see you're cash poor and style rich. It's my thank you gift. Promise me?'

Like I said, when you're this close to the coalface, there's no room for pretence, and there's nothing else to lose. How liberating that must feel.

'I promise.' My voice wavers as I speak, the clump in my throat I felt with Sam has now released as tears run silently down my cheeks.

'Good. Play me a song now.'

I call the nurse and let her know Phil and Katie must be summoned, and then I play the flower duet from *Lakmé*. Clara calms, and as my hands run over the strings I feel myself calm, completely present for Clara and, through the harp, I sing out her farewell.

'I do love them, you know,' she says softly. 'My family.'

'I know. And they love you, and this is how it's meant to be.'

'This time round,' she says and laughs. 'Now. Play Bowie. He can usher me out.'

By the time Katie and Phil enter the room Clara is pretty much delirious, though she hums along to 'Space Oddity'.

I watch her husband and daughter gather at the bed. Her friend Debbie – Phil's new partner – enters silently and stands nearby, looking uncertain. She's on her own precipice.

They kiss Clara. She kisses them. They exchange vows of love and thanks. She moans. She looks up, bright-eyed for a moment, and I can see the faces of the people who surround her are the faces she wants to see, and she is fulfilled.

She whispers incomprehensibly as her husband sobs freely over her.

I keep playing, though I know she's gone.

And in so many ways it's a perfect death. She had the faces she loved most looking into her with love, a song she enjoyed, she had confessed what she needed to, she had me promise to continue her dreams through my own. She completed and she departed with a smile.

I will miss you, Clara.

•

I head to June's room. She takes one look at me and raises her arms.

'Come here, darling.'

I sit by her bed and take her hands. My job is to help people let go but right now the thought of June going is unbearable. There is such comfort in her silken white hair stacked high on her head in big curls, in her smell of roses, her pictures and her beautiful hands. I want to plead with her to make a promise she won't leave. I know that's not only inappropriate but impossible.

'Was it Clara?' she asks gently. I nod. June takes my hands in hers.

'It was beautiful,' I tell her. 'But I'll miss her.'

'Of course you will,' June consoles. 'You're a bit like an old person, you say goodbye far too often.'

She pats my hands. 'But you help us so. Now, I'm going to tell you some more about Clem if you promise to play me some Bach then go and get some rest.'

I perk up at the thought of hearing about the mysterious Clem.

'I was dancing in a ballet in London,' she begins and I draw my seat closer.

FIVE

Dear Clem,

Quite simply, I am walking on air . . . not just walking,
pirouetting, leaping and gliding.

I had been losing hope, my days in the ballet are far too
arduous – the choreography, the music, the costumes, the
politics within the ensemble are so consuming. And this
ballet, Giselle, has been particularly taxing. To confess my
nose has been a little out of joint over Margot. Of course
she has the title role, she deserves it, Margot's dancing makes
me feel I should get on with my needlepoint and never
wear a tutu again. She is transcendent. She also possesses
more mettle than anyone I've ever encountered, which
has its moments in the dressing room. And we had quite a

run-in before the curtain went up for tonight's performance. Margot is only a year older than me but she is so sophisticated and men swarm around her. As was the case tonight. They were swarming in the wings so much so that getting on stage was a last-minute battle. To top it off I spent a lot of my performance attempting to conceal an errant ribbon that had come loose on my slipper, and my wig simply wouldn't stay put throughout the writhing in the swampland scenes.

Every time I bent over, said ribbon escaped me. I felt more like a member of a comedy troupe than the most esteemed ballet company in the country. I was expecting to be reprimanded, or worse, by the director, to be threatened, or to have my contract put to an end. I was preparing myself for it.

What a huge surprise that not only did my director not notice, but that I was approached by this handsome man with the smell of turpentine on his hands. You!

Clemency Lang. A painter from Boston. Only you hadn't missed the near disaster of my ballet slippers. That you willed them to remain done up and not cause injury, was so kind of you.

And now I keep going through it in my mind, Clemency Lang, the funny-sounding American with the velvety chocolate eyes and contagious grin. Why you chose me to chat to is still a mystery to me.

I did so appreciate your admission that you are a novice to the ballet. Your take on Giselle *left me with eyes watering from laughing so hard.*

I was and remain spellbound by your tales. Your world of America, your travels, your family, your art.

Oh, how I enjoyed your description of Boston on autumn mornings and your mother's apple pie. When my ballet mistress approached us and informed me it was after midnight and time to go, I nearly had a fit! It felt like only a minute had passed.

I'm not sure if you noticed but by the time you walked me to the car I had taken leave of my senses. My feet and head are firmly in the ether.

Why on earth did you choose me to talk to out of all the girls? Why not Margot? Was it the errant slipper ribbon that called to you – is it fate?

I wonder what your paintings are like. Oh, I want to jump up and down on the bed and wake everyone up. Marion is telling me I must turn the light off but I don't want to stop writing to you.

Clem, I am returning to my home for Sunday (our one day off), would you and your uncle care to join my family for lunch? You could attend church first with us if you like?

I will call Mother and Father tomorrow but I'm sure it will be fine. An American! I'm not sure I've ever seen the likes of one in Folkestone, certainly never in church!

How on earth am I supposed to sleep? I am certainly the luckiest girl in the world; I have met a funny handsome talented Bostonian and life will never be the same.

Please say you'll come.

June

SIX

LEXIE MAKES HER WAY THROUGH THE PILES OF CLOTHES THAT now fill my bedroom. I have spent the last day sleeping, and composing a piece for Clara.

'You're going to wear a dead lady's clothes? Eww. Oh wait, that's Versace,' she says holding a brightly coloured backless top.

'I'm taking them on holiday.'

'All righty.' Lexie looks unperturbed by my half-hatched sleep-deprived plan.

'Coming for a swim first?' she asks.

Tom appears, as he so often does when Lexie is around. He looks like he just woke up; correction, Tom always looks like he just woke up, which drives girls wild. Personally I think he looks like a cocker spaniel; brown hair with gold edges, not as curly as mine but wavy and always full of salt and sand, huge brown eyes, and an ability to get treats.

'Surf?' he asks her.

Lexie looks at me. 'Swim?'

'I'll meet you down there. I want to finish this first.'

'Please, Miss, play it for us.' Lexie pulls her Oliver Twist schoolgirl face and gently places one of Clara's scarves around my neck and another around her own.

Tom watches her appreciatively.

For Tom and Lexie I can play anything. I am near finishing this piece. The first few bars had been on my mind for the past few months, but since Clara's departure they've taken root and grown. June and Reg are both okay, so I have taken two days off. My rate of pay is so paltry that the hospital is at least flexible with my hours, which they also realise go largely unpaid. If it weren't for living in my family home for a nominal rent I wouldn't be able to make ends meet; that's an understatement, my ends have never met. I sometimes wonder what life would be like if they did. If it wasn't a constant struggle to keep my car registered and a credit card dance with the timing complexity akin to a performance in the French court.

When I grow up I will need to do other work. When I grow up . . .

The house in Ben Buckler, a non-refurbished weatherboard, had belonged to my maternal great-grandparents. I really am a local. My grandparents sold it to Mum and Dad at a greatly reduced rate – read gifted it as a wedding present to the newly-weds – and then moved to a little semi in Dover Heights that was inherited by my two uncles nearly twenty years ago and these days is a very ugly apartment block.

Dad, Tom and I stayed put after Mum died. And home remained home. Dad was a pilot, through and through. We had nannies, babysitters and stepmothers. While they were still here, my grandparents kept their collective eye on us. Dad moved out when we were in our late teens. And although Tom and I have moved out at various times, me for work and he for women, we've both ended up back here.

The house is two separate living spaces connected by the kitchen with a small central courtyard where we mostly eat and play. There's also a garage in which Tom, a surfboard shaper and magnet to all the hipster girls and surfie mates in the hood, works.

I wheel the harp in front of me.

I play my Clara piece, Tom listens and nods while Lexie plays with her phone.

'No good?' I ask. Clara's death and Ross's continual disappearing acts have taken their toll and I am most likely delirious to think I could compose something.

'Nup,' she replies still fiddling. I imagine it's Tinder time.

'Oh. I kind of like it,' I reply. I look to Tom.

'It's good, Zo,' he affirms.

'Not good,' Lexie says, 'it's fricking excellent. Do it again.'

I do, and this time Tom, who is never far from his board nor his guitar, accompanies me. It's a gentle piece but filled with the longing of Clara's hopes. Having Tom riff with me spurs me on. It's our way of hanging out together. I finish.

'Now, swim,' Lexie demands as she puts the phone away.

The other thing I am proud of, aside from composing a complete song rather than my odd bits that lead nowhere, is that I haven't called Ross. Aside from June, he was the person I most wanted to see and debrief with after Clara went. But I didn't because . . . Well, then what? An interaction with him, regardless of how intimate, tender and comforting in the moment, is never without a jagged edge, an uncomfortable fade-out, a longing that is becoming brittle.

I can wrap it up all I want, convince myself that because he doesn't sleep with Jeanie it isn't an affair, or because I won't sleep with him it isn't one. But the reality is we are doing something that is hurting ourselves and someone else. It's covert, it's secretive . . . it's an affair.

•

The cooling water soothes and revitalises me, each submerged minute provides the fresh hope of the ocean's magical powers. Lexie and Tom surf further out, while dogs splash and scamper for tossed tennis balls at the boat ramp, and snorkellers duck into the aquatic wonders beneath. I opt for a jump off Flat Rock and a swim around to the ramp, interspersed with floating on my back and staring into the cloudless blue sky above, listening to the muted squeals of delight, barks and laughter. A watery blanket of comfort fills my ears. I hear a voice of distant lands and mythical languages cooing a lullaby I can barely comprehend. A mermaid's song of surrender.

Later, while Lexie and I gather groceries for dinner – tacos and mojitos, perfect summer fare – Lexie homes in.

'Where is this holiday, what is this holiday, who is it with and how will you afford it?' Ah, the Lexie machine-gun line of questioning.

'Feel free to executive produce if you like.' I stay purposely vague, because I have no details to give her.

'Is it with Ross?'

She knows me too well. Of course that's what I'm hoping. I also know it's unlikely.

'Just me. Unless you wanna come?' I move our trolley towards the stack of limes.

'Can't – I'm in preproduction with *Haystack with a Heart* then, and there's the problem with the country vets.'

'There's a problem with country vets?' I stop bagging the limes and listen. I have high hopes of country vets.

Lexie throws her hands up in dismay. 'Complete divas! Don't fall for the R.M. Williams and the earthy smile; country vets make more requests than Liberace at a sequins convention—'

Lexie stops short and is rendered mute. She starts tapping my hand, which is now placing avocados in a bag.

'Look,' she finds her voice and stage whispers. 'Near the fresh herbs . . . fondling the dill.' I follow Lexie's eye line to a stunning redhead with skin like pearls. She smells dill absently.

'I—' I start but Lexie is already making her way there, calling to me: 'Coriander, need it!'

Lexie on the make is always worth watching. She skilfully manages to get herself close enough to the Beauty to smell her perfume and blast her into orbit with her Lexie megawatt grin.

'I love how they have the mist makers here to keep the herbs fresh,' she utters casually, almost to herself. The Beauty nods. The misting device on cue sprays a thin veil of fresh water over them all.

'Nothing worse than limp dill,' Lexie continues. 'Here . . .' She offers the Beauty an alternative bunch. Will she take it? She hesitates and then . . . yes, it's on.

There's no wedding band on the redhead's finger, so Lexie launches in with her charm offensive and I head over to the dairy section.

We meet back at the checkout.

'Is she joining us for tacos?' I ask curiously.

'No, but we're going to have a latte on Tuesday. Vivianne. She has to go to a funeral or something tomorrow. She's going through a divorce.'

'So, she's straight?' I attempt to clarify.

Lexie shoots me a look that informs me I should know better and helps unload tomatoes.

'This is the woman I am going to marry,' Lexie announces with the surety of a veteran news anchor.

'Oh good. Just don't be too pushy, people have a strange tendency to not enjoy it,' I say, unloading our bounty of fruit and veg.

'As if. Don't put the milk next to the avocados, what are you thinking, ning-nong? Do it like this.'

Lexie rearranges the shopping as my mind wanders.

We are all who we are, and given a minute we tend to revert to it. It's habit, it's programming. But we *are* capable of change.

And I need to change. I'm hoping a shift in environment will help me. My phone vibrates with an incoming text from Ross.

An invitation for dinner tomorrow night to my favourite restaurant, Fortune. One of the women I used to work with, Polly, my kooky anaesthetist pal, works there now and her husband, Charlie, is one of the chefs. Ross and I haven't been out together for months. I accept. I have to tell him about the holiday.

Lexie and I head home carrying our shopping and hopes.

SEVEN

THERE'S A CAR I RECOGNISE IN THE DRIVEWAY. THERE'S A MAN I know in the courtyard. Sitting under the Barnabas tree in the area we call the Barnabas nook. My father. Unfortunately, he isn't alone. Dreadful Tina sits beside him. As usual her face is hidden behind layer upon layer of expensive make-up. She chain-smokes, blanketing the cigarette with her coral-pink lipstick.

I feel sorry for the cigarette.

Since Mum died, Tom and I have watched our courtyard be possessed by a collection of babysitters, FOFs (Friends of Father), nannies and 'aunties' we weren't related to. We have also survived two 'serious' girlfriends and three new wives.

Tina has lasted the longest, a great disappointment to both Tom and me. Fifteen years. Dad's time with us since his wedding, which we weren't invited to, has become increasingly sporadic; weeks, usually months pass between visits.

To be honest, he checks out every time he finds a new partner – till the relationship melts down. It's been a bit like reverse parenting; when he has a fight, or a marriage ends, he takes up residence in his old room. We never know when that will be, of course. So my experience of him is inconsistent, though consistently inconsistent if that makes sense. From my scant recollections, he and Mum didn't get on well either. They were always fighting and then Dad was away flying. Mum was often on the phone with her girlfriends, speaking in a muffled voice about him.

After Mum came Anna, a Swedish air hostess. I remember, not long after Mum's funeral, seeing in the courtyard this woman with blonde hair and then Dad driving us all to Watsons Bay for a posh lunch at Doyles. Dad had a haircut and a new shirt. He told me to 'frock up'. I was wearing my fifth birthday shiny black shoes with long frilly white sox and a dress that billowed out when I twirled, it had bluebells on it and Mum called it my 'bluebell best dress'. Tom had his hair plastered to the side of his head with the hair gel he'd been experimenting with. I kept putting my hand on it because it was crinkly like sand and Tom kept pinching me to stop.

Dad played Roberta Flack and had his hand on Anna's lap. I wondered if Anna could be a member of ABBA. Sadly, she wasn't, though she did wear a lace hat at their wedding and I got to be flower girl. She lasted just under a year, till she asked for a divorce and a transfer. What I remember of her was that she drank a lot of black coffee, she had very long legs, she sang in the bath and my dad made her cry when he didn't come home.

Next came Ria, who wore a collection of scarves and too much perfume. She had a deep voice and used to tell everyone her hobbies were in the bedroom.

I went searching for her hobbies one day. I was seven . . . surely there had to be some skis hidden somewhere, or roller blades, or a sewing machine or something?

Then I found her hobbies. A large collection of what I thought were electric toothbrushes and torches. There were no bristles on the brushes, so I figured they were for massaging gums. I switched one on and set to work, until Dad walked in. He said yes, Ria was a dentist before she became a specialist in fine china at David Jones. Ria also retired from sales and took up drinking from a polished bamboo cup full time. She was really good at it. She started at morning teatime and didn't give a toss what Tom and I did . . . including cutting her hair to make a wig and drawing on her face. She told us we and our no-good dad were the reason she drank.

And then we killed her.

Not on purpose. I left the bathwater on and she went into the room, pissed, and fell over. She chipped her tooth and, despite her expertise in dentistry, she had to get it fixed. She left Dad for her dentist, whom she ended up marrying. They went on their honeymoon to the Amazon to kayak. This seemed a very ambitious activity for Ria, but perhaps she had turned a new leaf. Anyway, on the second day her kayak capsized and she was eaten by piranhas. That was the end of stepmother number two.

Then there were more girlfriends I can only see outlines of in my memories: Beverley, Jane, Lara.

Nina was my favourite. She had long plaits and was Jewish. Dad dated her from when I was nine until when I turned twelve. I think he fell in love with her. Nina was smart. She designed lights and was doing a PhD in community medicine. I didn't know what either meant but it seemed like it would mean she'd be travelling to war-torn places to make sure the infants there were fed enough, and I liked that idea. I figured we could be a family and all join in.

Nina wore t-shirts with university names on the front and hosted dinner parties with people who talked and played instruments and sang. She was a great cook. You could talk to her about anything. She had her own kids in high school who weren't very friendly. But she was cool. She lived in Rose Bay and smelt like Tasmanian lavender, as opposed to old-lady lavender. She encouraged me to make up songs, and for both Tom and I to play all our instruments.

Nina is the one who got me onto the harp. I had started on piano but wanted a harp from age five. From when Mum died. I think I thought it could help her get into heaven. And the sound of it is so pure and soothing. Nina made sure Dad got me one. She also helped me prepare for my bat mitzvah. She celebrated Shabbat dinners on Friday, something I still enjoy doing, and taught me about the kabbalah way before Madonna made it cool. My mum would have appreciated that, I think.

One day we stopped visiting Nina. Just like that. Dad didn't explain anything. He was extra grumpy, but it was the only time in my memory he was at home more. He played the harmonica a lot. He's very good.

Following Nina was a collection of more overnighters and short-termers. Then came Dreadful Tina. She worked at the airport, terrorising people at the check-in desk. I think she saw Dad, who by this stage was a handsome silver fox, and thought, *Eureka*. He brought her home. Tina hates Dad playing harmonica and looks at Tom and me as though we are illegitimate gypsies.

Dad moved to Mosman to live with her, and that was that. I was sixteen and obsessed with my music, so I pretended not to notice or care. I did care that Dad didn't invite us to his new home, and that his visits grew fewer. Dad was busy working, flying the skies and putting Tina's kids through university and her grandkids through private schools. Something that mystifies my brother and me, since for us he has barely provided lunch.

Dad finally retired a few years ago and since then Dreadful Tina has been on a spending spree. Mainly luxury cruises, a few overseas vacations with her kids and countless outfits involving sequins. I am not sure how old Dreadful Tina is but she must be bumping seventy. She is like a cockroach – she will live through anything. Meanwhile Dad has had a heart attack, suffers chronic hypertension and is a card-carrying alcoholic. Happy days. When my grandparents died it cemented the feeling I have that Tom and Lexie are my family. Tom and I don't talk about it, but my guess is he feels the same.

The last time I'd heard from Dad, a few months ago, he told me they were considering a move to the Gold Coast. And now here they sit. I am sure Dreadful Tina will take our taco-making as further evidence of our lack of sophistication.

Tom sits beside them looking pained. He pretty much jumps out of his seat with relief as we enter.

'If it isn't the prodigal father.' Lexie beams, still high from her herbivorous encounter at Harris Farm Markets.

Lexie and Dad get along famously, though she says he is a prize-winning limp dick. Lexie also loathes Dreadful Tina, whom she turns to now as Dreadful Tina offers each of us a richly pancaked cheek to smooch. Lexie takes a pass. I provide Dreadful Tina with an air kiss, it's as close as I can get without risking spontaneous combustion. The feeling is mutual, Dreadful Tina moves away, terrorised by being in such close vicinity to salty hair and un-Botoxed skin.

'I was just saying to Lou how hot it is,' she says. Weather – that's a good neutral start. 'You look gaunt, Zoe. You must be stressed,' she adds, weighing me up.

'Oh . . . umm . . . not really.' According to Dreadful Tina, I'm either 'stressed' or 'well', and by well she means fat. Whatever I am, it's wrong.

'She's just skinny, happens when you're active and pre-menopausal, Tina.' Thank god for Lexie.

Tina ignores this.

'About time you changed your hair, Zoe, it's been the same since I first met you.'

'Not really. I've had a fringe, I've had it up to my shoulders, I've had layers . . .' I drift off, why do I take the bait?

'No wedding ring yet.' She speaks in a flat monotone of statements.

'Nope.'

'No interested parties.'

I pretend that's a question rather than a statement and reply, 'Oh um . . . possibly.'

'I was just saying to Lou that I hope you haven't left it too late.'

Dad stares into the distance and Tom begins fiddling with his guitar.

'Her ovaries are fighting fit, thanks Tina,' Lexie says as she throws a supportive arm around me.

'You've been examining them, have you, Alexandra?' Tina counters.

'Drink anyone?' I head to the fridge. Dad follows me into the kitchen as I begin to unpack.

Dad wears a loose shirt over shorts and sports joggers. Except rather than the carefree retired look he's aiming for, he looks strained.

'So, all okay?' he asks. He seems nervous.

'Yeah. Good.' The only way Dad and I seem to be able to communicate decently these days is when we jam . . . and we've usually both had a few wines when that occurs. Which won't be today, not with the indestructible lipstick-loving cockroach in our midst.

'I lent one of your harmonicas to one of the patients. Reg,' I say as I unpack the groceries.

'No worries, can he play?'

'Not really – he's good with air though,' I respond.

I tell Dad about Reg, which makes him laugh. I miss Dad. After all these years, I still long for us to be like those dads and daughters who have actual conversations.

Dad can, however, make a mean mojito. I place the limes and mint in front of him and he sets to work.

I get the beef mince on for the tacos and join the others outside. Dreadful Tina doesn't drink. She sips on Coke and sinister.

Tom looks like he's ready to burst. He throws me a *She's going to kill us all* look and tinkers on his guitar.

'I was just saying to Lou and Alexandra and Thomas, the guitar is one of my least favourite instruments.'

'Do you like it more or less than the harp?'

'More.' She stares unblinkingly at me. Thank you, Dreadful Tina.

'Well, maybe there won't be any up on the Gold Coast,' I offer.

Dad clears his throat, and hesitates before he speaks. 'We're having some problems with the apartment there, actually.'

'We've run out of money,' Dreadful Tina adds.

'How?' I ask. Dad worked for the same airline for nearly forty years. His super would have been huge. They have a home in Mosman that Dad has paid off, I think.

'A few of the grandkids have needed some extra help,' Tina adds.

'Didn't they like their hotel suites in Monaco?' Tom quips.

Like a bull to a flag, Dreadful Tina's nostrils flare and she charges on.

'Sydney is expensive. You kids have been protected from that, being able to live in your father's place all these years.'

'You mean our family home that our grandparents gave our parents?' Tom fires up.

Tina shrugs. 'It belongs to your father.'

'It's our family home.' I can see Tom's face is flushed and he's holding his breath the way he does when he's stressed. Which is whenever Tina is in close proximity.

'It's on the market.' Dad can't meet my eye. His voice is thin and defeated. Where has my father, the fun-loving harmonica-playing skirt chaser, gone? Who is this? Like a true succubus it seems Tina has sucked the life force from Dad. And he's allowed it.

One of those terrible silences follows. The ones that arise in situations where you're in a school play and can't remember your lines; or where you realise the woman you just congratulated isn't pregnant.

'Oh, well done, Lou, you must be really proud.' Even Lexie's shocked.

'You kids need to grow up and lead your own lives.' Tina lights another cigarette.

'We've been doing that since we were teenagers.' Tom looks ready to crash tackle Tina.

'So, what's going to happen?' is all I can manage to quiver from my rage-filled throat.

Tina, now engaged in some kind of fantasy that sets her as head of a large real estate empire launches into an excited mono-logue. 'We've had a lot of interest, though as I was just saying to Lou, I hate Bondi. But all the hipsters love it. You're both too old to be hipsters. My grandkids are hipsters. Most of them are going to be doctors or lawyers. Mandy's boyfriend is a property developer and he's helping us. This is such a large block of land it could fit a lot of units. But we can't be bothered with building them ourselves. We want to get it off our hands so we can get on with our lives.'

She's unbelievable! Not one ounce of concern is apparent. I'm squirming in my seat, my heart is palpitating, and yet I am frozen.

'Sounds like a great plan,' heads out of my mouth and I rush back to the kitchen. Lexie follows. So does Dad.

I erupt into tears.

'I know it's a shock, Zo-blow,' is all Dad can say.

'How do you do it, Dad?' I am at the stove but force myself to face him. 'How do you stay married to that? You must love her. So, I won't say what I want to say. But she's a fucking nightmare.' I pause. 'Okay, that is what I wanted to say. This was Bubbe and Pop's house! They told you when you started dating everyone on the eastern seaboard that it was to be kept for us. You promised.'

'I just want some peace,' is his reply.

'She won't give you that till you're dead.'

He prepares another round of drinks.

'I've never asked you for a thing, neither has Tom. Please don't do this.'

Dad's crushing ice and doesn't respond.

I'm interrupted by the smell of burning taco mince. 'Shit.' I turn the gas off.

'It's already done,' he says, tearing mint.

I look at him. A broken man.

'I have to go,' I blurt. Lexie follows me as I grab my keys, stumble to the car, get in and start the ignition.

From the rear-view mirror I see Dad walk back into the court-yard. He doesn't call for me, or look back, or follow me to the car as part of me – the vulnerable aching, crying part of me – hopes he might.

I drive in silence. It's what I do when I'm really distraught. Which may not be the best idea. I head south to the lighthouse at La Perouse.

Lexie knows not to speak. I park the car and walk around the huge white cylinder of the lighthouse, looking out to the sunset of another day's demise and sit.

'I think what they're doing might be illegal. Did your grandparents put anything in writing?' Lexie offers.

I shake my head.

'It's not the house,' I say.

'Of course it's the house. Your and Tom's house—'

I shake my head and interrupt. 'It's Dad.'

'What?'

'His smell was different, he had that grey colour.'

'No, babe. That's the colour of weak, and he always had it. It's a weak father who leaves his kids to raise themselves and forgets to come to your graduation and Tom's twenty-first.'

Now I really lose it and sob. I know there's something wrong with Dad and I know he won't tell me what it is. They will sell the house and I will never see him again. Because that's who my family is and I hate it.

We finish our time in La Perouse, as we always do, with a chocolate milkshake from the nearby milk bar and a cartwheel competition. Lexie wins, as she has done since we were eight and I quit physical culture for a short stint in Miss Booth's ballet school. All through high school, if one of us was down we'd come to La Perouse, either on the bus, or later in one of our clapped-out cars, and spend hours dissecting the problem over a chocolate milkshake and seal its solution with a handstand. The problems from my side were unrequited love and parental concerns. Hers were frustrations over whether Romeo and Juliet deserved so much kudos and how she could turn both Nicole Kidman and Julianne Moore if only she could get five minutes with them.

We head home. Dad and Dreadful Tina have left and Tom has a crew of young Bondi starlets drinking mojitos and eating tacos. He is smashed. Lexie says her goodbyes and heads to the peace of her warehouse apartment in Surry Hills.

'He won't go through with it,' is all Tom says.

'He will,' I reply.

Tom studies his taco and the cleavage of a twenty-something who is fiddling with his guitar nearby.

'Shame we didn't kill Tina instead of Ria.'

I can't help but laugh.

'Or Mum.' He leans his shoulder next to mine and puts his arm around me.

'That's right. We killed Mum too.' A lesser mentioned, less funny anecdote.

On the morning of my mother's death we were out doing the shopping. I was five, Tom was seven. We were near the boot of the car and I was fighting with Tom over whether or not the exhaust got hot. I placed my hand on it and got burnt and began screaming. Mum put her hand to her forehead and said we had given her a headache. We got home and she took a few Panadol and went to bed. She suffered a massive cerebral embolism and never woke up.

Tom and I never told anyone about our fight. But we knew Mum's death was our fault. And then when Ria died we knew for sure. We were forces of death. This theory gradually faded and Dreadful Tina is a living testimony to the fact our special and terrible power has lapsed.

'What are we going to do?' I ask.

'Move out,' he answers. 'We'll be okay.'

He moves off to flirt.

Our sanctuary is going to end up being gazillion-dollar apartments for start-up gurus who think they can surf.

I head to bed, my ears filled with women giggling and Tom strumming. They morph into Clara handing me a dress, which I recognise as my mother's.

EIGHT

THE CHURCH SITS NEARLY ALL THE WAY DOWN MILITARY ROAD. It's full, half with designers and society fashionistas filling the pews with geometric haircuts and multiple shades of black. The other half is Clara's family – Katie, her partner, Phil and Debbie sit at the front occasionally speaking to each other or staring down into their programs. A few frail aunts and uncles are supported by younger family.

I search for someone I know who has space near them.

I recognise the latte hair and the peaceful handsome face.

Sam sits alone. I attempt not to trip over the pews as I join him.

'We have to stop meeting like this . . . palliative care wards, suicide destinations and funerals – you really are an unusual woman.' He smiles and makes room for me beside him.

'She was a patient.'

He nods. 'Good to see you.'

'You and Clara were friends?' I ask.

'Neighbours. We'd run into each other at the sea baths or the corner shop . . . she did the design on our renovations before Max's accident. She was a smart woman. Talented.' He pauses and then adds, 'I'm not sure if this is appropriate given the setting, but that's a great frock.'

I smile – Clara would approve. It's hers of course, a dove grey silk dress with a cowl neck and belt. I decide against filling him in on the dress's origin, though Sam seems like the type of person who would understand. I settle on: 'Thank you, it was one of Clara's favourites.'

'No harp?'

'No, they're sticking to the organ today.'

The ceremony commences. It's beautiful and hard and there's so much I'd love to tell the congregation about the hopes and dreams of Clara that I've become witness to. But as they say, funerals are for the bereaved more than the departed. I feel her through her family, and her dress, but she was ready for a new adventure. I picture her sailing some mythological Greek Islands of the afterlife.

I've been to so many funerals that I've often mused over what mine might be like and who might be there . . . which usually leads me to wondering what music would be played and who would play it. And if Ross would be there. And what if something happens to him, how I would even know about his funeral? I'm nothing official in his world. Maybe I'd find out via the obituaries in the newspaper, or one of the staff might mention they went to a funeral and then I'd discover it was Ross's and . . . what? Will it be the same with Dad? I can barely remember Mum's funeral, I sat in a corner for most of it waiting for the police to take me to jail for killing her. I stare at the white roses on the coffin at the altar and make another silent promise. I have to sort my life out.

Disrupting my epiphany, a dirge sounds from the organ – fittingly sombre for those of us left behind. We stand as our collective gaze turns to Clara's coffin. Tomorrow is Saturday and in the coffin's place there will doubtlessly be a wedding with two starry-eyed lovers looking into each other for the cure of all hurt, and the day after a baby will cry as water is splashed over its forehead to save its perfect soul from someone else's notion of sin. Hatches, matches and dispatches.

Goodbye, Clara. At the end of the service as they play Bowie's 'Changes' I take a sideways look at Sam. He has given up fighting back tears and allows them to flow silently down his face. I know it isn't just Clara he's farewelling, because when you have loved someone so deeply there is never absolute closure, just an infinite number of goodbyes. I take his hand. He squeezes mine gently before removing two perfectly pressed men's handkerchiefs, handing one to me and keeping one for himself. Old school. His chivalry is gratefully accepted. I am debating over the protocol of returning a tear-sodden hanky when I see her red hair. Vivianne, Lexie's latest target, exits the church mottled from tears. She's accompanied by a tall bald man who walks with his hands scooped as if he's been digging himself out of trouble for a while.

Is it okay to approach the woman your best friend ambushed at the herb station at Harris Farm Markets? I decide against it.

I smile at her and she returns a confused stare at me and then approaches.

'Hi,' I babble. 'I, you're my friend . . . I mean you're not my friend but you're friends with my friend. Well, not friends so much as you're having a coffee with her on Tuesday. Lexie? Oy vey. Sorry this is weird.'

The woman looks relieved. 'Sorry, Matthias said you were one of our clients, I couldn't place you.'

I hold out my hand. 'I don't think I'm anyone's client right now, but it sounds exciting. I'm Zoe.'

'Vivianne,' she says as she takes my hand graciously. Oh boy I can see Lexie will adore her, there's an emotional distance mixed with a vulnerability that will have Lexie doing flip-flops.

'Did you work with Clara?' I ask. She looks like she might have.

'Yes, I'm an art dealer. My husband . . . I mean Matthias is an artist that Clara particularly liked. You?'

'I met her more recently. I work at the hospice.' I notice her husband giving her a hurry-up look so I leave it at that. Except I add, 'Lexie is looking forward to seeing you for coffee.'

Vivianne looks bewildered, and just a bit excited as she leaves. We all pile out of the church, and watch the coffin with what was Clara leave for the crematorium and the rest of us head to her house for the wake.

Just like that, her body has gone. After a time it will be the same for all of us who have gathered to farewell her. But before that we have to play with all our might. Oh god, I hope I've lived before I die.

NINE

FORTUNE IS FULL AND BEESWAX CANDLES ADD A HONEY-HUED elegance to the space. How does one restaurant hold so many stories and make you feel like you are an integral part to every one of them? It's familial and glamorous, comforting and edgy – like the food.

I can hear a French accent singing in the kitchen as Polly, who has been ensuring I'm well and truly spoilt, tops up my glass with a chardonnay that has a melt-in-the-mouth butteriness and the softness of morning dew. Ross, of course, loves his wines and is happy for an 'old school' chardonnay. It matches perfectly with the lobster pithivier I ordered.

Right in this moment, life is perfect. I'm wearing another Clara creation. Ross's jaw literally dropped when I entered Fortune wearing the dress: emerald green, silk, with spaghetti straps that crisscross down my back – exposing most of it, dropping into a scoop-waist slimline skirt finishing just above the knee. My hair is in a loose fishtail plait down one side, and I added a pair of black strappy heels from the back of my wardrobe and applied lipstick. Clara is reminding me how much fun dressing up is. I did it more when I was in the orchestra – within reason and appropriateness – but these days it's the last thing on my mind. But here tonight, sitting on the newly upholstered chair, feeling the sturdiness of lead crystal in my hands, it feels good.

'How long are you going for?' Ross looks genuinely shocked, a bit jealous and very intrigued. An excellent combination.

'Not sure, maybe three weeks,' I reply.

'Do you have to use up your holidays?'

He speaks as though he had plans for my holidays. It's exasperating. Usually a line like that would put me on a detour back to the land of promises and possibilities. But I won't wait any more.

'Ross, I need to take a holiday, I need to get a life. I need to work out what I'm doing.' I own my words, shaky as they sound.

'But . . . you're fine. And you have work, they need you there.'

'I've organised Morgan to fill in.'

'But your patients—' Ross says in his voice-of-reason tone.

'Have promised to do their best not to cark it till I get back. Besides I'm partly going for them.'

He's shifted from annoyed to curious.

'I made a promise to Clara and I intend to keep it. And there's June, there's someone she hasn't seen in years, I don't know if they're even alive.'

'Isn't that why google-stalking was invented?'

'Not everyone is online, especially not June's generation. I can't find any trace of this man outside a vague mention from the *San Francisco Chronicle*.'

'Was it an obituary?'

'An exhibition. At Berkeley. Apparently he taught there. Anyway. I'm going.'

'I'm coming.'

'Ha.'

I gulp my wine. Of course, in my fantasies, this is exactly what happens. At no point in my life so far has a fantasy intersected with reality . . . until now.

'What are you saying?' I seek to pinpoint the amorphous inhabitant of my heart.

'I'm coming with you.'

'What are you really saying?'

He throws me a look to answer that . . . which leads me to my next question.

'How?'

'I'm not going to miss out on being in San Fran with you.'

He leans in, takes my hand and kisses it. 'I'm an idiot but I'm not that stupid.'

I stumble for an appropriate response, which is taking another sip of wine and swallowing it without tasting any of the butterscotch or whatever it was Sam described at the wake. 'Ross, what's going on?'

'I want to be with you.'

'Are you leaving Jeanie?'

'This is the first step. I'll meet you in San Fran.'

'How are you going to manage that, what will you say?'

'San Fran has a heap of hospitals I've been wanting to visit, some of the most cutting-edge advances in emergency care are coming from there.'

I knew it was too good to be true. 'So, it's a work trip?'

'It's a Zoe trip. If you want it to be.' There's a dare in his voice.

I want that more than anything.

'And no lies?' I say.

'I want to be with you, Zoe Wylde. No lies. When are you going?'

I falter. I'm using Dad's staff travel for this holiday so there's no use booking or listing myself until just before I want to leave.

'I, umm . . .' I flounder.

'Too much?' Ross tops up my glass.

'No.' I shuffle and lick my lips.

Ross hums in a way that makes my body sway towards him.

'No?' He asks teasingly. 'Shall we get back to discussing world affairs?' As he says this he creeps his hand smoothly up my leg and under my dress and my cares about global affairs are moderated by wanting his expert life-saving hand to go higher.

Even through the superb aroma and flavour of our meals, I can smell him, his slightly lemony aftershave. I want desperately to be with him, alone. We kiss and order dessert.

He stays the night. Feeling Ross's body next to mine, encasing mine . . . time and reason wither and diminish beneath the weight of longing. Of searching for each other through a tangle of limbs, breaths and promises.

He's coming to San Francisco with me.

I will go on this trip; I will deal with my demons. I will take Clara's wardrobe to the places she never reached. I will try to find Clem, or at least his tombstone. And I will be in a real relationship with a man who travels on aeroplanes with me. I may be homeless upon my return but I will be okay.

Ross leaves before sunrise though his smile lights up the room.

TEN

12th February 1939

Dear June,

What have you done to me?

This was not on the cards. I only came on this trip to London to perform the role of companion to Uncle Hugh. His generosity is what got me here. Back in Boston, my own family are as poor as church mice. Truth be told I think he can smell war and so he's taken pity on me, wanting me to have an adventure before I enlist. Though like I told you I am keen to join the navy. Not as keen as I am to paint of course. But defending our countries from the Hun is something that must be done.

I don't know where to begin. I am not certain I will even post this letter but it felt the best way to continue our marvelous conversations from this evening. June, I must see you again. Watching you on the stage as you bravely did battle with your ballet slippers, I knew you to be the most beautiful creature my eyes have ever rested their gaze upon.

And then I managed to meet you at the party and, I thought this trip couldn't be any better, spending my days walking around your city of majesty. Lingering at the Tate and the Royal art galleries till close, marveling at Turner's use of color and form in morphing the industrialization of this country into brilliance on canvas. Sketching in Hyde Park and Kensington Gardens.

I have a confession, when Uncle's gout was playing up, I was hoping I would not have to attend the ballet alone. As I told you, I've never been before and didn't imagine I'd feel so moved by the beauty and the profound melancholy the performers' bodies expressed. But the stories! Why must the performing arts always tell stories that involve poor lovers who are doomed as they attempt to dart the perils of poverty or marrying the rich for the wrong reasons? Opera is full of them; my favourite is Violetta, the courtesan in La Traviata. *And now poor Giselle has sealed herself a similar fate. Surely in this day and age, we can marry whom we love? Though I don't suppose happy stories hold the drama we flock to.*

My mind is flooded with you, June, laughing at my American accent and my mispronunciations of balletic poses. You thrill me. Your cleverness, your fun, your sweetness.

I'm a mess. My feet were burning, now they freeze. Every part of me itches. My uncle noted my state of euphoric agitation when I returned. I excused myself so I could be alone to remember this evening and the glorious June.

There's no point denying it. I have the fever. I've watched several of my pals come down with it over the past few years. All were irreversibly altered. Not for the better I might add. The love bug. It has me in its clutches. Till now I've evaded it, till now I'd not met you.

I am enthralled by you. Waiting until our next meeting is torture. First thing at breakfast I must convince Uncle to come to your performance tomorrow evening. How many hours away is that?

My mind returns to every moment we shared, every glance, every word, every laugh. Now I hope the night will last forever, so I might spend it with the memory and hope of you, June. As I close my eyes I see the outline of your smile and I shiver.

Sweet dreams, beautiful June.

Clem

ELEVEN

A CAT WHO ATE NOT ONLY THE CANARY BUT THE ENTIRE
contents of the aviary is sitting opposite me at our local café.

'What happened?' I venture as Lexie dives into scrambled
eggs and pesto with the gusto of someone who has either swum
from Manly to Bondi or completed a two-day tantric sexathon
with flying colours.

'I'm in love.' She munches into her toast.

'You slept with her?' I say, incredulous. 'She's married.'

'One: she's separated. Two: I'm a lesbian and she is on her way
to being one, so it will be at least a month, maybe six, before we
kiss let alone lie naked together.'

'But what about all those other times?'

'Shh. I was young . . . I was drunk . . . and, like I said, this
is love. Three: you are hardly the person to be espousing moral
advice regarding marital affairs.'

Ouch.

'They don't sleep together!'

'And you really believe that?' Lexie continues to munch.

I look at her blankly. 'Of course I do.' And I do . . . of course I do. 'Anyway, I have news too: Ross is coming overseas with me.'

Lexie stops munching. 'Seriously?'

I nod.

'Properly,' I add.

She whistles.

'It's good, isn't it?' I ask. 'I mean, if Jeanie's okay, it's good.'

'It's good if it's real . . . aside from you being a homewrecker.'

'Lexie!'

'Honey, I'm kidding, I—'

It's too late, I've burst into tears. Lexie has jokingly articulated the silent elephant standing in the centre of my psychic living room.

'What? No, no, no, I was joking,' she soothes.

'But it's true,' I blurt. 'Ross has a sexless marriage with someone who isn't well and I'm making him leave her, and their son will be scarred for life and Jeanie will die and it will all be my fault.'

I sob freely now as the Bondi waiters provide us with a wide berth.

'Let's go through this sanely,' Lexie gently suggests. 'The sexless marriage, if it's the truth, is *not* your fault. And I am sorry, you are sorry, Ross is sorry and the world is sorry that Jeanie is unwell. We don't know exactly how unwell because, in spite of being an award-winning doctor, Ross remains vague on this subject—' I start to interject but Lexie stops me.

'Yes, I know it's an autoimmune issue, or a "perfect storm" of a combination of them, to quote you quoting Ross, and most chronic illnesses go up and down. But Jeanie remains a human who needs to make her own decisions. As far as I know, you are not responsible for her mystery illness. And as far as Josh goes, the poor kid is living with parents who don't share a real marriage, how good can that be for him?'

'But all kids want their parents to be together.'

'They do, honey, sure, and yet one in three marriages, many of them with kids, end in divorce. If your parents can't be together it sucks, we know that, but what sucks worse is not feeling safe because you don't know what the fuck is going on or having miserable, self-destructive parents.'

'Okay, but . . .' My lip continues its wobble. I fumble with my teaspoon.

'Are you scared this might actually work out? That after all these years Ross has found his till now non-existent balls and you might be real together? Or are you scared of being the scarlet woman?'

'Just globally scared,' I acknowledge. 'I don't want him to hate me.'

'If the past five years have shown you anything it should be that you are *not* responsible for Ross's decisions.'

'What if we all sat down together – me, Jeanie, Ross—'

'What, so the poor woman can feel even more humiliated, and so you can feel like shit? This is between Ross and Jeanie, not you. Trust me, she will get her revenge . . . financially, if she has any sense. And you will have the joys of being with a man going through a horrific divorce. Lucky you're in love. You'd better buckle up.'

I stop crying.

Lexie returns to the demolition of her green eggs. I watch her for a moment. Can I deal with being the support person for Ross and his divorce? I'm a professional support person, so I should be able to. And I love him, I want to be there for him.

'That's what couples do, isn't it? Support each other?'

'I'm just saying, there won't be much room for you or your needs . . . which is no different from the past five years.'

'That's not true.' I look to Lexie for an affirmation on the time-zone of her radiant face . . . it's a Greenwich Mean Time situation . . . she's neutral, bar her enjoyment of her breakfast.

'We get each other.'

Lexie nods, shrugs and gobbles her googs.

I sift through my Bircher muesli, but I can't eat.

'Enough about my sunny prospects. What happened with Vivianne?'

'We had coffee for over two hours, then we talked for another two on FaceTime.'

'She's definitely going to get divorced?'

'She is, she said he's a raging alco with a mean streak. They still work together, but she's going back to art school this year. They've lived separately in the same house for over a year.'

'And she knows you're gay.'

'I mentioned it in the first five minutes, but she already knew.'

'Has she ever been with a woman?'

'No,' Lexie replies dreamily. She has actually morphed into a five year old with their first puppy.

'So, it's months of organic farmers' markets, cycling to picnics and *Orange is the New Black* marathon nights ahead,' I tease.

'Ahaaa.' She is almost swooning. I've just read out her wish list and handed it to her with a red satin ribbon.

It's a treat to watch Lexie. For a moment, all her edges and the producer pushiness have dropped away. I want her to stay like this. Vivianne must be pretty special to have this effect on her.

'I will make sure Ross is sure before he gets on the plane.' I attempt to convince both of us.

'And how will you do that, oh powerful one?' Lexie ponders.

'*That*, is a very good question.'

TWELVE

BILLY HOLDS KIP'S HAND IN THE AMBULANCE. I'VE PULLED IN all my favours with the paramedics, Steve and Lesly, bribed them with coffees, serenades and a bottle of pinot noir. And now we are on our way to Bondi.

Kip remains on oxygen but sits up in his gurney. We pull into the car park at Bondi beach, the promenade lamps offering skeletons of light against the still dark sky.

'You go and warm up,' I instruct Billy.

Kip's breathing is laboured. I move beside him, wondering whether this was a good idea.

'Is it too much, Kip?'

'Yes. But let's keep going. Most excitement I've had in a year.' Gently we lower Kip to the outside world.

'Tremendous,' he whispers as he looks up. It's not like the dawn is putting on a show, there are no angels singing, no dazzling bolts of sunshine . . . just a softly lightening expanse. But to Kip, it is all that.

'Over here, Grandad!' Billy calls out.

Kip raises an arm to wave at Billy, who begins a series of heart-stopping tumble-dives, turns and flicks from one edge of the skate bowl to the other. Fearless and focused . . . minus a few fumbles.

'By jove, he's not half bad,' Kip murmurs proudly.

He performs a thumbs up for his grandson, which entices Billy to fly higher. Kip's smiling now as he looks at the sky.

'You gave me my wish.' He pats my hand.

Billy continues to turn and twist as the sun, coaxed by Billy's skateboarding antics, performs a glorious rise over Bondi beach; the waves are calm, the tide is out. Now it really is all that, and more, especially for Kip.

I watch him, watching his grandson and the day, treasuring the moment. I want him to have longer here, to have more days of this.

In years to come what Billy will remember, I hope, will not be the property disputes between his relatives, but that his grandad got to see him on his new skateboard and that they watched the sun rise together one January morning in Bondi.

If given the choice, most of us would choose to see one last sunrise, kiss one last lover, devour one last roast chicken, and dip one last chocolate bar into a piping hot tea.

The writer Colette once said: 'What a wonderful life I've had! I only wish I'd realised it sooner.'

That's what the majority of the dying people I've played for think, when they're not in pain. And that's the rub. I guess most of us spend much of our life in pain – sometimes self-created, mental and emotional pain – and it sucks the essential force from our lives. We all want to be right, to get it right, but what does getting it right give us? A perfect performance perhaps, but too much restraint leads to paralysis. I know; my playing suffered from an excruciating addiction to perfection.

But isn't there another way to live? Why can't we have the wisdom of the setting sun during the lunchtime of our lives? Really, what are we waiting for?

No one at the hospice worries too much about the accuracy of my playing. It's more about the moment-to-moment experience of the listener, so I'm engaged in a different way. And when I'm not so focused on myself and possible fuck-ups, things seem to play better.

Kip picks up my stream of thought.

'It goes too quickly and the time we spend worrying is too long. I worried about Betty, about my job, about the closeness of my shave and the miles on my car. My mind now . . . it goes to the strangest places, Zoe. Tiny little incidental moments: waiting in line at the bank, squeezing oranges, waving the kids off to school, putting my arm around Betty's hip in the middle of the night. All those moments make up your life. I wish I'd chosen them more, enjoyed them more for what they were. And I wish I could choose when they'd stop. I'm content now. I want to remember this, not the kids bickering over which real estate agent they should be listing my house with so they will get the most money when I go.'

He's tired now, the lightness on his face is greying. I wish with all my might his passing will be gentle and swift.

'Don't let them be there, if you can help it,' he requests.

'It's not really up to me, Kip. You can tell them.'

'They discount everything I say. They confuse dying with idiocy.'

I want to tell him everything will be okay, but I'm not in control of that.

'Kip, you deserve to have the death you want.'

'You reckon? Why didn't God create a button for us to switch off when we thought it was time to go then?'

'Tell me what and who you want and I'll let the nurses know.'

'God only knows . . .' he laments.

'Well, maybe now is a good time to think about it.'

'No, play that, the Beach Boys song, "God Only Knows", it was Betty's and my tune. I want Betty to be there waiting for me but who knows what's on the other side. Make sure Billy gets my wallet, will you, Zoe?'

'Okay, Kip.' I make a mental note to start transcribing the song.

'Can you sing too?' he asks.

'Not well,' I admit.

Kip hums a few bars. I know the chorus and join in, and he smiles.

'That's it . . .' He falls asleep.

Billy holds his grandfather's hand during the drive home. I know Kip won't be here this time tomorrow.

And he's not.

Kip chooses 4 am to leave us. I get the call at two and race to the hospital. Just as he requested, his family have gone home. I string a few chords, he stirs but doesn't regain consciousness. He thrusts forward and gulps, like a fish jumping back into the deep blue sea, only I hope in his case it's into Betty's arms.

And he's gone.

I drive home via a sunrise at the Gap: a brilliant one, in honour of Kip.

THIRTEEN

I MISS CLARA, I'LL MISS KIP. EACH DEPARTURE IS AN HONOUR and a form of heartbreak. Loss is the biggest part of my life, so why do I remain attached to so much of what is here? Design fault of humanity, I guess. But it feels like my attachment is one-sided a lot of the time. Mum, Dad . . . it seems like I'm always the one being left. And Ross – is it different this time? Will he really come overseas with me? Will he be mine?

Sam approaches with Harry and two mugs of tea. He hands me one and sits without speaking.

The birds fill the space with their early morning medley.

'Well . . . I went on a date.' Sam finally speaks.

I admire Sam's openness and his readiness to be my friend. 'And?'

'Tinder has a lot to answer for,' he replies.

He now has my full attention.

'Isn't that for casual hook-ups?' I blush feeling how much I sound like a headmistress. I attempt a fumbling rewind. 'Sorry, that might be what you want.' Now, I'm truly flustered. 'It's just I've heard the cautionary tales about married men who reside over the bridge and date women on Tinder this side of it. As a pastime.'

'It was a bum steer, a friend of mine met his partner that way.' He shakes his head at the horrors that have befallen him.

'Well . . . it's good you're dating?' I backtrack.

'If you'd shared my experience from last night you may not be saying that,' he reflects with an ironic smile.

'What happened?'

'She was more of a cocaine and boats girl than shiraz and strolls. I'm wondering now if she was actually a working girl. And she was on some kind of sugar-free diet, so the night consisted of vodka shots and stilted pauses.'

Sam manages to keep a straight face . . . just.

'How old was she?'

'I'm not sure she has an age, or an address. She knew her rising sign, though. And she is very mad at her ex, and her plastic surgeon. Then somehow it came out about Max dying. Dead son equals early night.'

'It sounds horrific,' I say, then look at him hopefully. 'Are you making this up?'

'Not a word of a lie.'

'Well, she's missing out, you make good tea. Real tea if I'm not mistaken?'

I am relaxed about most things but I am a tea snob. I love tea; real tea as in tea leaves, spooned into a warmed pot, and covered with water still on a rolling boil, topped with a tea-cosy where possible, left to brew then poured into a good china cup with a dash of milk. Real tea, in my book, is the best answer to the majority of life's ailments, mishaps and wrong turns. And Sam's tea is good.

We both sip. Then he turns and asks, 'How about you? Late night?'

'Early morning. One of my elderly patients. It was peaceful but . . . you know.'

'Yeah,' Sam replies, because he does know. 'Where are they now?' he says, wistful.

'Here, I hope.' I nod to the morning sky.

'They'd be cheering you on, Zoe. Telling you to keep playing.' His words of encouragement provide comfort that is appreciated as much as the tea. I feel my shoulders drop as I release the tensions of the past days.

'And what are they telling you?' I ponder.

'To give up Tinder.'

We laugh. He has crinkly eyes and an ease of being. Hanging out with him feels good.

'How's your romance?' he asks.

I don't baulk but I wonder at the question . . . how is my romance?

'Better than yours by the sound of it,' I kid. Part of me wants to confide every gruesome detail to Sam; he seems sane and kind and unjudging. I settle for: 'It's complicated.'

Which he doesn't fall for. 'In what way?'

Oh no, he's going there.

'Oh you know, adults, life . . .' I try and vague into oblivion.

'Yeah, I used to. But now . . . coming out the other end of complicated. I'm into simple and clean slate. Two main things I'm going by – one: they're either available or not. Two: they're either into you, or not. So what category does yours fall into?'

I meet his question with a sigh. 'Not completely available . . . but into me, I think.'

'In other words, a world of pain.'

'Pretty much. He's working it out though,' I say, somewhat feebly.

'Good,' Sam says, unconvinced.

'What, no advice?' I was kind of hoping for some.

'Not my style . . . and not my story. Everyone's different.'

'I can see a "but" on your lips.'

'I try to avoid buts.' He sips his tea and pats Harry, who places his head in Sam's lap, a manoeuvre designed to guilt Sam into continuing his walk. It works. Sam rises.

'Just don't underestimate your worth. You're a diamond.'

'Thanks. Hey, maybe eHarmony is better, or one of those sites you pay money to join?'

'Maybe.' He looks to the sky, in anticipation of watching a pig fly through it I expect, following his date last night.

'How did you know I was here?' I ask.

'Harry told me.'

'Gotcha.'

He waves and heads off before he stops and turns. Perhaps he's offering up advice after all.

'I'm doing a wine-tasting, buttery west coast chardonnays, a few from my little vineyard and some from the Napa on the weekend. At my place. Come. And bring your complicated romance, as long as he likes wine.'

'I hope you included that you have a vineyard on your dating profile.'

'It's a tiny ramshackle one in the Margaret River that costs a lot more than it brings in. Still, we made a decent chardonnay last year.'

'I'll have to check on Ross, but if not can I bring my hot gay bestie? She loves wine.'

'Hot gay bestie sounds essential,' he affirms.

Sam points to his house, down near Gibson's Beach, and takes my phone number to text the details. I look at the time and realise I'm late for yoga with Lex and Vivianne.

FOURTEEN

PULLING MY MASS OF UNWIELDY HAIR INTO A TOPKNOT, I attempt to stretch on the mat as Lex unfurls Vivianne's gazelle-like form in various stretches, all of which involve Lex leaning into Vivianne and asking if it feels good – oh, save us.

The class has yet to start but I'm already feeling the dread of the pain to come. Lexie demands we do an Ashtanga class, which is basically aerobics with Sanskrit names and a nap at the end. The class is about to commence when she walks in.

I don't know if you've ever experienced the pain, torture and continual agitation of a nemesis, but if you have you will relate to how unfortunate Gigi Maiers's appearance at the 8.45 am yoga class is.

Gigi – even her name intimidates and irritates me – is a percussionist. Not just any percussionist, though. Not even just a successful percussionist within the symphony. No, no, nooo.

Gigi is like a combined Bjork and Mozart of percussionists. She's released solo albums of her inner imaginings, all brilliant, that have landed on the hottest 100 charts. Everyone loves Gigi. She is a phenomenon. Her hair, her taste, her sexual confidence, her laugh ... *phenomenal*, phenomenal, *phenomenal*.

Gigi and I are the same age and both went through the Con. I am desperately hoping she won't recognise me, but before the instructor can say 'Downward dog', Gigi is flicking her yoga mat, drum-rolling her hands on her thighs and chanting my name.

'Zoe, Zoe, Zo-blow, the Wylde child of the harp, get here now, gurl!' Like a dog with few options, I take a step towards her. Gigi is also in possession of the world's hottest yoga body, one that would leave Lady Gaga and Charlize Theron sighing longingly (fabulous shoulders that look crazy good in tank tops, a perfect peachy bum, slender yet still feminine hips, smooth honey hair with blonde bits perfectly blended, perfect cheekbones, blue eyes, sassy lips, and high-riding circular breasts, not too big, not too small); she's basically heaven with a xylophone, and hell to me.

What happened in London was hard, it was traumatic, and it was deeply humiliating. And when I look at Gigi, all I see is her face in my hospital room afterwards talking about my replacement. She was so quick to have me moved on. Truth be told there's often rivalries between different sections of the orchestra and both the harp and the percussion take up the space of a special guest star or ring-in novelty act, depending on your perspective. Of course to us, and I imagine the composer, we're both essential at various times.

Did I mention she has a heap of Sanskrit tattoos on her fore-arms and some tribal African insignia over her hands? She is, in fact, from Coffs Harbour, but she has created this persona of herself as a siren of tribal mythology that even she believes. She kills me.

Gigi envelops – suffocates – me in a hug that smells like expensive oil blends with a dash of semen. Oh joy. She is also one of those huggers who holds on long after a normal healthy hug time has elapsed. Being in her embrace is a bit like being a dying fish struggling for its last few gasps for water before death. You hug back, she places her entire body against yours, particularly her pert breasts, tunnelling in. You do the pat on the back thing that usually indicates it's time to step back, rub arms and smile nicely, but Gigi is having none of that. The more you hug the tighter she grips ... it goes for an eternity until finally, when *she's* ready, she steps back and holds you ransom by the arms and looks into your eyes with what seem to be the solutions to all universal conundrums. She's the kind of person who loves 'truth circles'; she held them monthly (in harmony with her 'lunar cycle') at the Con and the more people who cried and 'expressed our authentic pain', the happier she felt.

I look to Lexie for help, but she's wading into the uncharted waters of Vivianne's child's pose.

'Now,' Gigi commands as she finally releases me. 'We need to get together and talk. There must be so much you want to tell me.'

'So much,' I echo wondering what the frick it is she is wanting to hear. She's so fucking patronising, I want to grab one of her pigskin drums and thrash it over her head.

Now she opts for the hand clasp. 'Your work with the dying is so brave, so good . . . it's the perfect career for you. A calling, an absolute calling, a fucking calling.' Gigi loves to say things thrice, perhaps because she fears the rest of us mere mortals are so moronic it won't go in the first two times. Or perhaps there's some tribal rhythm to it. 'It's perfect for you.'

'Thanks, Gigi.' Any moment now, I know I will be slapped with an insult.

'You were always much too sweet to be in an orchestra. Now you're with people who want you.'

And there it is. I'm not sure if Gigi has any sort of grasp on how hideously offensive her comment is. She smiles blithely.

'That's an interesting perspective,' I say. Interesting as in *I want to strangle you with my yoga mat in a fit of yogic rage.*

I throw Lexie a *Hand me a lifeline before I kill her* look just as Aurora, our teacher, gongs her brass bowl for the class to commence.

Lexie manages to peel herself off Vivianne's hips, where's she's been assisting her with a twist. The class is seven-eighths women – seriously, if straight single guys could get over their fear of not touching their toes, they'd see they could be surrounded by unbelievably beautiful women offering to help 'adjust' them, and they'd be coming in droves.

The bowl is gonged again. Gigi performs a namaste, solemnly bowing as the yoga teacher chimes the bowl with an omniscient smile.

'On the mat, Wylde child.' Lexie smacks my bum and grabs me. Gigi whispers a few Hindu words – some sort of prayer I guess. Continues moving her lips. I sit down on the small part of my mat that isn't taken up with Gigi. Trying to imbibe enlightenment in lotus position while your nemesis literally stands over you is like some kind of overt cosmic punchline.

I close my eyes, place my hands on my knees and follow the teacher in a series of *om*s. I'm on my third and just about to congratulate myself for my non-reactive interaction with Gigi when I feel and smell the Gigi blend descend, and her perfectly glossed locks brush across my face. Her warm breath, with a garlic edge, whispers over my eyelids.

'Let's spend some women time together.'

I nod while keeping my eyes closed, hoping that's enough to get her back to her own mat.

'Zoe, Zoe, Zoe Wylde child,' she anoints my head with some strange blessing with her hands. *Help!*

'As soon as I get back from the Euro tour and my "Timeout with Tea Tim",' she air-quotes. 'Or honeymoon, if you want to be exact.'

My eyes open a crack. She flashes a ginormous diamond ring before me. I'm not sure if she's expecting me to ogle at it or kiss it. I knew she was going out with Tim, the young hot hipster-cum-ecommerce-entrepreneur, who moved up from Melbourne after he made a killing on importing vitamin supplements before deftly turning his focus to tea . . . all the tea in China it seems. Tea Tim now has tea houses across two states that cool people who want to discuss blends for hours and drink green tea from glass teapots under low lighting while listening to Mumford & Sons flock to. And they buy it online internationally. He is the tea mecca, a hipster Twinings of sorts. And his tea is brilliant, in addition to being fair-trade friendly, eco savvy, and beautifully packaged. Of course Gigi Maiers is engaged to him. He's utterly gorgeous and he recently purchased a Bondi beach pad for a measly three million dollars, which no doubt Gigi is now residing in.

'Mazel tov,' I muster. 'Congrats Gigi, that's just great.' I wish I could mean it but my head is being flooded with a compare and contrast PowerPoint presentation of Gigi's life and mine. Gigi – cracking career, stardom, perfect breasts, and hot tea-loving fiancé. And me – soon to be evicted by father's nasty wife, in love with an unavailable man, running around in a dead lady's clothes, and considering attempting to unite a most likely dead man with a dying woman who hasn't tried to find him herself in half a century . . . Peachy.

Gigi gazes down at her monolithic bling. 'He's the most totally connected lover. Like, it's intense. We just love being naked in bed holding each other, looking into each other's souls and—'

Vomiting, I want to say. I have heard countless tales of Gigi's tantric abilities, including her talent for making herself come purely through her breathing technique when she is on long-haul flights.

Lexie throws me a *Sorry, babe, but I'm not going near her again* grin as the rest of the class commences their first sun salute. I remain paralysed in the vortex of Gigi's lack of personal spatial awareness.

'Yeah, we're going to stay with Jules in Notting Hill. You remember Jules?' she asks.

I do. Jules is the artistic director of the London Symphony. Jules is lovely. I hope he has a soundproof guest wing. I can see them all throwing dinner parties and Gwyneth Paltrow popping in for a yogic music jam or cook-up with Gigi, or maybe George Clooney and his wife will be there, cooking, singing, playing. Tim will tousle Gigi's hair as he brews everyone a Golden Emperor tea with the fountain of youth and global world glamour hidden within a chrysanthemum flower . . .

'Zoe, did you hear what I said?'

I look at her blankly. She is millimetres from my face, so the fact I managed to block her out is quite a Buddha-worthy feat.

'Jules?' I whisper.

'Yes, he was asking after you. They're going to be looking for a harpist while Gareth is on paternity leave.'

'Oh . . . I didn't think he'd remember me.'

'That's what I said, I mean, it's been years since you were a professional. Anyway, I told him you're nursing now. He said to pass on his regards. He knows you and I are close.'

She places her hand on my heart. She really believes we are close! How can someone who is so into 'conscious living' be so oblivious to the effect she is having on another?

'I'm not a nurse, Gigi, I'm a bedside musician,' I whisper in my best *this is a boundary* voice.

Gigi makes a humming sound and beats my chest several times before springing off back to her mat, giving herself a cosmic shake that ensures everyone notices her as she commences her perfect yoga practice.

I am reminded by our teacher of the benefits of releasing ego as Gigi manoeuvres her body into a series of impossible positions with grace and ease. No wonder the tea guru loves her. Gigi's legs rise above the rest of the class and her cupid's face remains perfectly composed as the rest of us mere mortals redden with the sweat and grind of holding our bodies off the floor with our forearms. Gigi stands on her head for a full minute longer than anyone else. Gigi, Gigi, Gigi . . .

Of course, Gigi's music is playing throughout the class.

Inhale. Exhale.

Breathe.

Fuck me sideways. What happened to my life? How did I end up here? Why am I such a wretched, jealous bitch?

Thoughts of the London Symphony fuel me. That was always my dream – to be part of their ensemble, to work with Jules, to live in London for a time. If only it hadn't all turned to porridge. Balls, balls, balls. Gigi knew what she was saying. What's she playing at?

•

'I agree.' Lex and I sit in the courtyard over a chai. One of Tea Tim's chai mixes, of course, after the class.

'You have to admit she is fucking hot, but she's a wanker.' Lexie tops up our cups.

Tom enters post-surf and eyes the two of us. 'Bitching in floral yoga pants and calling someone a wanker? Pot's calling the kettle black, isn't it? Who are you dissing?' he asks.

'Gigi!' we reply in unison.

Tom's lips twist into a smile, his eyes glaze over. 'Gigi,' he repeats with a sound of longing and awe.

'Oh Tom, please don't lick your lips, that's just gross!' I blurt and he shifts into a lip smack instead.

'What's she done now? Won the Nobel Peace Prize?' I may have bemoaned the perfection of Gigi once or twice before. Aside from Dreadful Tina, it's my Achilles.

'She's marrying the tea baron.'

'He surfs with me. He's a good guy.' Tom turns on the outdoor shower, which is a hose on a hook.

'Of course he is. Is he heading up Amnesty International yet?' I ask.

'No, but he's been invited on the board of UNICEF, and Julian Assange orders his teas and now they're mates,' Tom replies.

'Dandy.' I eye roll.

'Stop being jellyfish, Zoe. You don't want to be Gigi.'

That stops me as I bite into an errant clove that's been floating in my cup. 'I don't?'

'Nup. She's too perfect. You'd stuff it up, that's your charm.'

'Thank you and sod off now, please, dear brother.'

'We like you flawed,' Lexie adds. 'Vivianne thinks you're adorable.'

'Who's Vivianne?' Tom feigns casual interest.

'Lexie's new wife,' I announce.

'Straight?' His interest is no longer casual.

'In conversion . . .'

'Do I know her?'

'Not yet, but if you pop the kettle back on I might let you watch us hold hands,' Lexie coos.

Tom rolls his eyes and heads for the kettle. Eye rolling is a family trait. Many times Tom and I carry out entire conversations without saying a word.

'Are you working tonight?' Lexie adds more honey to her tea.

'Nope.'

'Good, you're coming to dinner with me to Vivianne and Matthias Drewe's place.'

'They *both* invited you?' I have to wonder at that.

'Yes, it's all very adult and civilised.' Lexie sits back up in producer mode.

'He seemed pretty pissed off when I saw him at Clara's funeral,' I say.

'Vivianne says it's all show. He's really a pussycat.'

'A pussycat whose wife has left him and is now seeing you,' I gently remind her.

'It'll be fun.' She shrugs.

According to whose definition? I wonder.

'May I remind you of New Year's night and the countless other times I've been your stand-in when Ross has flaked?'

I hear that and shift gears. 'You're right, it will be fun. Can't wait, where is it?'

'Birchgrove.'

'Ross's suburb. Perfect. I've got just the dress.'

'Dead lady's?'

'Clara's.'

'Nice. How's the itinerary going? Ross got travel insurance yet?' Lexie asks wide-eyed.

'He's sorting it,' I reply too quickly.

I'm not fooling either of us.

FIFTEEN

THOUGHTS OF GIGI RE-EMERGE AS I STAND IN LINE AT ADRIANO Zumbo's delectable patisserie on Darling Street, Balmain. An assortment of impossibly perfect looking macaroons and mouth-watering patisseries line the glass counter before me. As always, the shop is packed. It's a sweet-lover's heaven. If only the world were as lovely as this store. I think of how Clara used to enjoy her sweets and Reg loves to tuck in, and I decide to buy an extra salted caramel éclair and drop it off to him on my way home from dinner.

I don't foresee it being a late night; I foresee it being stilted and awkward, and I'm not sure why Vivianne thinks it's a good idea. Hopefully the pastries will be an ice-breaker. I mean, who doesn't like sweets? Gigi probably, she's too busy fermenting kombucha and soaking macadamia nuts in orange juice . . . she's also a raw foodist.

'That one's my favourite.' A sweet-faced boy in cricket whites points out a delectable-looking mini lemon meringue pie framed by the golden glow of the early evening. He looks strangely familiar.

'I like lemon too,' I answer and order a few.

'Any other suggestions?' I ask.

'Sure, the choc chip cookies with ganache in the middle are so good too.'

I admire his decisiveness. 'You sound like an expert.'

He chuckles. That laugh; I know that laugh . . .

'I live near here. Mum's been bringing me after school once a week since kinder. Now I come after cricket,' he tells me proudly.

Joshua! It's Joshua! Ross's son. Oh god . . . Lovely, sweet twelve-year-old, not-yet-hormone-fuelled Joshua.

He is gorgeous. His mum brings him here, his mum . . . Ross's non-sexual life partner Jeanie.

I feel my fantasy life shatter into tiny shards of glass. I am in no position to bitch about anyone, including Gigi. I am a fraud. A total fraud with myself.

All these years I have told myself that Ross was being kept in his miserable loveless marriage by Jeanie's manipulations, and that it would be better if the child (I would never let myself ask too much about Joshua) was free of their Machiavellian deceptions. But now, here in front of me, stands an angelic-looking boy with the charm and chat of Ross and two huge brown eyes and a sweetness . . . A child who seems loved and well-adjusted and I am the lemon-meringue-ordering threat to it all.

'That's nice of your mum,' I manage. I do a quick look around to see if Jeanie is here too. Jeanie, the former she-devil who brings her son to the world's best patisserie for afternoon tea. Images of tyrant Jeanie morph into a Carol Brady type who is adored by all. Oy vey.

'Yeah, she's cool,' he agrees.

'Cool.' I nod and, flustered, reach for the cash in my wallet. Only to open it upside down and spill the paltry contents of coins over the counter and floor.

'Here.' Joshua springs to action, assisting me to retrieve all the errant coinage. Shit, this is getting worse.

'Thanks, thanks so much,' I babble. 'You're a lovely boy.'

'Are you okay? Your face has gone red.' He looks concerned.

'Fine . . . sugar rush.'

'But you haven't eaten any of it yet.'

'Anticipatory sugar rush. Thank you so much for your help, Josh.'

His face changes into curiosity mixed with the outskirts of alarm.

'How did you know my name?' he asks.

'I'm psychic,' I blurt.

'Serious?' He looks stunned.

'Yep, big . . . fortune-telling family. Crystal balls, owls—'

'Owls?' He's gobsmacked at the Harry Potterness of it.

He follows me outside to Lex, who is waiting on her bike for me.

'What else can you tell me?' he asks.

'Um, my talent is with names. But you like Led Zeppelin and your favourite colour is . . . blue.'

'Wow,' he gasps. 'That's cool.'

'I have to go, Josh, but you're a great person.' I shovel my ridiculous fibbing red-faced head into Lexie's spare helmet.

'Thanks.' He looks at Lexie's Harley, clearly disappointed it's not a broomstick.

'Bye!' I wave and smack Lexie on the shoulder.

Josh studies me with a concentrated focus identical to Ross's.

'Go,' I tell Lexie as I continue to wave. 'Go fast. *Now.*'

Lexie shakes her head and pulls away. I wave to Josh as I go.

'Wait!' he calls.

Lexie brakes.

Oh god, he must know.

'You forgot your pastries,' he calls.

'Shit.'

Josh whips back inside the shop and re-emerges with the cake box of goodies.

'For a psychic, you're pretty forgetful,' he comments.

Funny kid. 'Thanks, Josh, you're really kind.'

'See you round.' He waves.

'Maybe, sure,' I reply.

'Well, *you* should know,' he points out. 'You're the one who can tell the future.'

'Just not her own,' Lexie quips.

'Oh,' Josh considers this before waving again as we ride away.

'Josh as in son of Ross?' Lexie of course has it all worked out.

'Yes.'

'And you told him you're a psychic?'

'Kind of slipped out, I said his name.'

'I guess a psychic is preferable to a pervy stalker.'

'Thanks.'

'You're going to have to—'

'Work my shit out. I know. Thank you.'

'I was going to say tell Vivianne. She's good at this stuff.'

'You've only known her for a week.'

'She's incredibly intuitive,' Lexie says, equal parts admiration and lust.

'She lives around the corner from Ross and Jeanie, she probably knows them.'

'If she does, she might know what the hell is up with them,' Lexie offers.

'I need a drink.'

'Right with you, sister.' Lexie nods as she pulls up in front of a beautiful and massive contemporary masterpiece of architecture with outrageously extensive harbour views.

'I guess he sells a lot of paintings,' I say, marvelling at the mansion of modernity.

Lexie nods, speechless for once.

SIXTEEN

WE ARE ESCORTED BY OUR HOSTESS THROUGH THE CAVERNOUS extravaganza of dizzyingly high ceilings, expensive rugs and major artworks. The residence of Vivianne and Matthias leaves anything I've seen on *Grand Designs*, or in *Vogue Living*, or any other out-of-date house and home magazine from the hospice, for dead.

But in some ways it's like a gallery – all the furnishings and wall coverings are subdued, taking a back seat to ensure the star of the show – the art – is centre stage at all times. From the bit Lexie has told me from what Vivianne has said to her, it seems like a metaphor for their marriage.

The house is big enough to cover several postcodes and it would be easy to come and go without seeing each other, though it couldn't be pleasant. Is that what Ross and Jeanie are like? I'd always imagined it that way, but now seeing Josh, I'm flooded with mental images of family barbecues and a beautiful woman eating salted caramel éclairs ... or being fed them by Ross as Josh discusses his cricket match at the end of the bed.

I'm snapped to by the arrival of Matthias. He seems like he's had a few wines already, though Vivianne has just opened a bottle of posh bubbles, Taittinger, which Lexie brought over.

Matthias sports freshly washed hair and a perfectly pressed white linen shirt with the top few buttons undone. Designer jeans and bare feet. There's paint and nicotine stains on his hands, a bulbous nose and the smell of constant alcohol just beneath an expensive cologne. He clumps to the kitchen cupboard and grabs several crystal champagne flutes with an ease that suggests this is a frequent occurrence. Potential art buyers, perhaps?

Matthias and Lexie circle each other, two dogs before a rumble. I sip my champagne but can't taste anything but fear and Matthias tops up my glass every time it dares to look in the slightest bit empty. He leads the charge of a house tour of sorts. Vivianne and Lexie follow but Matthias remains eye-locked with me, making me incredibly uncomfortable as I attempt to maintain my focus on his works of brilliance. And he is brilliant. A bit like the Wagner of the Australian painting scene, I imagine – not particularly pleasant, all his goodness seems to be saved up and delivered in his art.

'Vivianne says you work with dying people.' He speaks with an edge of torment.

'Yep. I play them the harp.' I gulp champagne.

He laughs and shakes his head and moves to the next work. Many of them are portraitures – some are more abstract – all huge and free and daunting. He's a double bass of sorts. Vivianne is his violin accompaniment. Though he seems to spend his time ignoring her.

'Look at this one, Zoe. Shit, don't you think?' He scoffs at one of his masterpieces.

'It's hard to tell what it is.' The champagne is taking effect. I didn't mean any offence, it's just I can't make out what the painting he's pointing to is. A cow? A disgraced politician? A tuba?

Vivianne audibly inhales. Matthias breaks into bawdy laughter and tops up my champagne, again. 'A truth teller – thank fuck for that.' He guffaws and turns to us all. Here we go. 'What are we doing here? We're like some fucking French farce with an over-budget set. Are we doing this or what?' he pretty much yells. Cancel that. He yells. I step back, onto Vivianne's elegant foot. She whimpers.

'Doing what?' Lexie steps forward, there's leather in her voice. Oh god, this is going to end in black eyes and an AVO. Lexie has been kickboxing for nearly twenty years, you wouldn't want to cross her in a dark alley, or a fashion scrum. Trust me, I've seen her encounter both.

'Eating, sharing a meal, shedding skin and offering up our guts to the gods of wine and song,' Matthias replies. I have never heard anyone who talks like this and still takes themselves seriously. I guess this is what successful painters do. Maybe I should introduce him to Gigi.

'I could eat,' I offer up. I am now feeling close to full-throttle pissed and my feet have that *pad, pad, pad* feeling of gliding above everything I know daily life to be. Everything is heard from the room next door rather than the one I'm in. Everything, including the prospect of an out-and-out brawl between Lexie and Matthias, feels not so bad. I am steaming drunk. I feel like eating Thai food and listening to Yo-Yo Ma and taking a dare. Dangerous.

'Yes, let's eat,' soothes Vivianne.

'Yep, let's do it,' Lexie meets Matthias's blustery challenge.

A chilled vichyssoise is served first. Matthias tells me he got the recipe from his old boss when he worked at Fortune as a kid. He may be an arsehole but he's a hell of a good cook; the soup is creamy and rich with its leeks and potatoes, but still light. Matthias has moved us onto a riesling to match. They are the kind of couple who have a dozen different styles of wineglasses to match a dozen different styles of wine. Sam would be impressed. I wonder if Ross and Jeanie have lots of different wineglasses?

Matthias moves an errant curly lock that has fallen on my face back behind my ear.

'You're very beautiful,' he comments.

'Isn't she?' chimes in Vivianne.

I get a weird feeling in my gut. One of those you-are-about-to-be-sacrificed-and-this-is-a-set-up feelings.

I look to Lexie, who is squinting, obviously pissed too. Thank god for Uber; there will be no motorbike riding for her tonight. That's if she's coming home. Vivianne turns to her and whispers something.

Matthias puts his hand on my bare shoulder, thanks to Clara's 'rip it off me' one-shouldered khaki and navy Yves St Laurent wraparound halter-neck dress.

'Come help me with mains.' His request has the edges of a demand.

I help him clear plates and head to the kitchen, which is a tribute to science laboratories of the future.

Vivianne and Lexie begin giggling over music selection.

'Don't do that!' Matthias yells at the top of his voice as I move to stack the plates in the dishwasher (which took some finding). I jump up and bang the plates on the bench in fright.

'We're still having dinner. Besides, you're a guest.' He kisses my hand. I withdraw it as subtly as possible, though I'm aware I look like a stunned mullet.

'Come on, let's have some fun.'

I'm not sure what Matthias Drewe considers fun but I have a hunch it involves him getting what he wants.

'I could paint you, little Botticelli angel.'

I'm relieved to hear Lexie behind me. 'You couldn't do her justice.'

Matthias laughs. 'That's true.'

'You should paint her, Mattie.' Vivianne looks quite thrilled by this prospect.

'Have you ever modelled, Zoe?'

'Never,' I answer. I look at Vivianne. How long has she had to put up with this? Matthias flirting outrageously with other women in front of her, her playing along to keep her marriage together?

Lexie and I exchange a look, I think she's on the same page as me. We are both pawns in some weird understanding between Vivianne and Matthias: he can flirt, she can enable, she can rebel by, say, dabbling in lesbianism, but at the end of the day they're a unit. Albeit a co-dependent toxic unit. Not that I'm in a position to judge. Anyone. Ever.

I excuse myself to go to the bathroom and grab Lexie to accompany me.

'You're smashed.' She giggles.

'So are you. What's going on, do you think?'

Lexie shrugs.

'They're playing us.'

I sit down to pee. The guest bathroom contains more mirrors than one single room ever should. The result is Lex and I reflected and multiplied to infinity against a backdrop of white orchids.

'No.' Lex looks shocked. 'He's just a big old sleaze who's had a few. Don't go there, will you?'

'As if! But Vivianne . . . I think she's trying to use you to make him jealous by pimping me.'

'You've been binge-watching *House of Cards* again, haven't you?'

'They're Machiavellian,' I persist.

'They're a miserable married couple attempting to untangle themselves and not lose their fortunes or careers,' Lexie corrects me.

'Well, I think she will break your heart.' I flush the loo.

'It's about time someone did. I'm sick of not feeling anything. I feel something, a lot, for Vivianne.'

'Lust.'

'Yes. And I care . . . I could really care for her.'

Lex's bottomless brown eyes pierce into me, in the same way they have done since we first confided in each other as little girls.

She is once more an eight year old sharing her dream to be an astronaut.

'What if you're walking off the edge of a cliff into an abyss? I don't recommend it. Take it from me, I live there. Are you sure she's leaving?' I realise I am being over-protective.

'Yes, he knows. They're like housemates. A lot of the money is hers from her family and she's the one who has kept Matthias together so he's been able to paint.'

'So, what's her life going to be when she leaves? Is his career their child, the one they remain together for?'

'Are we talking about Vivianne or Ross?' Lexie is onto me.

'I'm too drunk to know for sure,' I tell her truthfully.

'Fine. Let's get through dinner and I promise you won't have to see Matthias again. Just keep your clothes on.'

It's a balmy Sydney night, the cicadas of Balmain are chorusing. I wish there was some way to sit alone by the water while the others drink from their very adult wineglasses.

Dinner is fresh trout that's been marinated in chilli, ginger, kaffir lime and coriander, barbecued to perfection by Matthias.

It's quietened down at the table, and I watch the lights outside twinkle over the harbour. I feel a foot rub against my leg, but then it is quickly withdrawn. Vivianne blushes, obviously aiming for footsies with Lex. Matthias is right, this is like a French farce. I think of Ross and his other life just a few streets up. A life with a de facto wife and a son, probably a view and a home filled with family photos in which I have no place.

'So, have you two fucked yet?' Matthias asks Lexie as he tops up her wine.

Vivianne changes the music to Nina Simone and begins to dance.

'Come on.' She grabs my hand. I'm drunk enough to let her – we head outside, the stars are shining and Nina is singing 'My Baby Just Cares for Me' and all too soon this moment will be dust. Lexie and Matthias remain seated as Lexie reads him the riot act about women and sex and lesbian protocol. Vivianne swings and dips me in her tall elegance, and it's all so ridiculous. All of it – us, the house, the crossovers. I need a swim.

'Can we have a dip without them noticing?' I ask. Vivianne and I look at the other two. Matthias is chuffing on a cigar and lining up music as Lexie continues her diatribe behind the huge glass walls.

'He seems to enjoy being yelled at,' I note aloud.

'Yes. Perhaps that's where I went wrong,' Vivianne muses. 'Come on, they won't even know we've gone.'

She grabs my hand and I'm led to the cool of the pool, where we both strip. I imagine Lexie's insistence that I keep my clothes on wouldn't have included a skinny-dip with Vivianne away from Matthias Drewe's lascivious glare. We both stumble about as we remove our coverings.

She giggles. 'I haven't done this in years.'

'I'd be doing it all the time if I was here, it's divine, look up.'

I dip my toe in, the water is the perfect temperature, of course, and we both dive in and re-emerge.

Nothing like water to clear things. A skinny-dip is the perfect foil when life is too hard, when dinner parties get too stuffy, when tempers overheat. Sometimes I think Sydney summers were designed specifically for them.

'Are you really leaving Matthias – can you leave him? I mean, really?'

'You're worried for Lexie?'

'She's like a sixteen-year-old boy with his first pretty girl at the formal,' I reply.

Vivianne gazes up. 'Living here . . . It's like living in the doll's house of my dreams. It's perfect but I don't fit into any of it.'

'You seem to fit,' I observe as she waves her perfectly formed alabaster arms in circles on the water's surface.

'All part of the service,' Vivianne laughs. Then she stops laughing. 'You know, I have no idea who I really am or what my life is outside of Matthias and his art.'

'But you want to find out?' I ask as I wade and look up at the stars.

'I do. Lexie isn't the only fumbling schoolboy.'

We swim in silence some more before getting out. I borrow a towel and a designer kaftan from Vivianne, as you do, especially when there's a poolside cabana that's fitted out with everything imaginable, from Jo Malone body creams to an array of wraps and robes.

Vivianne was right – Lexie and Matthias have barely moved an inch since we stole away for our dip. They remain in a heated discussion about misogynistic objectification and titillation, which they are both clearly enjoying.

I think Vivianne is genuine. I watch her watching the conversation and we share a tiny conspiratorial smile before eating our till now ignored dessert of summer pudding.

I change back into my dress, book an Uber and drag Lexie to her feet.

I have sobered up enough to know I need to get her home to bed so she doesn't wake up as a headline for throttling Matthias in this beautiful home.

Matthias kisses me on both cheeks. His slurring has compromised his flirting abilities, which is a relief.

'You're a nice chick,' he manages. 'You don't need to be second fiddle to anyone.' He laughs at his musical pun, and I wonder how much he knows about me.

SEVENTEEN

ALTHOUGH SOBER ENOUGH TO COMMAND LEXIE, I AM STILL drunk enough to make our Uber driver, Oliver, a professional poker player who does the occasional acting gig, stop in front of Ross's, just for a moment.

I've never allowed myself to do this before. I'm rarely in Balmain. But seeing Josh has opened the Pandora's box; I'm not ready to close the lid just yet.

The house is a graciously manicured terrace with beautifully groomed gardenias and star jasmine that have been shaped into perfect hedges and are scenting the air as I roll down the window to peer into the world of Ross.

The other world of Ross.

You hear stories about deranged half-crazed ex-lovers appearing on doorsteps to set world-weary spouses straight on their adulterous husband or wife.

But this is a house with an automated sprinkler system and gauzy white curtains billowing softly through open doors. This is a house with a glow. Nothing so sordid could happen in this house.

Yet this is the house where Ross lives, with Jeanie and Josh. This is where he hangs his suits, opens the freezer and eats ice-cream from the container, and wakes up most mornings.

'This is the house where Ross lives,' I whisper to myself.

'What did you expect him to live in, a shoe?' Lexie quips. 'Of course he lives in a beautiful house with a beautiful wife,' she adds.

'That's a Talking Heads song.'

Lexie perks up and begins singing the lyrics to 'Once in a Lifetime'. I quickly join in.

To our happy surprise, Oliver chimes in as we lead ourselves into a drunk slightly rowdy chorus.

We keep the windows down and leave Ross's beautiful house, same as it ever was, and continue to sing full-voiced as Oliver drives down the road, back onto Darling Street, across the Anzac Bridge and through the city. I decide it's a good time to deliver the caramel éclair to Reg.

'I may be dwunk, but I know that's a terrible idea,' slurs Lexie. 'Give the bloody éclair to Oliver, he's a nice guy.'

'Do you mind stopping?' I ask Oliver. 'You are nice but the éclair already has an owner who will be thrilled to see it.'

'No, let's grab Tom and all go out!' Lexie protests.

'Or you could go home and take a Berocca?'

She pokes her tongue out. Like most of us, there's no telling her what to do while she's inebriated, or ever, really.

Lexie lets out a large moan.

'What?'

'How am I going to last till she moves out? I want to keep our promise not to have sex until then, but oh my god, she's so beautiful. Have you seen her?'

'Better than that, I've swum with her fully naked by moonlight.'

Lexie provides me with another groan and a faux smack for that.

Oliver drops me off and collects my eternal gratitude for promising to get Lexie back home safely.

•

Partial drunkenness creates a certain level of foolhardiness in me.

I *pad, pad, pad* my way down the corridor. It's a quiet night; the 1 am witching hour is yet to strike. I know Reg will be skyping with one of his online female 'friends' while studying the form guide.

I arrive in his room and wave, holding the cake up. Reg waves back.

'Dolly, I have to go . . .'

I hear thick Russian from the computer.

'That's right, doll face. Exactly. Call you tomorrow.'

He shuts the computer before I can see what Dolly looks like.

'How's your Russian?' he asks as I plonk on the end of his bed.

'I can't speak a word of it.'

'Me neither,' he says. 'Russian, Indonesian, Balinese . . . all on the to-do list, and I'm not talking just languages. You had a few?'

I nod and hand him the packaged éclair with a fork and paper napkin.

'Didn't bring a bottle to go with the cake, did you? Never mind, this looks good.'

He hoes in.

'What's up, buttercup? Not like you to have a night on the turps.'

'I think I need a new life,' I confide.

'Blimey Charlie, you been drinking gin?' He whistles.

I hiccup on cue. 'Bubbles and wine.'

'Bubbles and wine make you feel fine but liquor is quicker and good for the ticker,' Reg quips then gets out the harmonica I've lent him and blows.

He plays a bluesy kind of tune. He's definitely improving. I applaud him.

'If you're not happy, change so you are. You're a long time dead, buttercup.'

I knew he'd say that, which is why I have elected to visit him.

'Stop whingeing, start doing. What about this holiday you keep harping on about?'

'But I'd miss you.'

'Listen, doll face, we will miss you too, but you need to get cracking with your own life. If you want to go on holiday, bloody well go. Stop treading water.' Reg checks his watch. 'I have a 2 am FaceTime with Saskia in Slovenia.'

'How do you meet these women?'

'Thank god for the world wide web.' He smirks then finishes off the éclair.

Hanging out with Reg makes life feel lighter.

'Where are you going, again?' he asks.

'San Fran, New York. Maybe London.'

'When?'

'I haven't booked.'

'What are you waiting for, toots? Stop lollygagging and get to it. I promise not to croak or get married till you get back.'

'Married? To whom?' I marvel.

'There's a long list, doll face. I'm narrowing it down.'

I grab the harmonica and give it a clean, then blow a little tune into it.

Reg offers his applause by way of an appreciative burp. 'What do you call that ditty?'

'"Tune for Reg on a Saturday night".'

'That's what you need to be doing, kiddo. Forget the trite shit. Get into your music.'

Never a truer word was spoken. Which is always a challenge to hear. I, of course, respond by wanting to avoid any further truth speaking. 'Thanks, Reg.'

He grabs my hand and pats it. I squeeze it back and head to see June.

Another great thing about palliative care wards is you can eat cake at 2 am, listen to Marlow at 3 am, and no one turns their head. This may be the last chapter of your life, so you're encouraged to live it as you choose.

June is sitting up, gazing out the window, when I enter the room. With her white hair piled on her head, and her pale pink silk gown with lace edgings, she looks like an elderly film star from the golden years of Hollywood. Her bright eyes tell me she's been spending time with her memories and enjoying the company they provide.

'Hello, darling, what a lovely dress. Where's your harp?'

'It's my night off.'

'Then why on earth are you here? Why aren't you with your romance?'

'June, would you like to see Clem again?'

'In Folkestone?' She asks with a tease. We both know she won't be travelling anywhere again.

'Why Folkestone?' I ask.

'It's where we had our day, the day by the seaside I told you about.'

'Of course. If you did get to see Clem what would you say?' I ask.

June laughs gently. 'Oh darling, you really are a hopeless romantic.'

I persist. 'Indulge me, please.'

'Well then, let's see . . . I would like to know what his life has been like all these years. I would like to sit in the sun with him. I would like to feel my hand in his; I wonder if it's still the same? I would like to see his face and I would like him to know I never stopped loving him.'

'That's quite a lot,' I say, taking it all in.

'I've had the luxury of time to think about it,' she reminds me.

'June, you know I'm thinking of taking a trip.'

'You must go, darling.'

'I'm worried about leaving you, and the others.'

'Well, you mustn't. We're going to be the ones leaving you when it's time. I'd be cross if you used us as an excuse for not having your own adventures. You must get on with your life, Zoe. We've had ours. Mine has been wonderful.'

'But Clem?'

'Clem is a wish, not a regret.'

'I can't find him listed in any obituaries I've looked at online,' I tell her.

'Well, then . . .' She allows a small smile but doesn't seem surprised.

'Though there were all those earlier years, before the internet,' I think aloud.

'He's alive in my memory. That's where I spend most of my time these days.'

'I will keep looking, June.'

'Only if it doesn't stop you living your life.' She turns to me. 'Where is that man who makes you cry?'

I'm put under the spotlight for the second time tonight. Perhaps it's because I don't have the harp as my buffer.

'Probably at work. Or at home with his beautiful . . .' I trail off. *Where is he?*

'Will he be with you, on your voyage?' she asks in a knowing tone.

I hesitate, because the answer feels so out of reach.

'He'd be a fool to wave you goodbye,' June continues. 'So many atrocities in the world, why make more when we needn't?'

What she says is so simple and true, it resonates.

'Humans are tricky, June,' I respond, though it feels a tad feeble.

'Indeed.'

June's eyes close, leaving me to wonder what she's referring to with her last comment. The war? The nightly news?

'Isn't the moon lovely tonight, Zoe?' she whispers.

'So lovely. I went swimming and watched it from the water,' I confide.

'I used to love night swims too.' She smiles, and I hold her hand as she falls asleep.

I wish with all my might I could find Clem for her. But where in the world is he? Is he even in the world at all?

EIGHTEEN

London, 20 December 1939

Dear Clem,

It's hard to believe how much has changed since you were here just a few months ago. How can this be happening? Unfathomable really.

Our plans to meet in America and share time together are now so fraught. I hate to sound selfish but it feels so terribly unfair.

All I want to do is come to you in Boston for Christmas, though if you have followed up with your idea and are in the navy as you said you might, you will scarcely know where you will be, and that scares me terribly.

Since that dreadful day in September when Germany invaded Poland and our country declared war, all has tumbled upside down, so many young men, like you (but none quite like you) have enlisted, trained and been deployed. Each night we listen on the wireless to the latest atrocities. Word is the Germans plan to bomb us! We have been undergoing drills and practising going under to the shelters when the sirens sound. It's a nightmare, like the Munch painting, The Scream, *we discussed. Human life, what does it mean, why isn't it valued more? Still, I believe that Hitler underestimates the British morale, we are a people who galvanise in adversity and will not be bullied by the like of him. Oh heavens, what a high horse I am on, forgive me, I do so long for our chats.*

Our ballet troupe is going to Holland still, and I am now going too. To dance for people feels a feeble thing when lives are being destroyed but Mother and Father insist it is the way I can help. My feeling is they think it will keep me out of trouble.

Can you believe we are performing a ballet called The Zodiac? *I have to laugh really, of course I am Sagittarius, half man half horse . . . typical, you know who the virgin is!*

I have knitted you (poorly, I'm afraid) some woollen gloves and will send them with this note. I do hope they find you, if nothing else they will make you laugh.

I would give anything to be with you, Clem. Each morning when I awake I spend my first few minutes remembering our day in Folkestone. How we promised ourselves to each other. The shine in your eyes. The look on your face when I made you try a whelk. The very moment my eyes closed and my lips received yours. It's my own private ritual. The memory of our day is sacred to me. I pray this war ends swiftly and we will be reunited soon. Most days I spend plotting how to find my way to you.

I hope you feel the same way too.

Merry Christmas, dearest.

Yours,

June

NINETEEN

ROSS MEETS ME IN THE CAR PARK OUTSIDE EMERGENCY. HE holds his phone up to me and speaks in the flat tone he uses when unimpressed. 'What's the deal?'

He examines my still wet hair, my bare shoulder.

'I saw Josh,' I blurt.

He looks alarmed. 'Where?'

I feel the light giddiness of alcohol still working its magic and I charge off the edge of my emotional cliff. 'At the patisserie. I saw your son, I saw your house, and I don't want this anymore. I haven't wanted it, not like this, ever.'

Ross looks both relieved and annoyed. 'I can't keep having this conversation. I told you I'm doing my best.'

That does it. Tears of frustration erupt. 'And you really believe that? We're a . . . a worn-out slogan from a defeated political campaign. You have a lovely son, Ross, a gorgeous house with a sprinkler system, and, from my attempts at google-stalking, a beautiful wife,' I stammer.

'Zoe, I can't keep telling you . . . Jeanie and I—'

I jump in before he can finish. 'Are *married*, that's what.'

'Well, no, we're not.' He uses his, *I am the head of emergency and I am telling you your arm isn't broken* corrective voice.

'You're de facto, same thing.'

He looks down and says quietly, 'I want to marry *you*.'

He said it. The thing I have always wanted to hear him say. He actually said it. I stumble a bit, losing my balance in my heels. Does he mean it?

'Tell her, then. Tell her, *tell her* for Christ's sake, please.' I choke on the intensity of my passion.

'It would kill her,' he says under his breath but loud enough for me to feel the impact of his words. Zoe the selfish de facto wife-killer.

I begin to gasp for air; there is none.

'Zoe, I want a life with you.' He places his arms around me.

I speak in starts. 'You want a life with me *and* you want your other life. I get it, Ross. You have a great life. Stay in it. Don't come to San Francisco, just let me go.'

'I can't.' He whispers to himself.

'Then, fuck you.' I'm out of words and sobs erupt. He holds me tight. I inhale the world of him. I hear the pounding of choruses within his chest. His own opera of heartache.

There's nothing else to say. He holds me till my sobs subside. Kisses the top of my head.

'You smell like chlorine, and alcohol. It's kind of sexy on you.'

We half laugh, the laugh you allow to escape when your heart is feeling torn apart but a tiny part of you can appreciate the absurdity of it. I can imagine the pair of us years from now recanting the anecdote to each other: his proposal in the emergency car park the night I was drunk with wet hair; we would remind each other of the details in some seaside café over tea and time. Some café of eternity where we regale the cute young waitress with multiple nose piercings and plaits with our story, the one that seemed impossible but still worked out . . .

'Zoe?' I hear his voice on the other side of his embrace.

'I'm going home,' I say, stepping back.

He checks his phone and his pager. 'I'll come with you.'

'What for?'

I walk away; he remains where he is and watches me get into a cab.

The cabbies outside the hospital all know not to ask questions of the pale, wan-faced people who get into their cabs.

I arrive home to a humongous sign inviting expressions of interest in the house. And, not to my complete surprise, I find a poker game between Tom, Lexie and our Uber driver Oliver in play. Oliver is wiping the floor with them. A few Saturday night revellers have popped by to chillax, smoking pot and playing guitars. If only we charged an entry fee we could buy the house off Dad and Dreadful Tina.

Tom suggests they switch to strip poker, at which point I put Lexie in my bed. I wash the chlorine and the night off and go online. I look through old emails and find the address I'm looking for. With a steady hand, and an image of Ross at the hospital, I type.

Dear Jules,

It's been an eternity. Gigi tells me you're looking for a
harpist. I'm ready to come back.

Best to Sally.

Zoe

I press send.

Given the time difference, I know he'll receive it quickly. Most likely the position has been filled and I will never hear from him again. It's not like my last performance with the symphony didn't create a massive migraine for him.

I make myself a pot of Irish breakfast tea. Toast a crumpet. Wake Lexie up and make her drink a huge glass of Berocca and swallow a few Panadol.

Then I return to the computer to book my ticket to San Francisco – and I see that Jules has replied. My heart leaps up to meet the crumpet in my mouth.

I'm auditioning February 17th. Can you get your arse here?

A text from Ross chimes. *Should I come over?*

I ignore Ross and reply to Jules, set up an audition time and list for my ticket via Dad's staff travel.

I do it so smoothly it feels like the hands of many are guiding me: Reg and June, Clara and Kip . . . Mum.

Ross texts again. *Are you okay?*

I reply. *Going to bed, Lexie here. Go home, Ross.*

TWENTY

THE REST OF THE WEEK IS A BLUR. I PUT IN FOR LEAVE, WHICH is way overdue.

I pack up most of my things and put them into the garage. I doubt if the house will be sold before I return home and, if it is, there's always a settlement period. Dreadful Tina has ensured there's a major campaign and there's going to be hideous open houses every Saturday from next weekend. I don't want other people seeing my private world, particularly Tina.

I meet Dad for a drink at the sailing club in Rushcutters Bay. He's left Dreadful Tina in town doing some shopping and escaped long enough to grab a vodka tonic and sit in the sunshine as we look at the boats.

He is still off-colour.

'Is there something wrong or has Tina worn you down?'

Dad laughs. 'She wishes. I'm a bit tired, love, that's all.'

I'm unconvinced. 'You sure?'

Dad, in his typical Australian male stoicism, looks at the boats and changes the subject.

'So, you're all booked,' he says.

'Yep. All booked. I don't want to be around for the auction.'

'I don't blame you,' he says softly.

He smiles his small smile that has been increasingly weighed down with lines of regret over these past years. Sometimes it's hard to recognise the man who used to pick me up over his head and fly me like a plane in moments of simple childhood joy.

'I'm sorry, Zoe, this wasn't part of my plan.'

'What was in your plan?' falls out of my mouth before I have time to rein it back in.

'Dunno, really. Planning was never really my strong suit. I kind of fitted into the tune that was playing.'

Like father, like daughter. I am so glad I've flight-listed for the ticket.

'I hope you get in. You're talented. Always were,' he says.

'I'm not sure I can do it, Dad. And an audience would be . . .' I feel the stabs of terror of being put on trial before a large jury.

'Cross that road when you come to it. Do a good audition. Focus on the music. What will you play?'

'Bach.'

'Bach will see you through. If it doesn't, tell them to get stuffed and play one of your own. They're good.'

'Dad, you haven't heard anything I've composed since I was eighteen.'

'I know you're good, Zoe. Really good. Play and compose. Bugger everything else.'

It's the most honest conversation we've shared in years. He looks away again. I'm convinced there's something he's not telling me. I decide to escalate the honesty, but he beats me to it.

'I'll try and see that you and Tom get something out of the sale. It won't be much, you know what Tina's like.'

'Why do you allow her to be like that to you, to us?' I ask.

He laughs the answer to himself. It's the laugh of someone in a lot of pain.

That does it, something is definitely up.

'What's going on, Dad? You're either about to dump Tina and marry a twenty year old or . . .' I cannot bear to say what I already know.

'A twenty year old sounds good,' he says wryly.

There's a long silence. In it, I hear Willie Nelson playing 'Bird on a Wire', I see Dad in the backyard jamming, and I watch Dad dance with Mum at the end of a party.

I'm going to have to say what I am dreading.

'What kind is it?' I know very well it's cancer, I knew the other day when I smelt him. I just haven't allowed myself to admit it to my consciousness.

'Pancreatic.'

Shit. I want to take this moment back, but all I can do is nod. We both sip our drinks.

'Fucker,' I finally manage.

'It's not fun,' he notes.

This is the worst. Pancreatic cancer is aggressive and there's no way out. I know from the patients I've played for that most of them have been dead within a year of diagnosis.

'Is chemo an option?' I say, knowing I am clutching to a broken straw.

'Not really. Just pain relief.' Dad speaks with the impersonal tone of a bad physician.

'Dad.' I grapple with my desire to howl and squeeze him till he comes back to life properly. Instead, I place my hand on the back of his shoulder blade for a nanosecond.

This is not the scene that was meant to play out when I arranged to meet my father today. The man I've barely spent time with is leaving.

He provides an ironic smile. 'Bit of a bummer really. Though I'm not sure I would have lasted in retirement with Tina anyway.'

'Does she know?' I ask.

'God no. I couldn't stand it.' He sips his vodka calmly.

'Why don't you move back home? You don't need to stay with her, Dad. I'm not sure what it is between the two of you but it's not love.'

'Love is a funny thing, Zoe. Kind of elusive if you ask me.'

'You do love her?' I have always wondered.

Dad shrugs. The last thing he wants is a lecture and I'm not in a position to throw stones.

'Let me take care of you, Dad,' I offer.

'Nup. No thanks, kiddo. I've made my bed.' He speaks with that false bravado of his that never convinced anyone.

'Is that why you're letting her sell our home?' There's more rage in that comment than I'd hoped for, but Dad takes it.

'This way you'll at least get something. As long as I don't die before the sale is finalised.'

'I want you with us. Does Tom—'

'Haven't told him yet. Bit too late, Zoe. I'm sorry.' He laughs at the joke the universe has seen fit to play on him. Tears of anger and shock sting my eyes. I swallow them down. Dad shifts uncomfortably in his seat.

'I'll cancel my trip.' I feel the rush of wanting to find some as yet undiscovered cure, some out clause for him.

'You'll do no such thing. You go.'

'But Dad, this is it . . . this is it,' I blurt. 'This is the only time you have left. I want to be here with you. I can help.'

'No, Zo-blow, you can't. I want things to change but I haven't got the guts for it. I'm not prepared for it. Never was. I just want peace.'

'So, what?' I implore him.

'Status quo. See how I go. I won't be gone before you get back from your trip.'

'Come with me then! We've never had a holiday together. Leave Dreadful Tina to her own devices and come with me.' Dad can see that I'm begging, and he falters.

'Never had a holiday together? What about Adelaide?'

I think for a moment then I recall.

'I was four, all I remember was the windscreen on the car shattering, getting it replaced, you and Mum singing the Beatles and getting in trouble for picking some old lady's flowers.'

'Well, it was a top holiday.' He nods, satisfied.

'Come, Dad.'

'I'll think about it.'

'Really?' My heart leaps.

Dad takes a beat and then nods, keeping his eye on one of the gazillion-dollar yachts being left behind for the day.

'We all have to die from something, Zoe.' The yachts continue to tinkle and whisper to each other with their own nautical language of escape.

He heads off soon after. He's already thinning (another symptom), fading before me as he heads to his car.

I get into the Mini and bawl. Images of Mum and that terrible day she left flood me. How can life be so dismal? How can Dad not be braver? I want to call Ross, but I don't. Instead I get back out of the car and take a walk around Rushcutters Bay Park, admire the harbour, pat other people's dogs and calm down.

I deal with mortality daily and what upsets me the most is the amount of disappointment that surrounds it. Beneath the loss and pain, there's a slow sad disappointment from some patients that they didn't live more while they could. That's Dad. For all his flying and womanising, I get the feeling it was all a bit of a dress rehearsal and he was waiting for his real life to begin, the one where Mum didn't die and he was a good father who came home after work and took us on camping trips. I'm guilty of doing the same thing with Ross, and even with Dad . . . I figured some day he'd leave Tina and get to know who his kids were.

I dial Ross and then cancel the call.

I head home and swim and swim and swim, each sweep of my arms is an attempt to rebalance and soften the pain in my chest. I'm seized with the sadness that, no matter how old you are, you're still a little girl or boy who longs for their parents.

•

'Shit.'

I've just told Tom. I waited for him to finish his surf and join me on the shore. He's stopped fiddling with the leg-rope of his board. Dad would have known I'd tell him.

'What can we do?' I ask.

'Nothing. It's up to him.'

We sit beside each other. Both dripping wet from our time in the waves, watching them now from the shore. It's late afternoon and the sun shines over North Bondi, casting a golden glow over all who inhabit her glorious bubble.

We drip little beadwork patterns of saltwater into the sand. I make a well and wring my hair into it.

'You think he'll come with me on the trip?' I ask.

Tom shakes his head slowly. 'No, but he knows the only way to get you on the plane is to say he might.'

Salt tears add to the patterns on the sand.

We say nothing for a long time. Just watch the procession of Bondi beauties make their way along the sand. Their coiffed, spray-tanned glamour is beautifully eclipsed when they re-emerge from the waves like drowned rats with wedgies. I love that about the ocean. She is the great social leveller. We all look pretty much the same after five minutes in the sea.

'We'd better have a big bon voyage party for you . . . and Dad,' Tom finally says.

I agree. The one thing our family knows how to do is host good parties. We stand to head home when Tom, in his imitable style, remembers: 'Shit, I told this chick I'm into that you'd play for her cat.'

And that marks the end of our special sibling moment. Thank god for Tom.

TWENTY-ONE

I AM NOT A CAT PERSON. I AM AN OUT AND PROUD DOG DEVOTEE, and one day when I own an integrated French-door fridge, I hope to have a dog who loves to inspect it every time I open the door. But that doesn't look like being any time soon, not now I've committed my paltry savings to this trip. Here, in real life, I will probably be living in a bedsit when I get back.

I am not a pet musician. And yet here we are inside a vet's surgery in Tamarama playing for Tamba's cat, Mr Waldorf.

I appreciate pet love and if Mr Waldorf were facing the end of his days I'd probably understand a bit more. Mr Waldorf, however, is recovering from the removal of a small tumour on his hind leg. Tom, my darling brother, met Tamba at the North Bondi rocks and they 'bonded' (what that means I'd rather not know) over an impromptu party and Bob Marley and mojitos last weekend. Since then Tom tells me he and Tamba have been getting to know each other, deeply and importantly; my hunch is that it has involved a lot of texts with emoticons and snap chats.

Tamba is a beauty with bronzed skin, henna tattoos and waist-length thick auburn hair. I have no doubt she loves her cat . . . she excels at expressing this love. She has created a Facebook page to keep her friends abreast of Mr Waldorf's operation and spends most of her time updating that. When she hasn't got her head in social media she is busy making 'the best juices' at one of Bondi's swankiest health food shops. The one that's won interior design awards, charges $6 for a latte and is filled with bouncy bliss bombs convening over activated almond milk frappes, spiralina smoothies, space age yoga mats and electric bicycles.

She takes photos as Tom strums his guitar, looking handsome and earnest, and I fumble along on the harp. Blondie's 'Call Me' is apparently Mr Waldorf's favourite tune.

The vet, Abigail, enters. She and I exchange a look that expresses our joint discomfort, embarrassment and amusement at the scene. Abigail has the calm no-nonsense vet vibe down pat.

Tamba begins filming herself as she talks to Abigail.

'Dr Abigail, would you mind telling us all of Mr Waldorf's progress . . . if it is progress.' She speaks with an earnest bleakness that will make her live feed viewers sit forward in their seats.

Abigail clears her throat.

'If you don't mind, guys,' Tamba signals to Tom and me to stop playing, 'we need a bit of hush.' She throws us a look that informs us she is polite but we have clearly overstepped her boundaries. We obey. I look to Tom, who shrugs. For his sake, I hope Tamba is fabulous in bed.

'Well, Tamba, like I explained earlier, Mr Waldorf is going to be a bit sleepy but he is fine. It was elective surgery,' Abigail states clearly.

Tamba takes this opportunity to ramp up the drama rather than slink out in embarrassment. 'You say elective, but any animal lover will understand our need to ensure our furry friends are living pain free.'

I don't think pain free is an option with Mr Waldorf's current owner, who begins to wail, while still filming herself at a flattering angle.

Abigail the vet has had enough too. 'Tamba, Mr Waldorf is fine, really the surgery was cosmetic more than anything. I have quite a bit to do, so I think you can take Mr Waldorf home now.'

Tamba sobs and nods her head slowly. 'Sorry, just the thought of anything happening to Mr Waldorf . . .' She trails off to allow us to see her wipe away tears of anguish from her extended eyelashes.

Tom leans in and holds her hand. Oh dear god he's falling for it.

Abigail and I exchange a look as Tamba grabs Tom in a passionate embrace.

'Oh Tom,' she sobs. To my amazement, Tom begins to cry too. Obviously the news about Dad is setting in. Either that or he's giving his own Oscar award–winning performance in the hope Tamba will provide a tremendous amount of gratitude off screen. But I doubt it. Tom's anguish is real. He begins sobbing from his guts. Tamba couldn't look more delighted. She goes into mother mode.

'You feel it too. But, Tom, Mr Waldorf's not leaving us yet. Let it out, Tom, let it out!' She nods to Tom and then back to the camera. 'Mr Waldorf lives!' She attempts to wail more but she is no match for Tom. Abigail watches on, clearly intrigued.

Tom moves away from Tamba's nubile comfort and places his head in his hands. Abigail, clearly concerned, addresses him. 'Have you had Mr Waldorf a long time?'

'It's not the fucking cat!' He explodes with a ferocity that makes Abigail take a step back and Tamba shift camera angles.

'We found each other!' Tamba proclaims, attempting to shift the focus back to her.

'You and Tom?' I ask.

'No. Me and Mr Waldorf. It was a cosmic connection from the beginning.'

'Which was when?' I ask to divert the conversation and give Tom a moment without an iPhone in his face.

'New Year's Day.' Tamba gives the camera a look of misty reminiscence.

'Which year?' I ask.

'This year.' She speaks with rapture.

'You've had Mr Waldorf for less than *three weeks*?' Abigail looks as astounded as I feel.

'Time is meaningless when it comes to soul mates,' Tamba states matter-of-factly. 'Tom gets that.'

'Actually Tom is crying because he found out today that our father, who Tom has known all his life, has been diagnosed with pancreatic cancer,' I say quietly.

'Oh,' is Tamba's cosmic response.

'I'm really sorry.' Abigail sits down beside us. 'My dad died a few years ago. It sucks.'

'Thanks,' Tom, who has stopped sobbing, manages. Tamba begins checking how many people have liked her download, upload, shitload. Clearly she's not one for the boring tragedies of life, only the film-clip montage version of them; too many gigabytes of reality otherwise.

Tom and Abigail continue chatting as I pack up our instruments. There's something sweet in the way they speak to each other. For once Tom isn't being smooth.

As we make our way outside, I get that twinge you get when you realise you forgot an important person's birthday. I think through the patients . . . nothing. I look at my phone. Nothing.

I head back to Tom's car, load up the instruments and wait with the cage containing Mr Waldorf as Tom and Tamba exchange mouth-to-mouth resuscitation and a hug that would make Gigi proud. Tom makes his way over to me.

'What? No!' I utter as Tom places Mr Waldorf in the back seat.

Tom shrugs and smiles. 'Tamba says Mr Waldorf told her he needs to be with me for a while. She said their healing journey is complete.'

'Seriously?'

'And she's letting me pay the bill as a sign of completion,' he adds.

'No.' I am officially gobsmacked.

Tom nods and we both laugh. And laugh and laugh until we cry.

Then it hits me. Sam's wine-tasting.

'You fancy some chardonnay?' I ask.

'I guess. Mr Waldorf definitely does.'

'My friend has a wine-tasting tonight. We're really late, but I said I'd go. It's just in Watsons Bay.'

Tom veers the car down Old South Head Road and we head towards Sam's. I have an inkling that part of the reason Tom has taken Mr Waldorf is to both free himself from Tamba and have a reason to contact Abigail the vet again.

I look at the cat, who seems relieved to be free of Tamba too. Perhaps Mr Waldorf is a bit magic after all.

Sam, closely accompanied by Harry, opens the door of his classic home to Tom, Mr Waldorf and me. He greets us with his usual casual warmth. Harry is less casual when he gets a whiff of Mr Waldorf.

'Perfectly timed, we've just opened the best wine of the evening.'

He thrusts his hand to Tom. 'Good to meet you, Ross. Welcome.'

'This isn't the bad man of my romances,' I announce.

Sam raises an eyebrow. 'No? Certainly doesn't look like your lipstick lesbian bestie either.'

'This is Tom, my brother. We've just been at the vet . . . Tom adopted a cat.'

Harry and Mr Waldorf commence requisite whines and hisses.

'It's all for show, he loves cats really.' Sam remains unfazed. 'Welcome all, good to meet you, Tom.'

We enter a warm home filled with books, timber, windows and dog toys. It's stylish and relaxed. It possesses an understated quality – like Sam, who is wearing a sky-blue linen shirt with rolled sleeves over faded canvas shorts and bare feet. About eight of Sam's friends, who also match the ease and warmth of the house, sit around a huge Tasmanian oak table on which sit various open chardonnay bottles and big round glasses.

Tom and I are immediately provided with wineglasses and platters of olives, cold meats, home-baked sourdough with dukkah, and warm grilled haloumi with honey drizzled over the top. It's the perfect soft landing to such an intense day.

I vaguely recognise some of the faces around the table from when Sam and Lisa were with Max at the hospice. Everyone is chilled, and before long Tom has his guitar out, which after another glass of wine leads to me picking up the harp that Tom placed in front of me and we're performing an ad lib recital.

Sam studies me as he fills my glass with more of the buttery chardonnay that's like sunshine and cream. It's the same one I had at Fortune, which I know now is from his vineyard.

'Big day?' he queries gently. Other people's chats and Tom's strumming continues around us.

I nod, then reveal what's happened with Dad and Ross and the trip I've booked.

Sam takes it all in, then whistles slowly and refills my glass. 'You need pasta.'

'That's not exactly what I thought you were going to say.' I smile.

'I'm honoured to break with predictability.' He rises and heads to the kitchen, which is well used by the looks of things, pans hang from hooks, a huge oven . . . I follow him.

'Nice fridge,' I think aloud.

'Why, thank you.' He smiles at me curiously.

'Need a hand?' I ask as he opens the door, gathering contents. Harry, just like in my fantasies, has risen from the depths of canine slumber and is instantly by Sam's side.

Sam appraises me. To be honest, I am feeling the weight of the day in no uncertain terms and wouldn't be of much help.

'Yes,' he replies. I ready myself to sous-chef. 'Your job is to sit on this stool.' He holds out a tall, well-loved stool with a worn leather seat. 'And drink your wine and be my executive taste consultant. Harry is hopeless, he thinks everything I make is excellent.'

Relieved and grateful, I take my place and watch.

It's evident Sam loves to cook. He chats away as he whips up a puttanesca that's restaurant worthy and the perfect salve. The punchiness of olives, capers and anchovies balanced by the sweetness of tomatoes and the expansiveness of spaghetti ensure it is devoured by all. Sam tells me that 'puttanesca' literally translates to 'prostitutes' pasta', because it was quick to prepare for the ladies of the night who had to work. Whatever its origins, here in Watsons Bay complemented with wine and easy company, it's pretty much perfect. I perform what's known as 'the Zoe Crash' after we've eaten. I've done it since I was a little girl but it's been more pronounced since the episode in London and being diagnosed with anxiety.

I can be flying high, mid-conversation, or even playing, and then suddenly, I need to be horizontal quickly.

I literally can't talk; I just have to go to bed. If this happens when I audition for the symphony I will be well and truly fucked. But here at Sam's there are sounds of laughter and Tom picking away at a Neil Diamond song and Harry snuggled up beside me on the couch and . . .

'I knew it was only a matter of time till I bored you to sleep.' Sam laughs. In truth, his company is anything but dull. He engages in ideas and freefalls through a variety of topics; he's wise without being a show-off. He's like the home you wish you had.

Eventually, Tom and I pack up and head home with Mr Waldorf, and I tumble into bed thinking about how Sam urged me to go on my trip. I glance at the list of vineyards he's given me to inspect in the Napa Valley should I get a chance. The Napa is two hours north of San Francisco – pretty close really, I could do a daytrip, but it depends what Clemency Lang presents me with. And Dad. I fall asleep rehashing my conversation with Dad, imagining various confrontations with Dreadful Tina where I save him from her clutches and he gets to spend the remainder of his time being happy with Tom and me. The question is, would he be, though? He never was in the past. Perhaps we're not what he wants.

Then my mind turns back to Ross, as it usually does before I release it from the waking day completely. Ross and the trip.

I dream I'm playing and the strings of my harp snap. As each one does it flies through the auditorium, which is full of people who look like my parents but refuse to look up from their programs. I reach out to catch the strings and plummet off the stage – falling, falling, hoping someone will look up.

TWENTY-TWO

IT'S THE DAY OF THE BON VOYAGE PARTY. OVER THE PAST FEW days, I have attended several doctors' appointments with Dad, and he assures me nothing will change so rapidly that I won't get to say my final goodbye in person. None of the doctors offers an escape from rearing mortality, just different ways to deal with the pain. I take Dad through the palliative care ward, which feels absurd and sad and comforting.

He and Reg hit it off. Reg is managing to stay on at the hospice even though he is clearly rehabilitated enough to return home. I get the feeling that, in spite of his myriad of online 'friends', there's no one at home to take care of him and, for all his bawdy raucousness, he is still frail and unstable on his feet.

I introduce June to Dad, and they talk about the weather and ballet and aeroplanes; not about death. They compare medications and share a chuckle.

And now it's here. The sun is setting on my last day in Bondi, possibly my last night in my childhood home. There's a cacophony of feelings. What about Dad? What if I get the gig with the London Symph? What if I don't? If I do, I will still come home and see Dad and pack up properly, there'd be a month before I'd need to go.

Dad hasn't mentioned anything else about coming on the trip with me. I asked the doctors if he could travel, and they said that for now he could, but Dad kept changing the subject and saying, 'We'll see,' which in Lou-speak means it's not going to happen.

I haven't spoken to Ross or let myself listen to his voicemails. Once I'm away I will, maybe, but what is there to say? Images of Joshua and the perfect house continue to flood me, though to be honest I miss Ross like a limb. I miss our chats, hearing about his day. I'd love his opinion on Dad and to hear him tell me I'd over-packed (I have). I fantasise he would beg me not to leave.

'Hurry up or you'll miss your own bon voyage party!' Lexie, looking stunning in a tight black silk halter-neck top and jeans, plonks herself on my bed, while Vivianne, exquisite in a silky sarong-cum-evening-dress, sits politely on the edge of it. I'm not sure how Lexie's pledge not to sleep with Vivianne till she has moved out of the mansion of modernity is faring. They pretty much engulf each other at any given moment.

Poor Tom, this will drive him wild, though there's half of Bondi's single female population in attendance in the hope of hanging, bonding or doing whatever it is they want to do with him. I believe he even asked Abigail the vet, which makes me happy. Mr Waldorf has taken to following Tom down to the surf and sitting on his towel awaiting his return. Even the cat has fallen for him. My brother the pussy magnet.

'Knockout!' Lexie calls at me as she plays with Vivianne's red tresses. Vivianne stands up and claps and squeals, tossing her sophistication aside for a moment of girly gaiety.

Clara has outdone herself for me. I am wearing a royal blue shot-silk Sonia Rykiel dress with a boat neck, three-quarter fitted sleeves and a full skirt. It's a bit like something from a Grace Kelly movie – Clara actually referred to it as 'the Grace Kelly' in her journal; she wanted to wear it on the Riviera. I figure the north of Bondi will meet her approval. I am completely over-dressed but I figure that now is as good as any time. I've piled my hair on top of my head with a few random ringlets breaking free. I've even applied some lip gloss and bought a new pair of heels. I feel feminine.

Dad enters and wolf-whistles. 'I forgot to say, Tina's girls wanted to come too.'

'Did they bring plans for the mega construction?' quips Lexie, who jumps up and kisses his cheek. 'You look all right, for an oldie,' she jokes. I've told Lexie about Dad's cancer but she knows not to say anything. And she knows not teasing him would make him wonder what's going on.

Lexie introduces Dad to Vivianne, at whom he marvels, of course, and then we head out into the backyard, where Tom hands us each a lychee martini. We've covered the courtyard with fairy lights, which we turn on as the sky retires from pink to lavender and night descends with a huge moon lighting the Tasman sea over the back fence. Most nights I hear the waves crash against the rock face; that's what the word Bondi means, the sound of crashing waves. Oh how I will miss this.

But for tonight the fairy lights shine, the candles twinkle, fire twirlers turn their waves of pretty flame on the cliff's edge. Music plays, people gather ... North Bondi still maintains a great sense of community and our neighbours, both the transient and longstanding ones, are always up for a gathering. It's never hard to draw a crowd when you live in Ben Buckler. It feels like we're farewelling not just me for a short voyage, and not just Dad for his longer one, but this tumbledown cottage that's hosted so many afternoons and parties for us all: my fifth birthday with the melted ice-cream cake, Mum's wake, Tom's thirteenth birthday (to which he invited all the girls from the girls' school up the road and most of them turned up), my bat mitzvah that Bubbe and Nina helped me with when I decided to pursue my Jewish heritage, eighteenths, twenty-firsts, beginnings of school, endless summers all celebrated in our ramshackle courtyard ... not to mention Dad's wedding parties (regardless of how bad the marriages turned out to be, the wedding parties were always knockouts – one went on for days, involved multiple skinny-dips down at the rocks and a makeshift raft that Tom and his mates made out of milk crates). Measles, crushes, hours on the phone to Lexie, marathon Monopoly sessions with Tom; and the playing, all the playing, the songs we learnt, the practice for the Con and the symphony, all the music I've written – it all happened here in this weatherboard haven. And now it's going. This time next year it will be in a skip bin as builders listening to Fleetwood Mac work through the plans of some excited architect.

As if picking up on my nostalgic moment, Dreadful Tina enters. She has gone out on a limb with the sequins this evening and her hair has been straightened in an Anjelica Huston style. I think she'd be more comfortable wearing a crown.

She holds her cheek out for me to kiss. I can't do it. Not even an air one. I step back. I don't want to see her. She knows it.

'You're going to miss this place.' She eyeballs me. I nod, it seems the nicest thing Tina has said in an age. Obvious but nice.

'The girls like your dress. I don't think it's the best cut for you.'

'Thanks.' Why can't she leave me alone?

She takes her time. Lights a cigarette. 'I'm not an idiot, Zoe. I know your dad's unwell.'

I sip my lychee martini. 'Okay,' is all I manage.

'He won't be travelling overseas. Not unless I'm with him. We have Fiji with the girls after the auction.'

It's too much. 'Well, heaven forbid we interfere with you and *the girls*, Tina.'

'You don't like me, Zoe.' Tina maintains her monotone but her eyes widen slightly.

'I don't even know you, Tina.' A bubble of exasperation surrounds my words. My cheeks heat, I feel my feet digging into my shoes as the heels sink slightly into the earth beneath. 'You never gave Tom or me a chance.'

'It's nothing personal, you know.'

I laugh at her absurdity. 'I'm your stepdaughter! How can it not be *personal*?'

'I have my family. Lou joined it. I look after what's mine. You and Tom have your own club.' She continues speaking as if she's announcing departure times for flights.

'We have our own *family*, actually, that Dad is part of – or doesn't that count?'

'He was pretty neglectful before I came along. Men are like that, they will go with the woman.' There's an edge of triumph in her voice now.

I'm stunned and I'm stung by her words, mostly because, in the case of my dad, they ring true. It's not all Tina's fault. Sure, she's an ignorant, opportunistic bitch with an air of kryptonite, but the case for Lou being father of the year was never on the table. No matter how much I wished it was different, he'd abdicated long before she arrived.

'He *is* really sick,' I tell her. 'He deserves to have the life he wants now.'

'He does have the life he wants. It's just not the one you and Tom want. He didn't choose you,' Dreadful Tina announces.

I want desperately to slap her. For her nastiness, her coldness, her greed. Sometimes I wish I wasn't raised with manners.

'Use an ashtray for your cigarette, please,' is all I manage as I turn away.

I spot Sam, looking dapper in a linen blazer with t-shirt and jeans. He approaches with a box. He looks at me with concern in a way that opens the floodgates.

'So glad you made it.' I try and smile between tears.

'Evidently,' Sam says gently. He places the box down and envelops me in a hug. Snot and tears pour out of me. He hands me another perfectly pressed handkerchief.

'Who does these anyway?' I gurgle as I blow and wipe.

'Rina, up at the laundromat in Vaucluse. My mother gives me a hanky every Christmas, birthday, funeral, Easter, firecracker night or time we change prime ministers . . . you could say I have a backlog. I can give you some if you like?'

That makes me laugh, which makes me cry.

'What's happened?' he asks.

'Dreadful Tina.'

'The dragon lady with the sequins?' he asks, looking around the rather large gathering that has now sprawled through the front and back yards and is spiralling through the house.

'She knows about Dad and she . . . she's so mean.'

'Well,' Sam offers, 'we have options. We can organise to have her dealt with, or I can spike her drink, or I'm sure if we remove her make-up she will run back under the bridge where she lives.'

'She lives in Mosman. And she's selling our house.'

'Are you sure she's the one you're upset with?' Sam says gently.

Lexie, armed with fresh martinis and Vivianne looking wide-eyed, join us.

'It's her hopeless dad she should be raging against – not the she-devil. But now he gets terminal sympathy. Lou doesn't know shit about being a good dad.'

Vivianne, in a fit of exuberance, throws her arms around me, catching my hand and stroking it rapturously. 'Zoe, you're so beautiful, a Botticelli angel and your skin, it's so soft, the skin on your hands, it's the softest skin I've ever felt, ever, oh this is

the best night, thank you, I am so glad we're all here together.'
She hugs me and begins playing with my hair.

I throw Lexie a *what's happening* look.

'Vivianne's decided she is taking the night off, she's always
kept it together for Matthias, but now . . .'

'I love you, Lexie,' she says solemnly to Lexie.

'E?' I query. Sam laughs.

Lexie nods. 'Just a half.'

'And the other half?'

Lexie smiles innocently.

Oh boy. Lexie and Vivianne launch into each other, feeling
each other's hands and looking deeply into each other's eyes.

'I was hoping it was the martinis,' Sam says taking another
sip of his and looking in it longingly.

'Let's lie on the grass and feel each blade caress our skin.'
Vivianne sighs and, before there's time for a response, they
are down gasping in awe at the gifts the prickly bald grass has
provided.

Sam picks up the box and hands it to me.

'Bon voyage gift.'

It's four beautifully wrapped bottles of wine, each with a
separate tag with a suggestion of when and where it should be
consumed. The first one says: *While eating clam chowder in San
Francisco with a view of the Golden Gate Bridge.* The second,
a bottle of bubbles: *Atop the Empire State Building, if they let
you . . . otherwise switch to bottle three and save the bubbles for
London to celebrate your brilliant audition.* The next is a bottle
of Tasmanian pinot noir, my favourite: *When you need a taste of*

warmth. And the final is another stunning champagne: *So you can continue celebrations in London . . . a bottle of chardonnay awaits you upon your arrival home to debrief. Play like you did for us in the hospital and you'll smash it, Zoe. Don't worry so much, it will all work out. All the best, Sam x*

I choke up. 'You've become a really good friend, Sam, thank you.'

'Same,' he replies and provides a deep bear hug. He smells like fresh laundry, leather and toasty crumpets; almost sandalwoody but not in a fire-twirling feral way.

I'm interrupted by the ecstatic lesbians, who decide it's time to dance. Now.

'Donna Summer!' Vivianne yelps. 'I feel love!'

'You certainly do,' I reply as she skips off to ambush Tom and the stereo system. Lexie, whose pupils have expanded to two chocolate saucers, looks after her.

'My bride.' She sighs.

'There's no rush, Lex,' I remind her.

'Give me a month and we'll be knocking on Tom's door with a turkey baster,' she replies, nodding proudly.

I pull a face as Sam laughs. Then I look closely at my best friend. 'Really?'

'She's the one, and that's not just the e; you know that, Zo.'

'I know.' We share our smile. A smile that only truly best friends can share.

'And I love *you*, Zoe Wylde,' she says as she headlocks me in a sisterly embrace. 'Love your guts, love your talent, love, love,

love you . . . and you too, Sam. I don't know you, but I love you . . . Okay, *that* may be the e talking,' she concludes.

'I'm okay with that.' Sam chuckles.

Disco erupts to mixed cries of dismay and glee.

'Oh yeah!' Lexie, a phenomenal dancer, makes her move to the centre of the yard and struts her stuff. Vivianne joins her, and men from three suburbs away seem to gather around to watch.

Sam grabs my hand. 'When on thin ice,' he says and spins me round, literally sweeping me off my feet. For that moment I am carefree and joy-filled and present . . . I see Dad watching and laughing. Pretty soon everyone is up, including Tom with an unknown young woman in a playsuit. Sam and I take a break and I decide to get Dad up. As I approach, I realise he's talking to Tina's granddaughter . . . he doesn't look tortured, he looks happy, so does she. There's an ease and an intimacy as they nod along with each other; they look like a family. Because as hard as it is for me to see it, they are. They are the family he chose. My stomach drops but they've already seen me. He doesn't speak but takes my hand and dances with me.

'Do you remember when you used to dance with me here in the backyard?' I ask.

'Mostly,' he says and turns me.

That isn't the response I was hoping for. 'Mostly?'

'Don't take it the wrong way, Zo . . .'

'Okay . . .' I attempt a light tone as we keep dancing, but I have an urge to push what I seem unable to restrain.

'What about when Tom sleepwalked to the garbage bin and thought it was his beanbag?'

'Kind of.' He stumbles.

'Or when you came home drunk and Mum was mad and put zinc cream on your toothbrush?' My voice is tight and rising with anger.

He grows awkward. 'Not really.'

'Or the night I lost my front tooth, or the day Mum got her hair permed and you said she looked beautiful even though she looked a bit like one of those Afghan dogs. Do you remember, Dad?'

We've stopped dancing.

'It's too hard, Zoe. I'm sorry.'

'For what? Neglecting us, abandoning us or not loving us enough?'

He hesitates and won't meet my eye. 'All of it.'

I'm winded.

'You and Tom, you're your mother's children.' He speaks slowly as pain rises in his own voice.

'We're yours too, Dad.'

'I know you hate Tina, but she and the girls, they don't remind me of anything. It's just . . . easier. I'm sorry.'

I nod. I pushed and I got my answer, the one Tom's known for years but I refused to admit. Now it's unavoidable.

'I'm sorry, Zo-blow. I love you, kiddo. You'll land on your feet . . . you always have.' He kisses my forehead. 'I'm tired, I might sit down for a while, hey.'

'Okay.' I try to smile but all the joy has been knocked out of me. I see Sam in my peripheral vision, he's standing still watching us both. I can't look at him. I feel too ashamed.

Dad wanders into the house. I turn so I can go and scream somewhere alone but instead I'm met by Ross, looking bemused.

'What's going on?' he asks.

'We're having a party,' I say numbly. 'Bon voyage for me, goodbye life for Dad and goodbye house for all of us.'

He absorbs this, wipes his mouth and chin with his hand, a move he makes when he's tired and frustrated.

'Why haven't you called me back?'

'I have nothing to say to you, Ross.' And in that moment I know this to be true.

'Well, you could at least call me to tell me that, or that you hate me . . . Your dad's sick?'

'Pancreatic cancer.'

'Shit, baby, I'm sorry.'

'I think he's relieved. He hasn't done so well at living multiple lives. Use him as a cautionary tale if you like. I'm getting a drink.'

Ross follows me to the kitchen, grabs my hand and leads me to my bedroom, which when we open the door, we discover is being well and truly optimised by the sonorous sounds of Lexie and Vivianne exploring each other's naked flesh.

'Sorry.' I close the door and lean against it, banging my head gently and repeatedly. *Just get on the plane, Zoe, get on the plane and never come back. Move to Positano and take up tai chi or go to the abbey in Jamberoo, or become a rabbi in upstate New York. Just get out and get away from everyone.*

'Zoe?' Ross's voice sounds light years away.

'What?' I travel through the quantum planes of oversized mattresses, searching for the pea of reality.

'You're really pale.' He feels my forehead and the cool calm of his hand makes me knock my head against the door again.

I push past him and head outside to the back fence, again. He follows but we're interrupted by the sounds of tribal drums and a triangle. I know its source immediately.

'You have got to be fucking kidding me,' I utter, feeling split from myself.

I turn to see the one and only Gigi Maiers setting up for a jam in the backyard. She spies me too and begins the chant: 'Zoe, Zoe, Zo-blow Wylde child of the harp, come heeere, gurl.' She drums faster and faster till everyone has joined her in a drum roll.

I'm thrust forward by the crowd . . . and am accosted by another full-body hug and a kiss on the lips by Gigi, who holds my head in her hands like I am her beloved newly born child.

'Angel, my angel,' she whispers – in a way that ensures everyone hears.

'Hi Gigi.'

'When Tom told Tea Tim you're off to London, I knew the universe had provided me with her answer.'

Everyone leans forward a little.

'Oh . . . okay. What was the question?'

'Do I have the big wedding that everyone is urging me to have? Or, do I take Tea Tim to the tribe in Papua New Guinea who have anointed Tea Tim and me as king and queen of their tribe by way of thanks for assisting them with their artisan recycling program? And have something so much more sacred, private, so much more us, much more us, so much more us.'

'Mazel tov. Sounds good,' I muster, unsure of what she's actually said.

'Thus allowing me to be present for the celebration of Zoe returning to her musical fold, her family, her home. And meeting her in London and helping her prepare for her audition with the London Symphony.'

'Wow,' I stammer.

'Who's my gurl?' she calls as she meshes me in another crushing hug.

There's applause from the guests.

Gigi performs a series of tribal howls and concludes with: 'Zoe, Zoe, Zoe Wylde child, let's play!'

I throw Tom a death stare; he smiles and begins plucking the guitar. My harp appears compliments of a ruffled-looking Lexie and a glowing Vivianne.

Gigi takes her place at the percussions, while Dad holds his harmonica, and his eyes hold her cleavage. Tina smokes, her granddaughters attempt to be subtle as they make mental notes on potential floor plans. Ross and Sam and Abigail the vet chat amicably.

There is nowhere to run. Lexie takes her place as lead vocalist and, figuring I have absolutely nothing to lose here in my backyard, I join in the music as a version of Neil Young's 'Heart of Gold' which I transcribed years ago for harp sounds out. We follow this with Nick Cave's 'Into My Arms'. I can't look at Dad, or Ross. I can't look anywhere. I focus on my playing like it's all there is.

No wonder I like fridges; I feel like one has fallen on my head. Dad cannot love me like I need – never could – and there will be no happy ever after in this tale. He can't be made to feel something he killed so long ago, because of someone I killed. Mum.

The song finishes – Lexie has a sweet voice, and everyone minus Tina joined in on the chorus.

Gigi, who I have to admit did an outstanding job on both songs with her percussion, recites a Rumi poem – of course she does – and makes us unite in a 'circle of love'. Ironic, really. She leads, hugging everyone to within an inch of their life, and it does make me laugh watching her capture Tina; fearlessly Gigi plunges through the layers of cosmetics to kiss her actual cheek.

I can hear Tina calling in a panic. 'Lou, Lou, I was just saying to the girls it's time we got going, singalongs aren't for us.'

Locked in Gigi's grip, I make my way around, accepting everyone's love and goodwill . . . and then I come to Dad. All I can do is cry. Everyone reads it as a lovely intimate father and daughter moment. But, as we hold each other, we know that it's a commiserative embrace of regret. I look up and see Ross heading off into the night. He stops, turns, catches my eye and holds his hand up in a still salute of farewell. How can so much pain be so completely anticlimactic, so the opposite of what made our hopes soar?

How can life be so disappointing?

The party continues – I perform customary chats, Sam farewells me with a warm, strong embrace, and says nothing about what he witnessed with Dad and me. He tells me he's proud of me. Then, as people settle in for the night, I escape to the sanctuary of my bedroom, now free of the loved-up lesbians. I turn, as I always do at times of fear and loss, to my music collection. I play a Wings LP that my parents used to like, and I fall asleep to it. *Open the door and let me in.* I dream of fire twirlers and Sam's son Max teaching me to catch a spinning globe in a sunny playing field of eternity.

TWENTY-THREE

London, February 14th, 1941

Dear Clem,

Happy Saint Valentine's Day dearest. Sometimes it feels like this war will never end. It's been over a year since I have heard from you and my last letter was returned. I can't stand to think of what might have happened. I feel selfish for missing you so much. Missing your eyes reading my words and responding to them. Miss seeing your words that so beautifully capture your experiences travel over the Atlantic and find me and make me believe that there is hope in these terrible times once more.

I pray to God you are okay.

You won't believe what's happened. I went on tour, as I told you I would and while we were in Holland, at

The Hague, the Germans invaded via parachutes! We had three days of being held hostage before we were smuggled out as stowaways via the stinking hold of a cargo ship. Clem, I can't tell you, it was terrifying. What horrified me the most was the thought of not seeing you again.

Now our company dances around England, through the air raids, I think it brings some kind of relief. I love that ballet is no longer for the tiara wearers, though we are performing seven nights a week. We have to always keep an ear out for the whistles, not wolf-whistles! One means we must be careful, two means get to the shelter and three means scramble to the stairs. I am literally dancing through the Blitz. My heart pounds onstage as much as when I come off, but I do believe it offers a service of sorts.

I've also been assisting as a nurse, mainly rolling bandages and holding hands. Nothing like what I imagine you're doing. Anti-submarine Warfare Unit, Boston, is where I have been addressing your letters.

Oh, Clem, every day I still hope I will hear from you, that you are safe. I am desperate for this war to end and yet I curse each day that passes for removing me further from you.

The mail is erratic, we are always on the move. There is so much I long to share with you but another performance beckons.

I hope this letter finds its way to you. Please, whatever else is happening, know my thoughts and prayers are with you.

Yours,

June

TWENTY-FOUR

I HADN'T ANTICIPATED ABIGAIL THE VET BEING THE ONE TO drive me to the airport the following morning, but when I awake to the detritus of the party, she's sitting at the table with a pot of tea in front of her and sporting Tom's PJs. How this came about I have no idea; Tom was last seen lip-locking with a fire twirler.

Abigail – Abi, it seems – remains unruffled. She wraps her hands around one of my Bubbe's china teacups, her legs crossed under her. She suits this place. I hope she will hang out with Tom while I'm away, these next few weeks of open houses won't be fun. Tina's granddaughter let it slip that they've had a handful of offers already, so chances of it actually going to auction are slim to nil.

We eat crumpets with honey and chat. Abi is forty, divorced and in no hurry to enter another relationship. I lend her some togs and we head down for a swim. There's a warm wind that heralds bushfires and the need for shade ... strange to think that I'm about to be on the other side of the globe, rugging up, watching snowflakes fall.

I return home, prep my harp for the journey, shower and pack the last of my things. Right on the dot, Lexie appears, Vivianne still entwined with her, both still slightly heightened and feeling the love. I take one look at Lexie studying the pattern of the china teacup in awe.

'You can't drive me,' I say.

'Agree ...' She pulls me aside as Vivianne shares her enthusiasm for Mr Waldorf, and life in general.

'Best sex of my life ... universes exploded, new galaxies were formed.' She is starry-eyed.

'Yay, sounds cosmic and chemically enhanced,' I reply.

But Lexie is on a roll. 'Come on, Zoe, you've had sex like that, haven't you?'

Damn her for reminding me. 'Yes, and it's got me heading overseas alone this morning,' I squeeze down on images of Ross.

'But the act of the two uniting as one ...' Lexie drifts off in her reverie.

Knowing Lex, it would have been a full-scale production.

'And her taste ... she's the sweetest nectar, mmm-hmmm,' she continues.

'Okay, Lex, got it ... she's flavoursome.'

'It was like returning to the life force.'

'Do you think it will be as good when you're both sober?'

'This is the beginning of the biggest romance of our time,' Lexie announces with the confidence of Winston Churchill.

'No superlatives then. And you're not worried about it going so fast? What about waiting till she moved out?' I remind her.

'I know. I blame the e. Still, this will fuel it. We've agreed never to spend a night apart for the rest of our lives.' Lexie picks up my teacup and sips from it dreamily, before realising it doesn't have sugar.

'Hmm, practical,' I reply.

I know ecstasy was originally introduced as a marital aid, to help pent-up, strung-out married couples chill out and feel the happy vibes via a huge surge of serotonin . . . I wonder if anyone has conducted a study on its effects on horny lesbians starting a new relationship? It's a wonder they aren't on the next plane to Vegas. Catching my thoughts, Lexie chimes in.

'I proposed.'

'Of course you did.'

'As soon as she's divorced we are going to fly to New Zealand to tie the knot. So you'd better start looking for a bridesmaid's dress.'

She walks round to Vivianne, who is still focused on stroking Mr Waldorf's back. She smiles up, ecstatic.

'I'll drive you,' Tom ventures out, looking green. He eyes Abi with Lexie and Vivianne and looks confused.

'Did we?' he stammers.

'Oh yeah.' Abi smiles sweetly. 'The four of us. Remember, you said it was the best night of your life.'

Tom looks bemused and more than a bit excited as Abi puts a hand over Lexie's.

'Damn.' He does a mental retracing, looking desperate for a crumb of this memory to resurface.

'And us all moving in together is like a dream come true, Tom. Of course, you'll have to come and meet my mother first, since she'll be living with us too.'

There's a long awkward beat as Tom's focus becomes clearer. Vivianne plays with Abi's hair. Finally—

'You're taking the piss,' he whispers.

'Correct. You were about to choke on your own vomit after a flaming Lamborghini, so I put you to bed and crashed next to you to make sure you didn't become another statistic,' Abi announces, finishing off her crumpet.

'Right . . . So we didn't?' He looks at her with the hope that he got closer to her than his pyjamas.

'If we did, you'd remember it. Trust me. Okay, Zoe, leaving in ten. Tom, you'd be over the limit. Anyone else want to come for the drive?' Abi is so centred we immediately anoint her as queen of the day.

Ten minutes later we've piled my gear and myself into Abi's old Land Rover, which is full of multiple animal scents.

We stop in at Bourke Street Bakery and line up for their freshly baked pork and fennel sausage rolls, which seems to help Tom over a hurdle of nausea. He's a vomiter from way back; long car rides with him always involve an ice-cream bucket and a head out the window. He sits in the back seat with the window open, occasionally throwing a longing look Lex and Vivianne's way, or an intrigued look at Abigail. I check my phone. Nothing from Ross.

Gigi has sent me a YouTube clip about orgasmic meditation. She gave me (verbally) a few pointers for her in-flight climaxes in case I found the journey arduous. She has already left this morning for Papua New Guinea to be wed by the tribal chief, and I will be seeing her all too soon in London. I should thank her really; I would never have emailed Jules if she hadn't pissed me off. I fear her 'assistance' will push me over the edge and I will implode in another anxiety attack, but there's so much prep to do before then. Music and Clem are what I need to think about . . . and whether I will actually get on my flight.

I check the flight again on my phone. It's still showing a dozen open seats in economy, but travelling on Dad's staff travel means a variety of issues can have you bumped from flights for days on end – overweight flights, last-minute changes, bad moods from the check-in attendants over the harp . . . I'm at the mercy of all of them and I won't know if I have a seat until the flight is almost off the tarmac. But it's about a third of the price, so here goes.

I thank Abi for the lift, and make Lexie promise to catch her breath before she books a reception venue or organises the menu. Vivianne is beginning to look very tired and drained; the problem with a huge surge of endorphins is the massive lack of them for the few days after.

'Spend some time with Dad,' I urge Tom as I hug him farewell. 'And don't let anyone sleep in my bed.'

I wave my party of four farewell and head to the purgatory of customs, security and duty-free shopping. A few hours later I have multiple layers of different hand creams and age-reversing mois- turiser testers lathered into my skin. I make my 'one day' retail therapy wish list. The longer you spend in the airport the more absurd it becomes: rainbow-striped Coogi jumpers, didgeridoos,

sheepskin steering-wheel covers, royal jelly capsules from aristo-
cratic bees, sunglasses with ridiculous price tags, mega bottles of
Baileys Irish Cream, pastel nailpolish and shimmering lipsticks.

Watching the board willing my name to be called is like
awaiting medical examination results. I watch as first class
boards, then business, platinum economy, brass economy parents
with children, prams, Birkenstocks and then every other imaginable category board . . . waiting, waiting. My heart falls quietly
as I clutch my ridiculous head cushion and check my melatonin
tablets are still in my pocket, and then, finally . . . I am called.
My seat screams middle of back aisle but I'm euphoric to have
made the flight.

A very sweet couple embarking on their honeymoon look
horrified when I front up with my ticket that seats me right
between them. I offer to shift seats, and get reprimanded by a
flight attendant, so I sit between the sparkling ring-wearers who
lean forward to share saliva. I do my best to be as non-existent
and small as possible in the hope they will be able to erase my
presence from their recollections of their first day of marital bliss.

I listen to a trio of 'Soave Sia il Vento' – 'May the Wind Be
Gentle' – from Mozart's opera *Cosi Fan Tutte*. When I was with
the London Symphony all those years ago, I would listen to it
before we'd embark on any journey. It has a soothing harmony
that uplifts as it calms, unlike the actual libretto, which is full
of men and women betraying and tricking each other, in a light-
hearted manner of course. Funny, these little quirks and habits
we embroider into our lives and our identities.

Just before take-off, I receive a tap on my shoulder and the flight attendant, Sue, asks me to vacate my seat. The entire cabin looks at me with dismay; am I holding up the flight? Am I a would-be curly-haired terrorist? I smile apologetically. No one smiles back. My guess is I am being bumped last minute. A palpable look of relief floods the newlyweds as Sue instructs me to collect my cabin luggage and follow her.

I perform the walk of shame through the mammoth aeroplane. We near the entry and Sue stops and turns.

'Upstairs, please,' she says.

'Upstairs? As in upgraded business class upstairs?' I gasp. In all my years of travel I have never been upgraded, never worn the special PJs, never had drinks in real glass and, especially, never been horizontal. How did this happen?

Sue hands me another boarding pass, this one with single digits and a window seat. I yelp, hug her and race up the stairs before anyone changes their mind.

Upstairs everything is quiet. I think they pump more oxygen into the air; the lights have a different hue. After the withering glares I received just moments before, I am blissfully ignored up here. Passengers busy themselves with headphones, menus, doonas, newspapers – the passenger in the aisle seat beside my new one is submerged in *The Australian*.

My seat is in the front row, so my appearance has no impact whatsoever. I sit, rid myself of my neck pillow in the spacious window side bureau and look out at the tarmac. Maybe Clara or Kip or one of the others who have passed is responsible? Otherwise, it makes no sense. I settle into the huge throne-like seat, try not to squeal as I play with the setting, receive a glass of bubbles, wriggle my ankles and my toes, silently toast to absent friends, and look out towards to the city hosting Summer to its residents and visitors.

'Cheers, big ears.'

Ross appears from behind the paper.

'Shit!'

I jump up, spilling expensive bubbles over both of us.

He chuckles his deep amused laugh. 'Thought it would be best if you travelled with a doctor, just in case. Rumour has it you're prone to chaos.'

'How'd you get here? How did you know I was here?'

'Your dad flew for Qantas, they only have two flights to San Fran today, I bought our tickets and the guy at check-in is a hopeless romantic.'

'More champagne?'

Surly Sue has been replaced by Radiant Rupert who has the pucker and cheeriness that makes you feel like he could smile through a tsunami and keep you calm. He hands me a wad of napkins and some PJs.

I stare at Ross, move my mouth, but am rendered speechless so opt to lock myself in the loos so I can think as I change. Excitement and confusion thrash it out. Excitement wins.

I re-emerge moments later looking like a grey bunny rabbit covered with a huge kangaroo insignia.

'Cute.' Ross is scanning the movie guide.

I stand over him.

'Why don't you take a seat? We have fifteen hours to repair the state of the world.'

'Are you here, here, or just a bit here?' I ask as I sit down.

He checks himself. 'All here I think.'

'Ross . . .'

He leans in and kisses me. 'I'm all here,' he replies.

We kiss again.

'I have us booked into my favourite hotel, right near Berkeley for your sleuthing, and then we head to the Napa.'

It all sounds so incredibly good.

'And then?'

He smiles the smile that says, *I knew that's what you were going to ask*. 'And then New York City, baby. Then London, then home.'

My heart is pounding. 'And you're going to be with me for all of it?' I am so excited I begin to wheeze.

'Soup to nuts,' is his reply.

My mind races, my head spins, I gulp for air. I don't want to ruin this precious moment, though I want to know more. I, I, I . . . take a large sip of champagne. I tell myself to breathe.

Ross watches me, amused. 'I'm open for questions,' he chirps.

I study him, wondering if he ingested some of the e the girls had. He looks relaxed and happy; a man with good commerce with the world, as my grandfather would have said.

'Josh? Jeanie?' I stammer.

He takes my hands in his. Kisses them. 'I've been dealing with it for the past few weeks. I couldn't bear you not being in my life. You didn't give me a chance to talk to you after your strange interaction with Josh; you made quite the impact on him, by the way – I caught him trying to read his palm the day after you met him.'

'Oh god, I must have seemed mad.'

'Charmingly eccentric.'

He kisses me. 'How are you going with your audition pieces? I can't wait to hear them,' he continues. I try not to notice he has changed the subject without actually answering my question.

I look around. To the rest of the world, we are a normal, happy couple sharing our lives.

Champagne flutes are collected and we prepare for take-off.

'You sure?' I ask Ross as the cabin crew are told to arm doors. It's his last chance to run.

He entwines his fingers with mine in reply.

And we are up and away in a bubble of bliss. The flight is a dream and, unlike my usual efforts at counting down the minutes till landing and staring relentlessly at the flight path, Ross and I giggle over films, eat sundaes with hot chocolate sauce and nuts, and find ourselves locked together in the lav as I attempt to share my scant knowledge of orgasmic meditation, which he recipro-cates as he introduces me to the mile-high club . . . life really is different in business class.

I don't want the plane to land; I want to preserve the bubble of us. We are an out-and-out couple. No more lies, no more waiting. Here he is with me and everyone knows. I feel like I can do anything.

TWENTY-FIVE

WE ARRIVE; JET-LAGGED AND JOLLY WE CLEAR CUSTOMS, collect luggage, hop onto the BART and check into the hotel. Fluffy matching bathrobes, room service, I feel like I've been zapped into someone else's life. Ross speaks to Josh to tell him he's arrived. All seems bizarrely above board and fine, which leaves an immense amount of space for us.

I am treading carefully around the Jeanie topic. I'm hoping she is okay; perhaps it was a joint decision? I practise some audition pieces for a few hours while Ross takes some work calls, lines up some meetings for his conference the following day and then listens to me play before devouring me again. I want everyone in the world to feel like this. We sleep enveloped in each other. I breathe him in and wonder where his slumber takes him.

The following morning I make my way to the Berkeley campus of the University of California. As I approach the imposing white buildings and pass people intently walking to class I feel a twinge of longing to be a student again – what an amazing institution of education and growth. I imagine what it must have been like in the sixties when Clem taught, as newly liberated females found their voices. I am met by a member of the faculty for fine arts who kindly shows me through their teaching roll and photos. Clem's tenure lasted from 1955 to 1972. I am shown a photo and, from what June has told me, I know that it's him – the strong jaw, the piercing brown eyes, the thick black hair, the beautiful hands. Clemency Lang.

There is no information about his private life, but one or two of his paintings hang on the walls. They are abstract and a product of the era; something about them indicates a desire to dive into ideas not emotion, stark masculine lines, almost geometric. Though one stands out. It is labelled with a date and a location – Alaska, 1942. In it, flames erupt from a still mountain, it's done in oils and feels heavy and intensely visceral, unlike the other pieces. Through the mountain is a face, a young man; perhaps it's him.

Further photo albums show pictures of Clem with his students, standing with fellow faculty members in thick-rimmed glasses, cigar in hand, making a lithograph, cutting tiles for a mosaic, pointing to a slideshow. In all these pictures he's smiling, but there's no sign of a wife or family, and there's no badge saying *I love June too*. It's possible I have got this completely wrong. Have I heard what I wanted to hear from June, taken on the reunion of two lost lovers as my own salute to *Cocoon* or some midday romance I watched as a kid? What am I doing here? Why does it even matter?

Sure this little self-created adventure has introduced me to Berkeley, but where is Clem? Who is Clem? I'm given Clem's old home address from an old HR file, and I google it. It's still in existence but Woods is the name associated with it now. I catch the BART and a tram down the steep descents of Nob Hill and marvel at the architecture. I knock on the door of a rambling freestanding house that is faded yellow with a greying white roof and it's opened by a student. It's a share house now for a group of postgrads, the owner lives overseas, no one has heard of Clem. It's a dead end.

I meet Ross for lunch at the Ferry Building and follow Sam's instructions as we open his excellent chardonnay to accompany the clam chowder.

'Who did you say gave you this?' Ross asks.

'Sam, my friend, you met him at the party.'

'Oh right.' Ross goes vague. 'Tall guy, handsome,' he says, pretending to recall.

Sam is certainly that. And much more. I nod.

Ross shifts gears. 'Let's really go for it these next few days. Make them count.'

We toast to that. He tells me about the advances in emergency medicine he's been chatting to people about. So much of it depends on the availability of hospital beds and staff being on top of the latest trends, both of which take resources, something he is always bumping against with state and federal governments. So many promises.

I reveal my lack of results with Clem.

'Maybe let it go? You tried,' Ross reasons.

But an unscratched itch remains. Clemency Lang went to war, survived and taught at Berkeley; he might still be alive.

'He might be thinking about June this very instant,' I say.

'You can't fix everything, Zoe.'

But, oh, I can try, I respond silently, thinking of June.

I resolve to visit the department of births, deaths and marriages before we head to the Napa tomorrow afternoon.

We drink wine, we marvel at the Golden Gate Bridge.

I think of Sam again and the Gap and our strange reunion. 'You know this is San Fran's version of the Gap?'

'Are you suggesting this lunch isn't going well?' Ross jokes.

'But unlike the Gap some people have actually survived their jumps – and you know what they all said they thought as they were falling?'

'Ouch, this is going to hurt?' Ross offers.

'Exactly, and they had second thoughts. Do you think it's the same for people at the Gap?'

'Possibly. No way to check though.'

'You know Sam's dog sometimes starts barking and drags Sam up there when there's someone about to jump?'

'So, he's handsome, has perfect taste in wine and has a psychic dog. How can I compete with that?' He leans in and kisses me.

'Sam's my friend. I played for his son when he was dying.'

'Bereaved too. Is he out of a Jane Austen novel?'

'There's no competition.'

Ross kisses me again. 'Darling, when it comes to men, both gay and straight, there's always a competition.'

Maybe he's right. Funny, I've been so flat out hoping Ross would be with me, tap dancing in the hope he would 'choose' me, I've never considered being with anyone else, or that anyone else would want me. I know Sam kind of asked me out on a date that first day at the Gap, but I'm pretty sure it was a sympathy vote. I've never thought of Ross being jealous over me, and part of me likes it, feeling coveted by him.

The afternoon fades into evening as we walk hand in hand around the city in no rush, with no particular plan, in a way we never have before. We head back to the hotel to get ready for the symphony and ravage each other in the process. He makes a skype call while I do laps in the hotel pool. We both dress up for the evening ahead. I wear the first dress I fell for in Clara's closet, the Oscar de la Renta, with a leather opera jacket over the top. I coax my hair into a loose French roll, and I wear the glow of great sex and a day with my love. *Clara*, I whisper, *we're going to the symphony!*

The San Francisco Symphony has been in action since 1911. They've had the luxury of time to refine and solidify themselves, and it shows. The concert is held in a magnificent symphony hall. We sit in the stalls, row G – I love being able to watch up close. Part of me still gets a jolt that I am in the audience not on the stage making last-minute preparations. One of my favourite composers, Mahler, said a 'symphony must be like the world, it should contain everything'. I think this is true – each symphony is a world unto itself that connects us more intimately with the larger experience of life. Each of the sections are different nations, cultures bumping up against each other, resisting and yielding; the symphony contains within it the world of emotions and conversations we've been having since time began – and it's done without a single word.

We sit beside each other, entranced, the world of us intercepting with the passion and greatness of the San Francisco Symphony. It's a beautiful program. Beethoven's seventh, Mozart and, to finish, Claude Debussy's *Danses sacrée et profane*, a piece that highlights the harp in the most exquisite of ways.

The harp is a relatively new addition to symphonies, not joining the orchestra until the nineteenth century. I always find that curious. Why was she given a second chance so late in the game? I'm grateful she was.

I look around at the people I'm sharing this experience with, a great cross-section of ages and origins creating our own united experience. Ross is listening with his eyes closed and the lightest of snores, jet lag having her revenge. He will tell me later that he was concentrating and meditating, like musical fishing.

Watching the harpist, I'm filled with the most intense longing; for my hands to be making that music without fear, without panic, to abandon myself to it like I used to, to get out of my own way and let it soar. Can I ever do it again? The nearness of the audition crashes against my consciousness. I need to rehearse more, need to really get my head around what I'm going to do. And what if I actually score the gig? It begins in July. What about Dad and Ross? Oh humans, we are so feeble, aren't we? So silly the way we tie our brain in knots to prevent us from doing the very thing that sets us free. I make a silent pledge to practise with abandon until the audition. Everyone walks out of the symphony looking touched and rejuvenated. Ross's arm is around me. The healing powers of music have triumphed again.

•

Births, deaths and marriages doesn't provide much because I'm not family. The San Francisco library has a birth announcement for a baby boy, Leslie Norman, born in December 1946 to a Nancy and Clemency Lang. So he got married and had a child . . . a boy who would now be older than my own father. I google Nancy and Leslie . . . but come up empty. Where are you, Clemency Lang?

TWENTY-SIX

THE ROADTRIP UP TO THE NAPA BEGINS WELL IN SPITE OF US getting lost because of an errant GPS system. I am attempting to appear calm as I sit at the steering wheel on the wrong side of the car and drive on the wrong side of the road through steep, curvaceous mountain ranges.

They say roadtrips are a surefire way to really see how strong a relationship is. I am not sure of our current status as I look to the petrol gauge, realising we have emptied a tank and the map on the dashboard is showing there are many, many miles till we are near anything. I opt not to trouble Ross with this news. He is already experiencing a steep descent in his till-now buoyant mood because he left his phone charger at the hotel in San Fran and we don't have one in the car and he's running on empty.

'Everyone knows you're away,' I reason to deaf ears. 'At worst it will be a few hours.'

'Sure,' he says in a thin voice that suggests it might be best if I leave it at that.

'I shouldn't have played my music, you have a better range anyway,' he says, with an edge of narky. Okay now there's the implication it's my fault. Great.

'What do you feel like listening to?' I ask.

'Anything is fine.' He shrugs.

I pick Van Morrison.

'Not that.'

'Okay, you choose.'

He looks out the window then swears at the GPS.

Oh, the joys of travel.

Ross announces his bladder is about to burst just as the final petrol warning light turns on. Fortunately we have found a gas station amid what we are guessing are vineyards, so calamity is at bay.

We get directions, refuel and head on our way. Ross has purchased a new charger at the service station and seems calmer. I get it, being overseas and away from your child and your unwell, estranged non-spouse can't be easy.

He attempts to chat and spark himself up. I am daydreaming about getting into a hot bath and getting some dinner when a loud sound erupts.

We look to each other.

We're on a deserted stretch five miles from our home for the night, which is in a vineyard with a wonderful view, not that we will be able to see it till morning because it's already pitch black.

The sound is promptly followed by the smell of burning rubber as the steering goes skew-whiff.

'Shit, can nothing work out between us!' Ross has decided to take this opportunity to globalise the blown tyre to a metaphor for our relationship.

'It's just a tyre, Ross.'

I find myself finding the humour in the absurdity of our predicament.

I begin laughing. Hysterically. Ross looks at me with a mix of wonderment and disdain.

I try and stop, which makes me laugh more. Tears of mirth roll down my cheeks, he half laughs but he's pissed off. The edges of his lips are turned downwards.

He heads to the boot, taking on the role of Mr Fix-it. I begin dialling AAA roadside assistance.

'They won't find us here!' he yells, before losing a bolt to the tyre. He commences kicking it.

I choose to ignore him and explain our location to the assistant on the phone. She seems used to hearing people yelling in the background.

It's quite amazing to witness Ross's transformation – Ross, ever calm and collected, on top of every emergency, is squealing and whining as he sits on the road with German instructions for our tyre change. He slams and throws things, he is in a fully-fledged three-year-old's rage. I sit with the car door open and quietly tell him help will be here within the hour.

'An hour? The kitchens will have closed, there will be no dinner.'

'Well, we can order room service.'

He looks unimpressed.

Within fifteen minutes, roadside assistance turns up and it takes a total of three minutes for the sweet young hunk to change the tyre. We wave him off.

'I should know how to do that,' Ross moans.

'You can save lives, so I think you have a get out of jail free card.'

We drive the rest of the way in stony silence, except for Ross berating himself intermittently.

What is it about fixing things, particularly cars, that gets men so worked up?

Ross strides to the check-in counter, and throws me a few furtive glances as he works out details and then comes back with two room keys.

'I thought it might be better to have separate rooms so you can rehearse.' He attempts cheery again. And fails.

'Okay . . . thanks. I was going to rehearse while you were having your jog though, there's no need for separate rooms.' I feel like I am beginning to lose my footing and the three-headed monsters of abandonment are rearing up.

'I have a conference call late tonight. I don't want to keep you awake.'

'Oh.'

He kisses the top of my head. 'Come on, let's go settle in.'

I'm not exactly sure what's going on, but it doesn't feel great.

I reach 'my' room and run a bath, pour myself a glass of Napa Syrah and play Bach. Temporary heaven. I then hop into my robe, plonk on the bed and look through the room service menu. Ross joins me. He's still dressed. He had some work calls, and he's stressed.

We devour our in-room burgers and fries, Ross has a glass of wine and chills out. We are lying beside each other on the bed giggling away as we watch *Seinfeld* reruns, when out of nowhere he kisses me passionately.

'I'm sorry, I can be a bit of a ham.'

'You're quite operatic.'

He laughs and we kiss again.

'Everything is still okay, isn't it?' I ask, attempting to keep the edges of desperation out of my voice.

He moves a stray hair from my face and studies me carefully before proffering his diagnosis.

'It's just a lot to digest, and this is the first time I've begun to wonder if what I'm doing is actually conscionable.'

'But you live with your conscience every day. I thought now you've made a break it would feel lighter.' I'm still trying to get him to choose me.

'So did I . . .' he mumbles.

Oh no, here we go, we're going to have another state of the union conversation. I steel myself but we're interrupted by Ross's phone. I can see it's Jeanie calling.

'I'd better . . .'

'Of course.'

'I might come back later, after the conference call.'

'You'd be very welcome,' I offer, hoping to calm him.

He nods and heads off.

As I rehearse I am back in the company of June, Kip, Reg and Clara. I'm with Dad, and with Tom and Lex and Vivianne. I'm swimming in the sea. I'm flying around the vineyards. I'm making love to Ross and I am completely free.

TWENTY-SEVEN

'ANOTHER SAM RECOMMENDATION?'

We are halfway through our vineyards day. The wineries around the Napa are stunning, each one more beautiful than the last. Some with amazing gardens, others show incredible sculptures, all with impressive wines and so many restaurants I wish we had a week here.

Ross is definitely getting into the wine-tasting. He's squarely pissed. I am the self-nominated driver; Ross is a terrible driver and we both know it.

We're having lunch at the vineyard where the grapes are grown for Mumm champagne. As usual Sam's suggestions are spot-on; it almost feels like he's guiding us.

'And it's all about the chalk,' I say in response.

'What is?'

'The quality of the champagne. As well as the wine-making processes the chalk in the ground determines how good a grape it is. And there's heaps of chalk in the ground around here.'

'Well, cheers to chalk!' We toast and sip our bubbles. They are so good.

'I'm sorry I've been a bit weird,' he proffers as he finishes his glass.

'This must feel pretty surreal, separated and in the Napa with your new partner.'

He studies me with an inscrutable look then leans in and kisses me.

'I'm sleeping in your bed tonight,' he whispers.

'Glad to hear it.' Our next kiss is interrupted by my FaceTime sounding. It's Lexie.

'Go ahead.' Ross laughs at my excitement. 'You haven't spoken to her since you left Sydney; that must be some kind of record.'

I press accept and am connected. 'Lexie, I'm in the Napa, *with Ross*.'

'What? Don't tell me limp dick grew a few?'

'Yes, and he's right here beside me . . .' Ross leans into view and waves.

'Oh, hi.' Lexie looks unperturbed.

'How's Vivianne?' I ask.

And that's all it takes. Lexie, who epitomises stoicism and doesn't believe in crying in front of anyone else, including me, begins to blubber.

'She's gone. All over, red rover. She dumped me.' She bawls.

Lexie is not one to be dumped. Nor is she one to bawl.

'What? Oh sweetheart, what's happened? It must be a misunderstanding, she is really into you.'

'Was,' Lexie spits.

'What? How?'

Ross looks amused but receives the look I throw him with grace.

'I'll leave you alone,' he says and makes to leave the table.

'No!' Lexie bawls. 'You might as well hear it too. Maybe you can help.'

She is definitely not okay.

'Okay . . .' Ross looks slightly terrified. 'Talk me through it.'

'We got together and it was good, *so good*. The best, and I was taking it slow, mostly; you know what I mean.'

Ross nods in a way that I know means he has no idea what she means.

'And it was beautiful. She's separating from her long-term arsehole, but they work together. Separate bedrooms, like you pretend you have.'

Ross swallows hard.

'And it was all going to plan but then, but, then . . .' She stops to cry some more. I find myself making cooing noises and rubbing Ross's back. Ross mimes to the waitress an order for another two glasses of champagne.

'Take a breath, Lex.'

She does. And heads back into the fray. 'And then at Zoe's party we split an e and we went from first base to homerun.'

'How was it?' Ross now looks intrigued.

'Amazing! I mean . . .' She stops crying to laugh in astonishment at her and Vivianne's sexual feats. 'Absofuckinglutely mind blowing. She came like a woman released, over and over, it went on and on for over a day. We were sore, we were raw, we were . . .'

'E'ing off your heads?' I offer.

'No, we were one, really, it was unbelievably phenomenal. You heteros have no idea, but it was beyond sex and gender, it was . . . oh, *fuck me.*'

Lexie continues to wail, while Ross takes a deep breath and a big gulp of champagne.

'What went wrong then?' I ask. 'It was all turkey basters and touching souls at the airport.'

'I know, right!' Lexie sobs freely. 'She went home and, apparently, Matthias sat on the end of her bed and said he's been a fuckhead husband, which we all know is true, and that he loved her. That they're real soul mates and he doesn't want to lose his marriage. He thinks this thing with me is her way of getting revenge and it's just a fling.' More sobs.

'Do you think there's any way he might be right?' I ask gently.

'Harsh.' Ross shakes his head.

'Of course he's not right, he's a drunken brat who is realising life will be harder without her. And he's scared because he's starting to see just how amazing she is. But it's too late, it's too late . . . isn't it?' she implores us.

'I don't know, darling. I don't know them well enough.'

'But she's my soul mate. She's the one. She's really *the one*. Oh god, why was I so hard on you, Zoe? This is unbearable.'

'Lexie!' I feel appalling for her. 'Do you want to come and join us for the rest of the trip?'

Ross throws me a look, which Lexie catches.

'No, you have your cheat-free rendezvous, I don't want to crash that and work is full on. Besides, I'm not giving up on this.'

'So, what's your plan?' Ross asks.

'I'm going head to head with stupid Matthias. I'm not backing down.'

'What does Vivianne want?' I ask.

'She says she wants me but she's scared.' She bawls again and Ross now looks truly sorry for her.

'Maybe she needs some time and space?' I offer.

'I shouldn't have slept with her. This wouldn't have happened if I'd kept my pants on.' She sobs with abandon some more.

'Maybe it would have happened anyway. Leaving a fifteen-year marriage, there's got to be some major adjustments.' As soon as the words are out of my mouth I realise they apply to Ross too, and that they haven't been lost on him.

'But you said they were informally separated way before you. Perhaps you're the catalyst for what already needed to happen?' I backtrack.

'Well, this catalyst is going to have to stop the deadshit husband taking my girl on a round-the-world trip.'

'He's offered a round-the-world make-up trip?' Even Ross is taken aback by this. 'He's good,' he adds.

'He's too late, he has to be too late, right?' Lexie entreats me.

'I don't know. Is she going?'

'I'm seeing her for a "walk and talk" after work.' Her voice wavers like a carelessly closing accordion.

Lexie looks behind her. 'I have to go and wrangle some three year olds for a pull-up nappy commercial.' She blows her nose and shakes herself like a newly bathed dog.

'Can you handle it, Lex?' I ask. I have never seen her so unhinged.'

'I can handle it,' Lexie regains some of her mettle.

'Okay, call me after you see her. I'm so sorry, honey.'

'It ain't over till the fat lady sings and I'm not hearing an aria just yet.' She ramps herself up with these words.

'That's my girl,' I say, cheering her on.

We bid farewell and I hang up.

Ross seems a bit shaken.

'Sorry, that's probably a bit close to home for you.' I see his already empty flute.

'I'm not sure if it's the conundrum or Lexie's description of lesbian sex,' he jokes.

We finish lunch and meander through the gardens then head to the next winery.

The winemaker, Stephanie, is one of the only female wine-makers in the region. There's something about wine, like music, that brings out such big passion. What we like, we really like, and what we don't like (in my case sav blanc) we want no part of. Stephanie speaks of her wines tenderly, just as Sam does. I text Sam letting him know where we are. Ross hovers over the wines further down the bar while I chat with Stephanie.

'And the paintings, did someone you know do them?'

'Mum's the artist. She passed the winery and the paintings on to me. She's into everything. So talented.'

My mind turns to Clem.

'Did she train anywhere?' I think it's worth a chance.

'She was too busy on the farm. She's a huge art buff though, belongs to the San Fran art society.'

I explain my search for Clem.

'I'll call and ask Mum. I don't know the chances, but she might know something.'

She heads off and returns five minutes later, smiling, and hands me a piece of paper.

'Not only did she know who you meant, she knows his sister, she was in the food and wine magazine industry here before moving to New York. She's still alive, in her eighties, in a retirement home. They still exchange Christmas cards.'

My heart leaps. Finally a real piece of Clem is in my hands. 'You're kidding?'

'See for yourself.'

I look at the piece of paper: Dorothy Andrews and a New York number.

I head back to Ross to share the great news. He has befriended a smart-looking couple in their sixties who nod politely and look relieved when I introduce myself.

I realise Ross is smashed and ranting. 'The whole of civilisation is going to porridge . . . already has really, just look at England since Brexit.'

The couple, who are Scottish, have obviously been through this conversation before. Multiple times.

'And the States, we may blame Trump but it's run by the banks . . .'

'But you live in Australia, it's better there surely, the health system?' the wife asks in a broad Glaswegian accent.

'Ha, don't believe a word of it, it's all guff. Hospital bed short-ages, gap between public and private health care, the nightmare continues, all of it. The Western world has collapsed but we don't want to hear it, so we ignore it and visit wineries and pretend we understand what a nose of blackberries actually means.'

The couple step back from him. I've never seen Ross quite like this before. Roaring drunk Ross is quite the extrovert. He waves his hands and arms around, spilling wine.

'Okay,' I interrupt. 'I think we need to get moving, nice to meet you.' I put my arm around Ross and head him towards the door.

'All of it's a ruse to fool us into believing we're not going to die, but we are. Alone probably.'

'I agree but maybe now isn't the—'

'They were swingers, you know,' he bellows.

'Excuse me?'

'Without a doubt. The wine world is full of them.'

'And you know this how?' We're standing in front of the hire car now. Perfect mountains and valleys with perfect vines frame the scene for the collapse of modern civilisation and relationships.

'They were totally checking us out.'

'They were being conversational.'

'I'm a doctor, I know conversational.'

'You're a smashed doctor.'

'They were totally up for it, and if you hadn't rushed us off we could have had some fun.'

'Sorry?' I feel myself lose my emotional footing.

'Monogamy doesn't work, Zoe, I'm living proof of that. Deceit doesn't work, relationships don't work, so what is wrong with consenting adults opting to have a bit of swapsie fun?'

'Oh my god you're really drunk.'

'I mean it.'

'You want to be a swinger? With them? With me? Sorry, but the husband was in his sixties and even if they were in their thirties . . . that's just not me.'

'The wife was pretty cute.'

My uncertainty switches gears and shifts into anger.

'Ross, get in the car and don't speak.'

He obeys, not out of choice but because as soon as he sits down and puts his head back he dissolves into an alcoholic snoring, farting coma. Sweet.

What's going on with him? Why is it so hard to talk about our feelings with each other? Am I just a fantasy who isn't living up to his expectations? How can he go from wanting to marry me to swinging? Is it all about Jeanie? Is any of it about us? Is there an us?

When we get back to the hotel I wake him and help him as he stumbles to his room. I remove his shoes; part of me wants to fling them at his head. Feed him a few Panadol and a litre of water.

'None of it works out, Zoe,' he mumbles. 'You want a fairy-tale, invented by romantics a few hundred years ago to keep the peasants under control.'

'I want to be with someone who wants to be with me. It's not that complicated, surely?'

He raises his hands in the air. 'This is me, glorious, sunny me. Aren't you glad you waited?'

I sigh and make my way to the door. 'I'm going to practise for a while.'

'I'm not saying this because I'm drunk. People are more themselves when they're drunk.'

'Not this drunk,' I murmur.

'We could call a hooker, have a threesome. Lexie got me all worked up.'

He looks down at his non-existent erection then collapses back on the bed and immediately starts to snore.

This roadtrip is beginning to feel like a clusterfuck of bad ideas. Is this who Ross really is? I've had my fair share of drunken moments, but if this really is Ross, we are going to have to work through the symphony of his feelings. I have a sick sensation in my stomach. What if this all happened because I was stupid enough to fall for him, and all he wanted was sex? Conferences have a lot to answer for. Is this my karma?

TWENTY-EIGHT

Alaska, June 10th, 1943

Dearest June,

I'm writing this as I look out over the Aleutian Islands. I had no idea where they were, it seems few other than the Japanese know of their existence, but they are near Alaska and in need of protection.

My job, however, is to paint them. I'm here with the Naval Arts section. It sounds a happy gig, I know, but truth be told it's colder here than a Boston picnic in January; I have the choice between painting well or preserving my hands from frostbite. So, I have donned gloves and my painting has developed a muffled quality.

I finally got word of the ballet's near miss from The Hague. Were you part of it? Oh June, my heart was in my mouth as I read of it in an outdated news article. I swore in disbelief as I read of something so calamitous happening so close to you and me not knowing as the whole incident was reduced to one column. The thought of anything happening to you is unbearable. I want with all my might to protect you. The world must not lose your bright light, June.

I haven't heard from you in the longest time. Letters arrive, some for me from my family but nothing from you. I will write to your family again. The London Blitz is beyond my comprehension. Oh god, I wish I'd brought you back to Boston with me. Where are you, June?

We will be here for at least the next twelve months. Ship life is wearying, and at times I hunger to be on the frontline. I fear we all feel impotent in the face of war.

It's a comfort to think of Folkestone's shoreline and imagine you gracing it as you stroll on the promenade. Oh what I would give to be beside you once more.

For now I am to depict the attacks from my foxhole. There is little joy in recreating the loss of life. How long will it continue?

I think of you each day, mostly when I wake.

I remain yours,

Clem

TWENTY-NINE

ROSS APPEARS AS I GET OUT OF A HOT, SUDSY BATH A FEW HOURS later. He looks contrite.

'How's your head?' I ask.

'Not great. Shall we go and get a bite?'

We head to the main street of Yountville to find somewhere to eat. Yountville is like an escaped page from a picture book mixed with the social awareness of Silicon Valley. Everything is both aesthetically delightful and eco-friendly, from the streetlights to the rubbish bins. The street is in possession of several separate Michelin-star restaurants, two of them from Thomas Keller, including his famous French Laundry. His farm gardens, complete with plump chooks roaming around and a maze of vegetable and herb gardens, are also on the main street.

Ross and I walk hand in hand. To anyone else it would seem we are a perfectly normal, perfectly happy couple, but I am beginning to see there really is no such thing. Like a symphony, every relationship is a world unto itself.

We find a little French brasserie and settle into mussels in an elegantly balanced white wine sauce, using freshly baked baguettes to dip our way through, accompanied by the waiter's suggestion of a chablis – Ross opts for sparkling mineral water and more Panadol. He pulls my hands to his lips and kisses them.

'Forgive me,' he says gently.

'It's not what you said. God knows, I've said a load of stupid things when I'm drunk. It's what you want that's worrying me.'

'I want you. Me and you.'

'Really?'

He looks away, shaking his head with one of those *Save me from another talk about our relationship* looks. I decide to ignore it and keep going.

'I get you are newly separated and you don't know which way is up, but maybe you need some time?'

'I thought you were over waiting.'

Stalemate.

'Maybe if you told me how you're feeling about Jeanie it would help?'

'I miss her,' he blurts. I feel a stab in my heart and a drop in my stomach but attempt courage.

'That's pretty understandable.'

'Is it? I feel like an arsehole being here with you.'

'You chose to come. You weren't coming, then you opted for the grand romantic gesture.'

'I'm worried I have nothing to back it up with,' Ross admits.

I nod, attempting to digest this. If only it was as palatable as the creamy mussels.

'Do you want a threesome with a prostitute?' stumbles out of my mouth.

'What?' His face crumples.

'It's what you asked for before. That, and swinging with the sexagenarians.'

'No. I . . . oh fuck, I don't know. I've been with Jeanie since I was twenty-one and now . . . Well, I know you want something substantial and it feels like I'm going from one woman to the other.'

'Because you are. I love you but I'm not down with swinging three-ways . . . not for a few decades anyway.'

'You've had so much freedom in your life, Zoe,' he says wistfully.

'True.' Of course, my words for it are 'abandonment' and 'loneliness' but I figure it's best not to split hairs at this stage.

'A few decades . . . really?' He's teasing, I roll my eyes and our conversation shifts to the Edith Piaf we're listening to, which of course is '*Non, Je Ne Regrette Rien*' . . . oh, the sweet irony of life. We eat more – roast chicken cooked to plump, juicy perfection; fennel and pomegranate salad; we share profiteroles – and then we wander home. We head to my room and kiss on the edge of the bed. Ross begins to remove pieces of clothing, and then his phone beeps. He looks strangely at me and tells me he won't be long.

I attempt to transfer my passion to the harp. I choose Mozart, because, as they say, Mozart fixes everything. Pluck, pluck . . . oh fuck, fuck, fuckery doo. I want to call Lexie, but she has enough to contend with. I call Dad; he's a bit concerned that

I've called – we don't do regular phone chats – but he says he's okay. I can hear Tina in the background warning him the call will be expensive. I FaceTime Tom, who is board-shaping and then going snorkelling with Abi the vet after work.

'We're just friends,' he informs me with surprise in his voice. 'I really like her, as a person,' he adds.

'Are you attracted to her?' I lightly press.

'Yeah, but I'm attracted to every woman I'm not related to. Nothing's going to happen with Abi. She's cool, that's all. I respect her.'

'I'm glad you're hanging out with her. How's the cat?'

Tom directs the camera to Mr Waldorf, who sits on the edge of the board Tom is shaping.

'Any house updates?'

'Yeah, you know Mick from surfing? He's with the company who've put in an offer. Five million.'

I almost drop my phone. 'Are you serious?'

'Corner lot, backing onto the cliffs, the last quarter-acre block in Ben Buckler.'

'Shit.'

'Tina will want more, you know what a greedy witch she is.'

'That I do.'

I begin yawning; talking to Tom has calmed me down.

'It's late, Zoe, put the harp away and get some z's.'

I hang up and change into my PJs then walk next door to Ross's room. I knock gently. No response. I enter. He's crashed out on the bed. I lie down next to him.

He holds me for a minute then opens his eyes and says, 'I wouldn't if I were you. Funny tummy.'

'Are you okay?'

He moves away from me, groans and falls back to sleep. I lie on the other side of the bed, not touching him, just watching.

What do you want, Ross?

THIRTY

WE HAVE THREE HOURS UNTIL OUR FLIGHT TO NEW YORK CITY. Three days there and then onto London. We're sitting at Chez Panisse, the restaurant run by Alice Waters, who was a pioneer in the paddock-to-plate local-sourcing food movement in America in the seventies. The restaurant is world renowned, Ross has talked of wanting to go here forever. I booked it as a surprise treat and our last hoorah in San Fran, but for all his forced gaiety it feels like he'd prefer to be getting the plaque scraped from his teeth.

'You don't like the food?' I ask, now on eggshells following a morning of monosyllabic replies to questions or observations on seemingly innocuous topics.

'Bit tasteless. I guess I built it up in my head.'

'I know the feeling,' I mutter and put my head back down to my breaded Alaskan salmon, which is anything but tasteless.

'Should we head to the airport?' he asks.

'If you like.' I signal for the bill.

'I'll get it,' he says with a certain level of misery.

'No, this is my treat. For you. You've done everything else.' In my mind, in my hopes, this meal would be the delicious finale to our romantic bonding in California.

'Because I earn five hundred percent more than you.'

'That's not the point.'

He rolls his eyes and hands the waitress his credit card. I feel like a reprimanded teenager.

'Well, thank you.' Now I'm squirming.

Ross makes a dismissive gesture. 'I have a few calls to make on the way to the airport. You okay to drive?'

I've been driving the entire time, I'm not sure why the trip to the airport requires a formal agreement. As I drive, I realise that he's avoiding me. He does a round of work calls to Sydney, which is just waking up. He laughs and jokes and finishes each call with a vague 'See you soon'.

We return the hire car and head into the terminal. As we make our way to the check-in, Ross stops me.

'Zoe, I've had to change my flight.'

I turn, blindsided. 'Huh?'

'Jeanie isn't well. Actually, it's more than that.'

'Why are you telling me this now?'

'Let's get a drink.' Numbly, I check in, receive my boarding pass and follow him like a lamb to the slaughter. He keeps his luggage with him.

We sit at a bar; he orders us both a double martini.

'What's happening?' I ask.

Ross downs his and orders another.

'I didn't tell Jeanie about us.'

The sounds of infinite other shoes echo as they hit the floor of my psyche.

'I told her I needed a break, from the grind, and that there was an opportunity to come to San Fran to check out hospitals here.'

I gape at him in disbelief.

'What about while we were in Napa?'

'I told her I was still in San Francisco. I don't like lying.'

My jaw drops even lower. 'You don't like . . . Ross, your entire existence is a lie.'

Ross readjusts his position, pushing the stool out from the bar, crossing his legs as a means of self-defence. 'You've never been married, you wouldn't understand,' is his retort.

'Technically, neither have you.'

My hands are shaking, my mouth is completely dry. I can't swallow.

'What did you think you were going to accomplish by following me over here?' The inside of my lips stick to my teeth as I try and speak.

'I love you, Zoe. I'm in love with you. The fact that I love Jeanie too doesn't contradict that.'

I feel like recent roadkill.

'Okay, so now you're lying to both of us? What the fuck is this?' This scene belongs to someone else. Not us. *How can this be us, Ross?*

'I'm just trying to keep everyone happy.' He grapples.

'Actually, I think you're just taking what you want. You obviously have no respect for either of us.'

'You knew I was committed,' he says quietly, knowing he's trumped me with his own ace.

'Unhappily!' I implore. 'Separate bedrooms on the eve of separation committed. Is any of that true? Is she even sick?'

'She has an autoimmune disease, yes.'

'Which one?' I challenge.

He refuses to answer, just stares at me blankly.

'Do you sleep together?'

He hovers then makes a decision.

'Sometimes.'

I down the rest of my martini. 'I'm a fucking cliché.'

I gather my things, but Ross is on a roll.

'I thought this trip would help me see what it would be like with just us.'

'And obviously I failed the test.'

'I have a family,' he pleads.

'I'm not the one who's cheating on them.'

'If I was single I'd be with you in a heartbeat.'

I'm speechless, but only for a moment. 'So, now what?'

'I need a few days to myself.'

'Good idea.' I pick up my boarding pass off the bar and stand to go.

'I still want to meet you in New York,' he says.

Oy vey. I have to laugh at that.

'You're either separated or you're not. You're either fucking her or you're not.'

'Jeanie wants us to get married.'

I sit back down.

'Excuse me?'

'I think she knew I was distancing myself. She's always wanted more of a commitment from me. She wants to do it for my fiftieth birthday.'

His fiftieth birthday is in less than a month.

I order another martini.

'This just keeps getting better.' I feel myself leave my body. I can see Ross and me. The bar, the terminal, the screen with boarding times; I'm floating above it all. He can't touch me here.

'Even you can't be party to that. Considering you proposed to me a fortnight ago, it would be reprehensible.'

'I said I wanted to marry you. It wasn't an actual proposal.'

'Oh my god.'

'I love her, perhaps I owe it to her?'

'To make up for having an affair and deceiving her? That's just great, Ross. What's my gift for being strung along for five years, are you going to ask me to be Jeanie's bridesmaid? Play 'The Arrival of the Queen of Sheba' at the service? Or better still, give you away?'

'I can't leave her,' he whimpers.

'You don't want to leave her,' I correct, finally understanding that truth.

'I don't want to leave her,' he echoes.

'So, fine. Marry her. You have hijacked my trip, my life, for what? Just stay the fuck away from me.' There's nowhere left for me to go. I am not sure I am going to survive. He has destroyed us, destroyed me.

'Zoe, I've had to think about hurting the least number of people. This is the only decision I could make. Unfortunately, it hurts you most, but you're young and beautiful, you have everything going for you. You always land on your feet.'

His mouth keeps moving, but I don't hear a thing. I swallow the rest of my martini, pick up my bags and head to my boarding gate.

'Fuck you,' are my parting words.

He follows, but I continue walking, deaf to him. I feel beyond humiliated, beyond ridiculous, beyond worthless. I want to curl into a ball and die. Instead I get on the plane, turn off my phone and stare out the window, demolished.

THIRTY-ONE

ONE OF THE TRAITS OF ANXIETY, AND THERE IS A PLETHORA OF them, is that it can be reignited at any time or place, at any seemingly insignificant incident.

The car ride to our Airbnb accommodation is a blur, as was the flight. White noise in my ears. I cannot digest anything. I cannot speak to anyone.

I cannot play.

Time passes and I wake. It's dark but the lights and buzz of the city fire around me. I finally absorb where I am. SoHo, New York City. One of my favourite places on earth. I hear a saxophone, a steady stream of pedestrians and the slosh of cabs driving through the sludge remaining after the last snowfall.

I'm in a gorgeous brownstone. African artifacts surround me, rugs and wooden bowls, they've even carried the animal print motif to a few of the chairs. In the centre of the living room sits a huge white leather couch with, you guessed it, animal print cushions. A tiny kitchen. A huge bed with a studded leather headboard. The perfect apartment for the happy couple.

I look to the fridge. A huge stainless steel number with an ice dispenser on the outside. A grown-up house. Inside the fridge is a tub of yoghurt, a carton of egg whites and a bottle of soy sauce. The cupboard contains a few half-full cardboard containers of herbal teas. The freezer contains frozen peas and half a bottle of vodka. I take a swig and contemplate. I'm an okay cook but I am not inventive enough to come up with a meal out of the fridge's contents, unless it's a vodka and soy egg-white omelette with peas.

I can hide out and starve until someone – Gigi Maiers, knowing my luck – happens to notice. No doubt she will make an Emmy-winning doco titled – *Heart of the harpist, an exploration into the poet's voice.*

She'd do a good job too, I can imagine the interviews. Lexie would blow the whistle on Ross. Tom would blame Dad, Dad would blame Mum . . . Tina would say we were very close but the harp is not her favourite instrument. And Gigi would rightfully bring it back to personal responsibility and pose a poignant question of the muse, the magic and the madness of musicality.

I ponder the end credits until my audible stomach grumbles make them fade to black. I don't feel great but I'm not ready to die over being tricked by the man I fell for. Besides, everyone will think it's because I was too scared to audition, which may be partly true. And I haven't helped June yet and I still have that number to call. Death via SoHo starvation will have to wait. Instead, I opt for taking my broken heart and rumbling stomach to the streets of New York.

I'm slapped with the adrenaline of the city the moment my hatted, gloved and coated self leaves the house. It is fricking freezing, which feels great. The apartment is a close walk to Prince and Spring streets. It's not late – 6.30 pm – but it's pitch black. I wander into Dean & DeLuca, withdraw my hat and buy coffee and some cheese and bread. All things I should have been doing with Ross . . . whoever he is.

From there I venture up past stationery shops, tourists marching into H&M and Prada. I take the corner and am relieved to see Balthazar is still there. Such a stalwart. It's been a decade since I've been here but on entering I find it largely unchanged. I look in my wallet. On account of Ross supplying the accommodation and the Chez Panisse dinner, I decide to splurge and eat here. And eat well. I know heartbreak makes you lose your appetite, but sitting in the warm restaurant watching plates of food bring delight to full tables provides a temporary balm of sorts. I am seated and order a pinot and the duck confit. I take my phone out of my pocket and switch it on.

There's a load of messages. Mostly from Ross. Regretting the way we parted. Wanting to meet me in New York. Declaring he was just scared, he *does* want a life with me. I begin skipping and deleting them; he has ruined enough of my trip, besides he knows where I'm staying.

Lexie, reporting in. Vivianne is not going to go around the world with Matthias. She is going to Bali with Lexie. They are reverting to handholding for the next few weeks then going to the villa Lexie owns in Ubud. I have a sneaking suspicion Lexie has promoted the villa as being of the luxury spa variety, not in the thick of the jungle, with no air-conditioning and bought as a bizarre investment with an ex kind of villa. Still, I'm happy for her. So happy for her. Lexie goes on to say she took Matthias out for a beer and a 'talk'. I can just imagine how clear she was. And how terrifying. No blurred boundaries there. I wonder if Vivianne will move out of the mega mansion. I text Lex to say Vivianne can stay in my room till I get back. Which Lexie jumps on.

More messages from Ross. A text saying he's coming. Another saying he might have to fly back to Sydney. All telling me how bad he feels, none asking how I am.

An email from Sam, checking in on winery progress.

And a voicemail from the retirement home where Dorothy Andrews resides: she will be happy to see me, though I should be warned she has vascular dementia that is rapidly advancing. The caller, one of the nurses, gives the visiting hours and the address. I write it down. Even through all this crap at least tomorrow I will know where Clemency Lang is.

I text Reg, who texts back that none of my patients has 'carked' it and to kick up my heels and he will say hi to June for me.

Somehow the search for Clem is making everything else bearable. I jot down a rehearsal schedule and makeshift itinerary for the next three days, though New York isn't one for plans; like me, she is a believer in spontaneous providence and certain derailing, but walking round the park, visiting the Met and the

Guggenheim, and scoring a cheap seat at a play or an opera are on my list.

I scan the profiteroles. My favourite, but no Ross to share them with. I opt for crepes Suzette instead, which are also a pretty coupley dessert.

I walk home via Wholefoods. Unpack my harp.

And play.

THIRTY-TWO

London, September 1945

Dearest Clem,

It's finally over! Where are you? The news has been met with a fevered euphoria and relief. There was dancing in the streets and we stayed awake all night.

I am still recovering from a broken leg, it was shattered in a fall at work. Though I didn't allow that to stop me.

But now home come so few compared to all those who left to protect us all. I have never been one for mathematics but the arithmetic of it is heartbreaking. The answer is loss. Loss of life, loss of limbs and, in far too many cases, loss of love.

Are you still with the navy?

Are you painting? What is it you draw?

In all likelihood, these letters will continue to be returned unopened. And yet to stop writing them is more than I can bear. I cannot stop hoping that we will somehow be reunited now the war is finally done.

I wish I was sharing this day with you, Clem. I wish I was sharing all my days with you.

If anything the war has increased my feelings for you. I know what loss is and how fickle the world can be, and it makes me cling to my feelings for you even tighter. I know not what has become of you. I pray to God you are safe and warm and know my heart remains true.

Yours,

June

THIRTY-THREE

HOW IS IT WHEN YOU GO THROUGH EITHER GRIEF OR HEARTACHE you cannot stop replaying your last moments, last conversations, measuring up their quality, their significance?

As I play, as I brush my teeth, lather on moisturiser, squeal and roll around in the bed to try to warm up, my conversations with Ross play out . . . and out and over and out.

At 3 am I replay the few messages from him I haven't deleted and I wail. What was I thinking? I should have known this wouldn't work out. I should have asked for more details, questioned him more, and made him sign something in blood. I make Pollyanna seem like a realist with my persistent optimism bias. By 5 am I am constructing various replies and deleting them, because they all end up with the responsibility being mine and me wanting what he so obviously cannot give: himself.

Yes, he used me; yes, he disrespected me; yes, he's an arsehole
. . . but I should have known he couldn't be trusted, I should have
dug deeper, asked for proof, read the signs.

Why did I trust him so blithely?

Why?

Really? *Why?*

Because I was in love with him.

And now?

Now there's nothing.

•

The retirement home is one of the nicer ones I've been in. It smells
of decent food and fresh linen as well as bleach.

Dorothy is sitting in the drawing room. It has velvet-covered
Jason recliners, side tables with fresh flowers and doilies, and
paintings in the style of Dorothy's era.

The nurse, Emma, introduces us.

'She's been looking forward to your visit,' Emma tells me.

'Have I?' questions a wide-eyed diminutive figure with faded
red hair that's been recently curled and teased. She sports a Pringle
cardigan, pearls, and a kilt-style skirt. She has apples in her cheeks.

Emma pats her arm. 'We've been talking about it all morning.'

'She didn't sleep well . . .' Emma smiles at me. 'Not having
the best day.'

'I'm out of sorts,' Dorothy announces.

'I'll get some tea sent to you both and leave you to chat.'

I feel panic rush through me as Emma walks away. I must
seem like a strange guest.

'Ms Andrews, I'm a friend of one of Clemency's old friends.'

'Who's Clemency?' she asks with a prickle.

Oh god, this is a disaster.

'Clemency Lang, your older brother, he's a painter?'

'Poor old Clem,' Dorothy muses, then looks at me sharply. 'If it's money you want it's too late for all of that. He's gone.'

I stop short. Is this my answer?

'Dorothy, I don't want any money. I'm just trying to help my friend June get back in touch with Clem. If he's alive?'

Dorothy eyes me suspiciously. 'What'd you bring that thing for? Are you going to cart me away? Well, I'm not going anywhere, not with you.'

I've brought my harp because when I called to confirm my visit I asked about musical therapy and if they'd like me to play.

'Dorothy, it's my harp.'

'You turn up from heaven knows where with a harp? Good grief, missy, who do you think you are? My guardian angel?'

'No. I'm just a musician.'

'A musician!' Dorothy pretty much screams this and I am sure I will be asked to leave for disturbing her. But then her entire demeanour shifts and she smiles gaily. 'Well, why didn't you say?' She resettles herself. 'I like musicians. I dated one once, nearly married him, but mother said no and I married George instead. He's dead and he wasn't much chop when he was alive. Couldn't play the fiddle like my young man, but he could whistle all right. Now you sit next to me and tell me what you will play. I should have organised for some tea and cakes.'

The fact I am sitting beside her already and a tea tray with fine bone china cups has been placed nearby does not deter her from playing the magnanimous hostess. Dorothy is as far down the rabbit hole of vascular dementia as Emma warned.

'Oh look, the tea's arrived. Shall I be mother?' She claps her hands and pours tea with an expert hand.

'Lemon, milk, cream?'

'Just milk, please.'

'And just one cube of sugar, don't want you losing your figure.' She pops it in before I have a chance to say I don't take any.

She hands me my tea, then takes her own and sips.

'Well, now, where were we?'

We are obviously going to begin the whole conversation again.

'Clemency,' I say.

'Is that your beau's name? I had a brother called Clemency, my big brother, he took care of all of us. Poor old Clem.'

'Yes,' I say, spilling sweet tea over myself in my excitement. 'Clem, Clemency Lang.'

Dorothy's look sours. 'Well, you're not going out with him, are you? He's married. Was. Poor Clem.'

How do I get through? 'My friend June went out with him, before the war.'

Dorothy nods significantly and says nothing.

I wait.

'He used to carry me around on his shoulders when I was little. He was already in the navy when I was just a little girl.'

'He painted?' I ask gently.

'He painted me! I was very pretty. I still am.'

'Yes, you are. Like a model. Is Clem still alive, Dorothy?' I'm leaning forward on the edge of my seat hoping she will stay with me long enough to answer.

'Poor old Clem, it wasn't fair what happened. Still, life isn't. Look at me and George, no kids. Now, enough chatter, play something cheery.'

I wait for a moment, hoping she will say something else about Clem, but nothing happens. The least I can do is play for her.

'What would you like?'

'Strauss,' she answers. 'And Bing Crosby, he's marvellous.'

I play Strauss's waltz, 'The Blue Danube', which Dorothy hums along to and loves. The only Bing Crosby song I know is 'White Christmas', so I play that. Dorothy doesn't seem to mind. She sings along blissfully, remembering every word. Apparently music helps us access our brain through a different angle, firing different neurons, I've seen this happen time and time again.

The conversation continues to circle and backtrack and repeat; it reminds me of Ravel's 'Bolero', so I play that too. One theory is Ravel was in the first stages of Alzheimer's when he composed it, hence the steady and haunting repetition brought forth and escalated by the increase in volume; it's also associated with sex and the female orgasm, thanks to Bo Derek and *10*.

As I finish, Dorothy's eyes shine. She smiles warmly. 'Yes, you did that well.'

'Thank you. Dorothy, may I ask you a question?'

'Well, of course, my dear.'

'Did Clemency, your brother – did he die?'

She looks squarely at me. 'You know very well he didn't. Really, Rita, your memory is getting worse than mine. Clem moved after Norman was killed and Nancy . . . poor Nancy. But what mother could live without her son? If men gave birth there would be no war, mark my words.'

'Norman died in the war?'

'Why do you keep making me go over this? After all Clem survived, he didn't deserve that.' Dorothy shakes her head at me with disgust.

'Where is he now?'

Dorothy chuckles. 'Late for dinner as usual. Mother will be cross but he works to keep us in school and you going to ballet class. He's still sweet on the British girl, moons over her, Mommy says. Shall we read her letter again? Her handwriting is so pretty and she is in Holland dancing with Nijinsky. Imagine!'

It's like having a conversation with the Mad Hatter. Anyone who has experienced losing a loved one to the horrendous vacuum of Alzheimer's and dementia knows the true meaning of exasperation . . . and heartache. Where is it they recede to?

Dorothy, still holding her teacup, closes her eyes. 'I was one of the first female magazine editors in the country and now I cannot hold onto the string of a sentence. Silly, isn't it?' She laughs and then leans her head back and sighs.

'You've been really helpful, Dorothy, thank you so much. Will Clem be in to see you later?'

It's a long shot but you never know.

'Hardly.' She laughs again. 'He lives in Australia.'

I stop putting the cover on my harp. 'Really? Where?'

'You ask a lot of questions. Some place with space and sheep and surf. I wish he'd come back and visit. Long flight though, isn't it?' Suddenly she's completely calm and lucid.

'Really long,' I agree.

'Well . . . next time then.'

She pats my hand. 'You mustn't give up, dear heart. Never, never give up.'

I hold her warm vital hand as Dorothy begins to snore.

I play one more song as she sleeps, pack away the harp and head out.

Emma is playing checkers with a group of sprightly elders in a recreation room that's well heated and full of plants tended by residents. If only aged care was this good universally. I tell Emma what I can piece together from what Dorothy has told me. I hadn't mentioned Clem's name to her when I called.

'I think I have a number for Australia. Though there's been no calls for over a year, not that I know of.'

Emma and I head back to her office. She searches through her files.

'Yes, Clemency Lang, here.' She copies the number carefully. I'm still buzzing that he and June have ended up on the same continent.

Emma hands me the number – it has an 08 area code – Perth. I do a quick time check; he'd still be asleep. Hope beats curiously in my chest. Perhaps this will all be solved in just a few hours.

•

Filling a day in New York City is hardly a chore. I take my harp home and then head uptown on the subway, getting off near

Central Park, walking around the lake and the ice rink trying to overcome cold with brisk movement. As is always the way, there are couples everywhere: couples holding hands, couples Eskimo-kissing on the ice rink, couples nuzzling over hot chocolates. Lord Byron once said that happiness was born a twin; by all accounts he was a spanking narcissist, but he got that right. We are social creatures, we were born to share and co-create.

I walk up to the Guggenheim, the gigantic white snail of a building, recently renovated. I walk around and around, marvelling at both the architecture and the collections – the Matisse pieces, the Kandinsky and Marc's *Yellow Cow* are my favourites – colour and form make their own music for the eyes. How lucky we are to have art; it makes life bearable. I am daydreaming with the *Yellow Cow* when Lexie FaceTimes.

'You have to come to Bali,' she announces.

'Why?'

'Because it will be fun and Vivianne and I want you there and you can stop in on your way back, you're going through Singapore anyway. And you will stay with us, it's free!'

'Lex, does Vivianne know how rustic your villa is?'

'What are you talking about? It's got that beautiful bath and the electricity is on, mostly.'

'It's not quite the Four Seasons that's all. And Vivianne seems like someone who'd be fond of air-conditioning and running water.'

'It will be a tremendous bonding experience.'

I want to forewarn her of newly separated couples and travelling to bond but am not in the mood for an I-told-you-so sermon from the high priestess of Sapphic righteousness.

I uncoil my way through the Guggenheim trying to show Lexie the artwork as a means of distraction.

'What's wrong? Where's dingbat and why are your eyes swollen?'

'Art moves me.'

'Not that much. What's he done now?'

That's all it takes. I walk down towards the subway on the Upper East Side letting my tears flow freely as I provide a summary of the past few days.

'Holy fucksticks. Do you think I scared him off?'

'I think you provided a reality check.'

'So you should thank me.'

'Thank you, Lexie,' I blubber.

'Oh babe, it's not meant to be this hard,' she says calmly.

'How do you know? You're only at the beginning with Vivianne. It's probably going to be all uphill for you too.'

'I believe from both Vivianne and Matthias that they are truly separated. Matthias has death rattle regret, that's all. Ross was always so shady about what the reality with Jeanie was.'

'Maybe because he didn't know himself?' I manage while blowing my nose.

'Totally, but it's not a great foundation for a relationship. Stop crying, babe, you'll make yourself vomit. Tell me how your sleuthing is going, any updates on your international man of mystery?'

I nod as my lip quivers and I will myself to stop crying. 'I have a number for him, he lives in Western Australia.'

'Seriously?' Lexie is surprised and delighted for me. 'That a girl. Right, go home, take a bath, play your harp and list yourself to come home via Bali, then call me back, okay?' She says everything with a *this is so easy and do-able it will only take a second* tone.

I agree and head off on my mission.

THIRTY-FOUR

ISN'T IT STRANGE HOW THE CALLS THAT YOU KNOW ARE important need a sort of run-up to be made? Well, that's the case for me anyway. I am willing, I am visualising, I am praying that a chirpy senior voice answers after two rings and I can in some tiny way set the world to rights for Clem and June.

I take a breath and dial.

The number has been disconnected.

I try again. And again.

Still disconnected.

I look up the White Pages online.

He's not there.

I google again, this time leading with Perth.

No.

I try obituaries in all the Western Australian papers.

Nope.

He's disappeared again.

•

Lost for what else to do, I sit and retune my harp. Harps are notoriously sensitive to changes in weather and my poor girl has been through it all. Even though I always cover her in her blanket and protective case, I can hear the tuning is a bit off, like her mistress.

I change my flight to go home via Bali.

And then, as the late afternoon swiftly turns black and arctic, I compose a piece for June and Clem in the hope it can unite them in a way I have failed to do. Ross is in there too, of course. Longing and loss make good muses. The work helps me start to sort through the debris of my history with Ross. All that waiting, all that yearning, all those hopes . . . where are they now? There's just a big gaping space, another flag of grief to raise alongside the others from my life.

At least while I work and I play, I don't feel such abject failure. I continue working till the first light shines through the streets of SoHo and I dress and venture out for coffee and oatmeal.

My last day in NYC.

I score a cheap seat to the Met's latest production of *La Bohème*. I stand and marvel at the Chagall which has offered its colour to Lincoln Square for decades, recount the films with a scene set at the fountain and at the opera. Most of them involve romances. Well, opera is of passion. I lose myself to Mimi and Rodolfo's plight for the next few hours and watch as much of the orchestra working so hard down in the pit as the view from my seat permits me to. There are sighs, tears and the death of a dame. There usually is in opera; it's always the women who suffer.

From the Met I make my way to the Empire State Building to bid the city farewell. Wouldn't it have been the most romantic day had it been shared? Do I send a selfie saying, *Wish you were here, Dr Fuck-knuckle*? Tempting.

Instead, I take a small amount of the bottle of champagne Sam requested I drink there in a little sippy-cup. I toast him as the sun fades and I toast all the near-misses of the heart our memories revolve around.

Nothing dramatic happens. Ross doesn't appear, as my own operatic and fanciful imagination had inadvertently fantasised. He doesn't even get run over as he's getting out of a yellow cab and looking up at the Empire State, wondering if I'm up there, waiting. Nothing. Just tourists, mainly families, looking through the telescopes and sighing in wonderment at this city of life.

I'm too sad to send a selfie but I get my phone out to text Sam, after taking a furtive sip of his delicious bubbles. How does someone know how to pair wine with environments like he does? It's like he knew I'd be feeling alone and lost and provided a potion that would combat my sadness.

It's a big champagne and its breadth and yeasty sophistication match the Big Apple, but there's also the straw taste of home that provides comfort. I text Sam my appreciation. He texts back, he's out walking Harry and heading for a swim on the other side of the globe.

I scan my emails. Gigi has sent several expressing her excitement and her desire to 'significantly bond' in London. As well as a website link to the tribal wedding.

And there's an email from Ross, back in Sydney and full of mea culpa but then in the last paragraph:

> Know that I feel sick about it all. I hope we can resume a loving friendship when you're ready, because life without you would be unbearable. I have decided I will go ahead with a commitment ceremony of sorts with Jeanie, well I didn't decide really, a decision has been made and I seem impotent to stop what is now in motion. I owe it to her. We will have a small garden gathering and then I am taking long service leave so we can have the honeymoon I have till now denied her. Know that this doesn't change the way I feel about you. Break legs at the audition. I know you will. I checked in at the hospice, you haven't lost any yet.
> My love, Ross

I feel the heavy thump of more shoes landing, this time with taps screwed into the bottom of them. I look out to the city, providing it with my best *Can you believe this?* gasp. It answers back with a voracious grumble and twinkling lights that appear as the sun sets. A fait accompli. I finish the champagne. Swallow hard on my own stupidity. I only now realise I had maintained a dwindling hope inside – the *He will turn up when he realises he can't live without you* voice. That voice is silent now.

I tumble through my options as I descend in the lift and make my dejected way home. I check the time and realise it's tight. Flights aren't delayed on account of cheating men marrying their wives. If they were, my guess is we'd all be grounded.

THIRTY-FIVE

September, 1972

Dearest June,

After all this time you're still in my thoughts. I tried to find you countless times and then, well, life got in the way I suppose, as I hope it has for you too.

I'm in New York City. Today I took myself as a tourist to the Empire State Building. I'd hoped traveling to this great height could provide some clarity. Though till just now I've remained at a loss.

The contents of my house, which till now has been in San Francisco, are packed up and on a ship to Australia. A quick decision I made in the first week of grief. How will I fill the lifetime that remains of it, June?

I came to Manhattan to see my sister. I figured it would be years before I'll be this side of the equator again. I've already been to Boston, to see what remains of my family there and visit my parents' graves and those of the majority of my childhood pals.

My life seems to be one long lesson in loss. And yet buildings are erected, children hold ice-creams, fathers hold their daughters up to look through the telescopes and out to the future. Heavens, what a depressing note, I apologise, I'm just trying to comprehend what to my way of thinking is incomprehensible.

I have lost my son and now my wife and, truth be told, I went to the Empire State Building with a fancy to jump. But then what? Someone would have to clean up the mess and that's not fair. And I know now what lies beyond.

I decided there were no answers to be had on top of this gracious building. I was minded to depart when my eye caught on the elevator door closing. I spotted a lady my age, in a hat and holding a little girl's hand while a man and a young boy stood beside her.

She wore a yellow dress with flowers. The curve of her hip, the smile of curiosity and hope on her lips. I know those lips.

The doors closed. A new crowd of departing sight-seers stood in front of the elevator.

I must confess I have the flutterings of madness – this is my life now. But, there's no mistaking it, in that moment, that woman . . . it was you, June.

If only I'd called out, leant forward. But then, what could I have said?

My mind turns back to the two of us on the Folkestone promenade, your arm in mine. The promises we made as we kissed. The purity of us.

If it was you, and it was you, June, there was a smile on your lips. If it was you, and surely, it was, knowing you exist is the sign I needed to go on living.

All these years, all these tragedies, all this life and the desecration of loss have done nothing to diminish my love for you.

Thank you for saving me today, June. Thank you for being my bright light.

Yours,

Clem

THIRTY-SIX

LONDON. SMOKY, HAZY, GREY, GORGEOUS LONDON OFFERS HER steadfast presence of not too high buildings as I land. Restrained as always, minus her show-offy Eye.

I board the Heathrow Express to Paddington station and walk up cobbled roads through old mews to my second cousin's home in Bayswater.

They are a gorgeous, raucous British family. Four children, all under seventeen, all with instruments; their parents are first loves who met in medical school and still find each other refreshing and fascinating . . . in my observations anyway.

I am met at the door by a chubby red-haired boy, Fred, munching toast and holding a box of cereal. Thanks to skype, he is so completely familiar with me it seems I've walked back in from borrowing a cup of sugar next door, rather than returning after years.

'Come on then, you'd better hurry up or you'll miss our rehearsal.'

I enter the maelstrom of vivacity and life and couldn't feel more grateful.

Daniel and Sabrina look not a day older. He's reading something out of a medical encyclopedia sporting lycra cycling gear. Sabrina, not missing a beat, queries him on it, something to do with blood types. They shift to discussing drop-off and pick-up duties while hugging me, taking my bags, showing me to my room and fixing me a cup of tea. While this is occurring, Mary opts for a variation in hairstyle and a request to attend a slumber party this weekend; Len, the baby, gurgles; Fred requests a day off school in vain; and John asks about borrowing the car to attend a footy match. Within fifteen minutes they have all departed to various destinations and I stand alone with a teacup and incoming jet lag. They are the perfect balm. They are the family everyone should have, for at least a day or two.

Sabrina texts after I shower. *So sorry to rush off, please make yourself cosy, your friend Gigi has been trying to get hold of you, she said she will call round in a few hours. So glad you're here. You must stay this time.*

I'm too tired to reply with anything but a kiss. I do the same to Lex so she knows I'm safe, and Tom, then I tumble into bed and sleep deep and heavy.

I would have continued sleeping but for the steady rhythmic knock at the door downstairs syncopated with the ringing of the doorbell and the chiming of vocals. It can only be one person.

I drag myself into one of Sabrina's bathrobes and wander down the stairs, bracing myself for a full-body Gigi encounter.

But to my surprise waiting at the door isn't the yogic goddess, golden angel of percussion and tantra. It's my reflection.

Gigi looks wan, exhausted, drawn . . .

'I need a friend,' is all she says.

THIRTY-SEVEN

FOR THE FIRST TIME EVER, I DRAW GIGI TO ME AND EMBRACE her, she's like an owl who's fallen off its perch. She begins to cry, a sob befitting Gigi, a huge hailstorm of tears.

I gather her up and bring her inside, hoping the clutter of a happy family world will soothe her as it has me.

Gigi looks around her like she's just arrived in Oz. 'Where are we?' she whimpers.

'My cousin, second cousin, Sabrina. She's the one you spoke to on the phone.'

Gigi looks vague, an altogether unfamiliar look on her. 'Oh yes, I had her number from when you had your turn here all those years ago. I met her at the hospital.'

I put the kettle on and seat her among the school assignments and ironing.

'Thank you,' she whispers.

'What's happening, Gigi? You seem on top of the world in all your posts, podcasts, instagrams and snapchats. The wedding looked really . . . tribal.'

'It's a sham, all of it, and the chief – he knew it, he knew it, he knew it!' she blurts.

I attempt to digest this as I make tea. 'Who?'

'The king of the tribe who married us.'

'Oh.'

'You know what he said to me?' She quakes.

I figure this is a rhetorical question, so I pour tea and wait.

'He said I had a lying heart.' Now Gigi really loses it, I guess primal would be the best description. I put an arm around her as she lets it rip.

After a few minutes of full-throttle bawling that leaves my efforts looking like those of a simpering amateur, she eases up.

'Oh god, thank you. I needed that.' She sighs.

'Okay, so the chief didn't like you, that's upsetting you, yes?'

'He could see right through me and into my soul, and he could see . . . you know what he could see?' Her sobs build up again.

Another dramatic pause and another wait. She is earnest in her theatrics, I can see that. To Gigi the world *is* ending right now. I get it. I've had mine end at least four times over the past three days yet here I am comforting my nemesis. Life's like that.

'I'm a big fat phoney and he knew it. And you should have seen him, Zoe.'

'I did, in the pictures. Very impressive.'

'He would look at you and . . .' Gigi clicks her fingers.

'You fell for him?'

'It wasn't that. I mean, don't get me wrong: six foot four, body of iron, noble warrior and a psychic surgeon,' Gigi reports with awe.

'Gigi, I'm getting really confused, what happened?'

'Well, we were doing one of the tribal ceremonies leading up to the wedding ceremony; Tea Tim was off having "man time" in a hut nearby, I had been in a women's weaving, smoking, honouring circle.'

'Okay.' I have no idea what that is but I'm picturing baskets and pipes and Gigi hugging everyone.

'And the chief's son pulled up, he'd got a load of chickens from a neighbouring village and wanted to tell his mum.' Gigi looks at me with gravitas.

'Okay.' It's best not to stop her.

'And he is also a very, you know, hot tribal warrior, I mean . . . rippling, ripped, really hot.'

I'm now picturing muscles and chickens. I nod.

'I offered to help him put the chickens away and I . . .'

'Got plucked?' I offer.

Gigi bawls once more.

'Oh Gigi, I'm sorry, that's not great.'

'That's nothing, that's just the beginning of this nightmare!' she replies.

I pour more tea.

'The chief walked in when we were kissing. I don't know what came over me, it was his tribal earthiness I guess and everything was so raw, really, raw, raw, raw. You know, eggs, hens, dirt.'

She stops short and catches her breath. In my imagination the events move into close-up.

'And he was so sweet and had these eyes of endlessness and I . . . I wanted to feel him in every inch of me.'

'What about feeling Tea Tim? He's the one you married?'

'This was the day before my wedding. I thought, *If I just do this, this last naughty thing, I can sign off for the rest of my life.*'

'I thought you had amazing sex with Tim?'

'I do, but it's . . . I mean, I love it and . . . oh god, I just wanted the bejesus fucked out of me by a tribal warrior!' More tears.

'What happened then?' I'm biting my lip now, feathers fall freely in my own mini film of the event. Tribal drums are increasing in pace and pitch . . .

Gigi attempts to compose herself. 'The chief pulled me out of the chicken coop and took me aside. He said I had a lying heart and the only way out of it without Tea Tim knowing was if we were to make an astronomical donation to more of the community programs.'

I finish my tea. 'How much?'

Gigi looks blank. Pauses then speaks slowly: 'A million dollars.'

Ouch.

'So he bribed you? That's not very chief-like.'

'He could also see my underlying blackness.'

'Gigi, you're anything but black. Do you love Tim?'

Gigi nods. Her eyes puffy, her nose red, she looks like a little girl who got lost at the shopping centre.

'I came up with some crazy program involving percussion and nomads and herding. I was an absolute bitch to Tim until he agreed to donate the million.'

'And then you married him?' I ask quietly.

'I married him. The chief glared at me as he officiated but I'd organised so much fucking press. Tea Tim is at a loss, he knows nothing about it, and you know what's worse?'

'Not really, no.' I'm at a loss too.

'That's not the extent of my moral bankruptcy, because my lovely, kind husband and I are staying at the house of my ex-lover.'

'I thought you were staying with Julian?'

'We are.'

Boom. Gigi has truly outdone herself.

Lovely, fumbly middle-aged eccentric genius conductor and artistic director Jules . . . and his gorgeous wife, Sally.

'What was . . .' I can't finish my sentence.

'I love him, I fucking love him, I've been in love with him since I met him on that first tour.'

That first tour with the Melbourne Symphony was eight years ago.

'What about Sally?'

'I know,' she whimpers with a shame I recognise. 'She's lovely, so lovely.'

'But it's over, right? With Jules? When did it end?'

Gigi looks at me with blue-eyed desperation.

'Oh Gigi,' I stammer.

'What am I going to do?'

She hails and thunders in her own percussive one-woman show of wretchedness. I understand her so much more than I want to admit.

'Just breathe. I won't say it will be okay ... I don't know that, but you mustn't let anything happen with Julian ever again. Understand?'

She nods her head and continues to cry. 'You're right. I know you're right and I know this is all so retarded and ridiculous.'

'So painful,' I lament.

'Right?' She nods her head in recognition and continues. 'And you know the stupidest thing? All these years, with all my telecasting and promoting of Tea Tim – which by the way has helped make him the mecca he is today – but all the time I kept hoping Julian would turn up and rescue me. Save me from myself and say, "She's mine." Especially in Papua New Guinea. I didn't think he would be able to stand me marrying someone else.'

My karmic reflection looks at me with her wide blue eyes.

'I mean how ridiculous is that, imagining something that unlikely?'

My mind does a quick flashback to me on the Empire State Building a day earlier. 'Gigi, I get it. I am no better than you, but I can tell you it's not going to get you anywhere good.'

'I hate myself!' Gigi shudders.

'That's not going to help either. Has Julian strung you along a bit?'

'A bit?' She laughs with defeat. 'He's pulled every line possible ... I'm his muse; he couldn't bear life without me; we are creative soul mates.'

'But he never said he'd leave Sally?'

'Oh, he hinted at it but time kept passing and it was the kids then it was Sally's menopause, then it was his prostate.'

'Really doesn't sound that inviting,' I reflect.

'You're not the one in love with him.'

'I know.' With deep discomfort, I feel the repulsion Lex must have felt with all my Ross madness over the years.

The tissues Gigi clutches have all but dissolved in her hands.

I wish I had Sam's supplies on hand. Instead, I grab a nearby rumpled, un-ironed napkin and hand it to her and grab another for myself.

'Here, use this, some of the family's decency might rub off on us,' I say, sniffing.

'Zoe, we're musos, we're never around decency,' Gigi replies.

'True, but you got out there and met Tea Tim, he's decent and gorgeous.'

'Only to try to jolt Jules into leaving Sally and being with me.'

'But Tea Tim loves you.'

More tears. 'He really does and he's great. It's a fucking disaster, it's like having Ryan Gosling in love with you when all you want is to marry George Costanza.'

That makes us both laugh.

'I knew you'd get it.' She grabs my hand.

'How? We've hardly seen each other for the past five years.'

'You always seemed comfortable with ambiguity.' Gigi sighs.

'Thank you . . . I think. I'm probably not as good as you suggest; I've been in a moral wasteland myself.'

She looks slightly shocked and devastated by this.

'But you're out of it now,' she insists.

'Yes. Just.'

She squeezes my knee hard.

'What will you do, Gigi?' I ask.

'Keep clear of Julian.' She is like a five year old reluctantly agreeing to put the bar of chocolate back.

'And?' I press.

'I don't know.'

'Work out if you want to be married to Tim, quickly! You mustn't dick him around anymore. Could you love him if you freed yourself of Julian, do you think?' I hold my breath awaiting her reply.

'There are some excellent pheromone exchanges between us.' She speaks slowly.

'Okay.' I nod.

'He's very earnest.' Gigi bites her lip.

'Right.'

'But so am I usually. That's what I loved about Jules, he made me laugh at myself. And the sex . . . oh my god, the sex . . . I mean before the prostate obviously.'

The thought of Jules being sexual is three stations past alarming.

'Gigi, I once went to a tarot card reader at the Glebe markets. You know the best advice she gave me?'

'No.' Gigi never was one for rhetorical pauses.

'You can't ring it if there's no bell. It has to be there at a gut level. If there's anything we should both know from being in the orchestra and from our relationship detours, it's that relationships and marriage are not for sissies. You have to be in it together or it's not going to work.'

'In the trenches of the heart,' Gigi adds.

'Right down deep, in-the-sludge-with-soggy-footrot deep,' I say, realising I'm probably taking the analogy too far, but three-time Gigi doesn't mind that.

'In the trenches, in the trenches, yeah, in the trenches.' She absorbs it.

'Is Jules in the trenches with you?'

'Musically?' Gigi replies hopefully.

'No. Really. In life.'

She shakes her head.

'Well, that's a shame, because if he's stringing you along he's not in them with Sally either. Is Tea Tim?' I ask gently.

'He wants to be; not that I am encouraging the use of warfare metaphors, but he has the artillery and he wants to be there with me. And you know, part of me wonders if I am just scared of letting myself be loved, properly loved, by a great guy.'

'I get that. But take your time and think about it. This is it, Gigi; do everything you can do to be someone you like.'

Now I sound like a new-age desk calendar. I don't know how to word it so it isn't corny, but it's also the truth.

We sit quietly amid the tea, the ironing and the tears for a bit then Gigi resurfaces.

'How's your audition prep?' she asks.

'Up and down,' I reply.

'Want a hand?' Gigi sniffles.

'Really?'

'Sure, I do actually want you to get the gig FYI.'

'Even if it means I'll be working with Jules?'

Gigi shrugs. 'Time for you to get your skin back in the game, sister. I was just being a jealous bitch before . . . harpists steal my thunder.' She grins at me and winks.

'Thanks, Gigi.'

And then she makes me stand and, as anticipated, a full-bodied, full-throttle Gigi hug ensues.

Funny, I never thought I'd come to London through the hail of heartache to find myself becoming actual friends with Gigi Maiers.

But then, like I said, life's like that.

THIRTY-EIGHT

THE DAYS FALL INTO EACH OTHER. STRANGE HOW WHEN YOU return to a place where you've lived previously you kind of slip back into an alternate reality, like you merely walked into another room for a minute and now you're back.

It's been half a decade and yet, staying with the family, walking around Kensington Gardens and the chilly grey Serpentine, warming up in Granger and Co. in Notting Hill . . . everything feels normal.

Gigi has rehearsed me to within an inch of my life. I think it's a distraction for her; she is trying, wisely, to limit her time at Julian's. Tea Tim is working on another big ethically aligned deal involving a literacy application, so Gigi has taken it upon herself to be my personal coach, which both drives me spare and inspires me, as well as keeping me focused.

I play her some of my original pieces.

'That's what you should be doing,' is her proclamation.

'You said I should be in palliative care.'

'All of it, all of it, yes, all of it, I feel it all,' is her reply.

I take a day off practice, and off Gigi, and catch the train to Folkestone to try to imbibe some of what June loved so much about her hometown. I walk along the water's edge and sample the cockles (okay) and mussels (good) and whelks (disgusting) as ordered by June. I imagine June and Clem walking here arm in arm in their day.

How can one day with someone make such an impact on some people's lives while a lifetime with another can leave barely any impression at all? I guess it's like music; certain people transcend space, time and rationale and pierce your heart in such a way the moment or two you spent with them becomes the fixed point of the compass of your life.

I weave through the pretty little shops on the High street, and end up with multiple bags of boiled sweets for the kids at home. Anything to stop me thinking of Ross.

I know Clem married and had a son, I know something happened. I know he continued to teach and paint until he moved to Western Australia. I know his phone has been disconnected and his sister hasn't heard from him in a year. I know I haven't seen an obituary for him, so there's still hope. I also know the chances of him being barmy or ill or in a grave are higher than those of him being at the supermarket.

From what Reg tells me June is holding strong, but he's one for minimalising, he so wants me to find happiness on this trip I can imagine he wouldn't tell me anything unless it was major.

And time is always running out and we cannot control it and how am I going to get through this audition in two days' time? It's before Julian and a few board members and some of the key creatives. In other words, it's a big deal. A really, bloody big deal.

I long to overcome this debilitating sense of dread that I will freeze and it will happen all over again. They'd be taking a risk, I don't have a great track record from my last appearance with them, and every halfway decent harpist from all corners of the world will be auditioning. Oh boy. Silly, isn't it, you can talk yourself in circles about staying calm, keeping it in perspective, distancing yourself from the drama, but once panic and fear take hold it's like trying to give a drowning man swimming instructions.

I breathe in the sea air. I can see June as a little girl skipping up and down the water's edge. She has such a joy of spirit.

I begin fretting she will die, and Dad, before I get home. Perhaps I should just fly home now, forget this whole stupid audition. I'm a great bedside musician, what do I need to prove?

I stop and breathe again. It's like getting yourself to exercise or go to bed when you're overtired – what you so desperately need for the quality of your survival can be the hardest thing to give yourself. What if I do clam up? At least I tried. My life won't be over. Though it may feel like reliving the end of that chapter of my life all over again.

Why do I need this?

Because I do.

Because in my own murky depths, my fixed point is my music. I have always known it, and I am not ready to say I can never play with an orchestra again.

•

The following day I head down to my fabulously rambunctious family's farm, which is in a tiny hamlet outside of Surrey called Christmas Pie . . . truly. I attend their church with them, which is a tiny chapel that would do the vicar of Dibley proud, complete with an ancient organ. It's freezing but much warmth is in hot cups of tea and chat afterwards. I take my harp and perform for them as a practice run; considering there are only twelve of us in the congregation and six are my relatives, I don't find it overwhelming. I plan to practise the program I have, with the help of Maestro Maiers, coordinated for tomorrow's audition.

I wait a moment before I commence, then spot Fred mouthing *Hurry up!* as he rolls his eyes to the ceiling, in hope of a higher help. He is itching to get home to a promised James Bond film marathon this afternoon and has us timed to the minute.

This decompresses me and, to put him out of his misery, I begin with 'One Fine Day' from *La Bohème*, on to some Saint-Saëns, Bach and finally the piece I composed for Clara, to conclude.

It is well received, bar Fred, who felt the tempo was too slow.

Afterwards we all pitch in to make a huge roast for lunch, picking apples from the trees in the backyard for apple sauce to accompany a pig reared on the farm; fortunately I never met it before its happy life ended when the mobile butcher came to visit.

We all sit around and chat and delay washing up before the afternoon of James Bond in front of a roaring open fire with hot chocolates commences, then supper and the slow creep back in two cars to London on the M4 on a Sunday night. And my last sleep before the audition.

THIRTY-NINE

THE NEXT MORNING, I WAKE AND WATCH THE MINUTES PEEL away before my alarm sounds. I check emails. Part of me wonders if Ross will remember today's audition, though he's most likely too busy exchanging vows, hopefully ones he will keep this time, buttoning up a dinner suit, or flying to an unthinkably exotic location for his honeymoon . . .

Stop it, Zoe, he is banned. No more.

I snap to and shower and motor up. I catch the tube and wander around Covent Garden, finding a warm, steamed up café with drinkable (just) coffee. I am too early to walk up to the rehearsal studios where the audition will be. So my harp and I wander slowly through the main square, absorbing the history. June performed here too, with the Royal Ballet, what a feat.

It's too cold to stay out and I don't want the harp losing her tune. So I head in, press the lift button and travel up the two floors to the well-heated studios where I take my seat outside and wait.

I'm about to switch my phone off when the ping of a new text message arrives. I'm sure it's Ross . . . but no, it's Dreadful Tina.

My heart performs a steep descent and my breath catches. All I can think is: *Dad*. I'm terrified to read it. I hear Julian's voice nearing, he's about to open the door and invite me in. I freeze and read the message: *Just letting you know house has sold. Four-week settlement. Lou told me not to worry you while you're away but I thought you should know. Trust you're having fun. Tina*

At that moment the phone rings, it's Tom. I send the call to voicemail as Julian appears from the kitchenette looking like butter wouldn't melt in his mouth. A tear-stained Gigi stands beside him. Julian obviously has no comprehension of my insider knowledge.

'My two favourite antipodeans. Lucky me.' It's all hugs and pats from Jules. I catch Gigi's eye, she shakes her head subtly.

'Thanks for helping me with that,' is all she says. The fact they have entered from the kitchenette doesn't seem to occur to either of them.

'Well, we can work on it at home,' he replies. 'Sally is making spaghetti marinara tonight for us all. Fun.'

'Fun,' she repeats on autopilot. I know that look.

'Gigi tells me you're on form, Zoe.' Julian pats my hand, and all I can think is: how did Gigi fall for him? It would be like dating Elmer Fudd. He's dithery and bald. Sally organises his life because he's so into his music he'd go to bed in the fridge if left to his own devices. Genius gives you a big get out of jail free card sometimes.

Julian steps in to receive Gigi's pert cylindrical breasts in a full-body hug, but Gigi steps back and focuses her Gigi powers on embracing me; actually, it feels like I'm a lifeboat she's clinging to.

'I don't mind if Gigi wants to stay, she's helped me a lot,' I offer.

'No, my dear, I must focus all of my attention on the task at hand; too hard when Aphrodite is in close proximity.' He says this seemingly innocuously but I can see the little stab it provides Gigi.

'Call me when you're done and I'll take you for a chai.' Gigi attempts to sound bright and breezy but the tension in her voice pushes it to shrill. How the hell is she staying in the same house as him? She's only just keeping it together.

I watch her get into the lift and spy the tiniest glimpse of how her public face drops and her vulnerability and pain surface as the lift doors close. How can Julian not see it too? Perhaps because remaining oblivious is a much easier route.

'Shall we?' Fuddy-duddy Julian, sweet and unaware, escorts me into the rehearsal studio. I'm considering the fact he is possibly blind to any of Gigi's pain when I'm slapped by the reality of a long table of five of the head honchos of the British classical musical world awaiting me. They stand and the distance the harp, Julian and I must walk to shake hands and greet them lengthens to what feels like light years, my heart racing and the pounding amplifying with every step. It's a wonder there isn't a record player in the corner where I should be putting on the theme song to *Flashdance*.

Instead my esteemed betters of the industry stand, smile, shake my hand, tell me how well I look. Everyone elegantly avoids the fact that last time they saw me I was being carried out on a gurney as I embarked on a breakdown. There's a feeling of good-will, apprehension and straight-out nervousness for me, which of course increases my heart rate and shaking hands exponentially.

I try to visualise Fred rolling his eyes to stop my mind fare-welling my body, as happens at the commencement of an anxiety attack. I breathe . . . picture Reg burping the national anthem. I imagine how they'd rate his performance, though he wouldn't give a toss because he does it for his own joy . . . not that I know of anyone belching in tune as a serious vocation . . . I wonder if anyone has ever had a professional belcher as a wedding performer, as opposed to Elvis . . . Ross wouldn't get married in Vegas, would he . . . oh god—

'Zoe?' Julian gently pulls me back to the room. 'Take your time, Zoe, we're all just excited to hear you play again,' he reas-sures me.

'It's been a long time since . . .' Oh god I am going to fuck this up, royally.

'No pressure,' Julian says gently as the others lean forward, ready for me to get on with it.

I take my girl out of her case. Check a few things, like my pulse. Adjust my butt cheek positioning on the stool. Okay, I am out of faffing options.

Start, Zoe.

My fingers freeze. My breath catches, and the faces before me morph into Dreadful Tina. No, not Dreadful Tina, she can't ruin this for me. I squint and close my eyes for a moment, and I see Mum and Dad, Tom and Ross. Okay, so I have gone over again. Is this happening? Am I sitting here? I haven't started floating away yet. Of course the faces are of Julian, Laura, Ben, Misch and Viggo. Holy fuck, I must have a death wish coming here.

Sweat pours from every pore of my body, acute fire strikes my cheeks, my hands tingle and cramp. There is no sense of time, just the ghosts of my heart lining up. *Think of June and Clem, do it for them, give them this.* Okay, I bargain, I will do this for June and Clara and Clem and Kip . . . and fuck you, Ross and Dreadful Tina.

Story has it that Puccini had his heart irrevocably smashed and couldn't compose, couldn't listen to music, couldn't be anywhere near it . . . yet he'd been commissioned to write an opera. He was doing his own nosedive into depression and was sent off to the country, where he lived alone in a benefactor's cottage. He sat there day after day in a funk, then he started walking in the afternoons because he had zero inspiration or motivation. He walked and breathed and that was about it. He liked to wander down to a big lake near the cottage, and one day while he was there, he listened to a gentle warm summer breeze pass through the bulrushes. He listened more, and more, and that is where the first notes of the humming chorus, which led Puccini to write *Madame Butterfly*, arrived.

I listen to my short starts of breath, to Dreadful Tina's voice telling me about the sale, and Ross climaxing and Ross leaving and the rush of breath as Mum put her hand to her head and told Tom and me we'd given her a headache, and the sobs that came from behind Dad's closed door, and the last gasps from Clara and Kip. I hear Lexie's laugh, Dorothy's questions and Tom's singing, Vivianne's coo and Sam's whistle to Harry and Harry's pant as he places his head on my lap, and above this my own howl of incomprehension at my place within it all, wild and calling, hungry and scared. And I listen and I allow the heat to rise and rush to my fingers and I open my eyes and I commence.

I have no idea if there is anyone else still left in the studio, or whether I am in it either, or if I'm already lying down on the floor, being carried away screaming or . . .

I play, as though my life depends upon it. Because it does. This instrument is my lifeline, my bulrushes. And so it goes.

I finish. I am saturated with my own sweat and not sure if I have peed myself. I am terrified to see what existence I am in, but I slowly raise my eyes to the lights. They are the studio lights. I see there are people at the table. The auditioning panel, not my family, not doctors. They are out of focus but I hear Julian's voice among others.

'Thank you, Zoe.'

'Thank you,' I whisper. The faces seem to smile tightly. I have crashed, burnt and fucked this up. I am a mental health issue and a red flag.

'Zoe, who on earth was that final piece by?'

'Me . . . I . . . I am.' I try to speak but my mouth and voice seem incompatible.

'Thank you.' Viggo stands. The others follow. I am obviously meant to take my leave.

I rush to put my harp back in her case.

Julian walks to me, places an arm around me and escorts me out, a bit like when the nice ambulance man comes to escort you to the sanitarium, they know kindness is a better tactic to deal with loons like me.

I didn't check to see if I broke a string. Perhaps that's what happened. Or perhaps I spent the time belching the songs not playing them. My body begins to shake. I hide it as well as I can as Julian puts me in the lift. Wow, they really want to get rid of me quickly.

'And what's next for you, dear Zoe?' he asks as I get in.

'Fucked if I know, I'm not big on plans,' comes out before I have a chance to edit it into anything else.

I realise what I've said as he murmurs something then waves his hand as the doors close.

God I love kissing in lifts . . . Wait, that's not the next logical thought. I have completely lost my postage pack.

FORTY

I GET TO THE STREET AND ALLOW MY SHAKES AND SHIVERS TO take full rein as I don my gloves and beanie and stand on the corner checking my voicemail to hear what Tom has said.

'Hi sis. I bet bitchface has beat me to it but, yeah, it sold. Seven million, can you fucking believe it? Ah, bugger me. What would Bubbe and Pop say if they knew the place they bought Mum and Dad was worth that? What would Mum say if she knew? I'm sort of spun out. Need to surf, so . . . I might see you guys in Bali. I could handle a week in Uluwatu but I'll come up to Ubud for a night or two. I was going to move in with Abi, but . . . yeah . . . nup . . . that's a bit . . . not sure. Anyway, it's pretty random and Dad and I are going for a beer later. I'll tell him we reckon he needs to do a runner with the cash. He won't though, will he? Hope your audition went well and you didn't lose your shit and go all weird. Strange days, Zo. See you next week.'

I listen to the message a few more times. I love hearing his voice, sometimes a big brother can be the best anchor in life.

A text comes through from Gigi, and Lexie and Vivianne have sent a video clip they've made of themselves drinking espresso martinis at the airport all revved up for Bali.

But I can't speak to anyone. I just need to walk. Actually, I need to swim but the Serpentine looks completely uninviting, let alone freezing, but bless those few who brave it. So I lug my harp and I walk until I realise that walking London with a harp is possibly the most ridiculous plan I've ever had and I splurge on a cab to drop it off at Sabrina's.

From there I head to Kensington Gardens, passing the statue of Peter Pan and walking round and around to clear my mind. So, the audition didn't go so well. I didn't die, that's a plus. I managed to leave without the assistance of an ambulance. No one lost an eye.

I will have to find some other kind of work when I get home; bedside musicians do not get paid above the poverty line. And where am I going to live? With whom? I ponder what happened with Tom and Abi. He must've tried to shag her is my guess. I love Tom but perhaps it's time we live with other people, or alone.

Gigi texts again: *MUST SEE YOU IMMEDIATELY – meet me at The Carrot and the Rooster around the corner from your place.* X

Oh dear, she's been sent to break it to me. The fact my professional music career is officially over and I will be blacklisted from every professional body forever. And of course this will be told to me at a pub called The Carrot and the Rooster, though

I have a feeling it is actually named The Parrot and Rooster . . . still . . .

Gigi doesn't even drink, she is a temple-loving matcha tea and spirulina shake girl. She sits with something clear in a glass – mineral water.

'How bad was it?' I ask as I sit. Straight to the circle of truth for me.

'It was terrible,' Gigi admits. 'Just appalling.'

'Shit.' I gulp down my glass of pub red, Sam would not approve. I have really lost it.

'Oh Zoe.' She wraps her arms around me with abandon. I feel too miserable to say anything. I hold her though I want to hide under the table.

'What am I going to do?' Gigi gulps.

'What do you mean? Shit, I hope you didn't get in trouble for recommending me? I just . . . lost it, I guess. I didn't know it was that dire but I had to find out sometime.' Perhaps I could retrain and be a nurse. I feel so appalled, my patients must have been humouring me. A captive audience.

'What are you talking about?' Gigi stops her heaves of despair.

'My audition. I fucked it. Didn't I?'

'Did you? I have no idea, you saw Julian last. He's a professional, you won't hear till they've auditioned everyone else. What makes you think you fucked it?'

'What's going on then?'

She erupts, Mount Vesuvius with a cleavage. 'I'm pregnant!'

'Oh, Gigi. Oh shit. It's not . . .'

'No, I haven't touched Julian. I've been keeping my distance. Trying to . . . I'm going insane. What made me think I could stay there?'

'I meant the tribal chief's son.'

'No, the chief walked in before it got to that. No, it's Tea Tim's.' She sobs more.

'You're pregnant with your husband's baby. That's not bad,' I offer.

'But I still love him!'

'Julian?'

'Yes, yes, yes, stupid bloody bald Julian.'

'Oh, Gigi, that's horrible, I'm sorry. How many weeks?'

'Nine! I only found out today, my period has always been erratic, but my breasts!'

Gigi holds her golden cylinders of wonder. They are even fuller and rounder than ever, and riding so unbelievably high.

'They're so sore and so fucking huge!' She holds and circles and rubs them. 'Feel,' she demands.

She grabs both my hands and places them over her breasts, I get why guys are so fascinated with them. I'm flat-chested so have always marvelled at other women's flowering mammaries. If I were a straight bloke I'd definitely be a tits man.

A few of the pub patrons turn to us, watching appreciatively. I gently remove my hands from her boobs and place them on her hands.

'I thought I had a virus from the stress,' she continues. 'I mean I do mucal testing with Tea Tim.'

I am not sure exactly what she means.

'So you were telling Julian today? Tim doesn't know but Julian does?'

Gigi nods, misery and radiance oozing from each pore. 'Here I am. Up the duff. I went to Julian because . . . I had to know.'

'What?'

'If there was any, any, any chance of an us. Because this means I really have to say goodbye to him.'

'What did he say?'

Gigi stares up at the ceiling, reliving the conversation. 'Not much really. I pulled him out of auditions. He was worried I was sick, probably because my next concerts with them have sold out. Well, I mean he knew there was no chance it was his. You know, I don't believe he's ever really considered the fact I lie naked with and fuck Tea Tim; he's kind of oblivious to anything outside his own sphere, he only knows the bits of me that he inhabits. It's not even a healthy relationship.'

'No,' I echo, sounds familiar.

'He got all very English and said it was for the best and I'd be a wonderful mum.'

'You will be, if that's what you choose.'

'He doesn't want me, Zoe, he really doesn't want me. I thought he loved me, you know?'

'Yep, I know. And he does in his silly way, but if he *really* loved you, really, really the way you love him, do you think he would have ever kept you hanging on like this? Wished you luck and stayed married?' I am aware the words coming from my mouth are for both of us.

'No, no, *noooo*!' She cries and I cradle her. I can only imagine what it must be like having heartbreak crashing against surging hormones. I imagined Ross and I might start a family, one day when. But we were always careful there were no pregnancy scares.

After a while she settles.

'Gigi, do you want a baby?' I ask.

'Not if it makes me ordinary.'

'Gigi, you will never be ordinary.'

'Good, no, I didn't think so. Yes, I've always known I was a mother. And a baby, growing a baby . . .'

The tiniest smile emerges.

'It's very clever if you ask me,' I offer.

'It is a bit. A little being for me to play to.'

I can already see Gigi's world domination as the baby-whispering percussionist.

'And what about Tea Tim, how are things going?'

'You know he really is a god. He is adorable, and the sex has been . . . his oral, Zoe – sometimes I come even before his tongue reaches my clit.'

'Well, you're obviously very compatible.'

'You should see his tongue sometime.'

'Mmm, um, okay.'

'I mean . . .' She nods and sticks her own tongue out to show me. 'Much longer than mine, and it has a point.'

The patrons all watch again.

'Better than Jules's tongue?'

'Jules needs training. He can hum Beethoven's fifth in time

with fucking – before the prostate thing – but really that's his main party trick.'

'Good to know.' I feel I have been permanently scarred with that image.

Gigi clasps my hands. 'Tea Tim will be a magnificent father.'

'Absolutely.' I believe that's true.

'And he's so excited by what's happening with the chicken co-op companies.'

'You mean the chief's chicken coup?'

Gigi clasps harder, bringing my hands and hers back to her mothering jugs.

'I didn't tell you. The project the chief made me invent and us invest in is going dynamite, so Tea Tim is expanding it all across Asia. It's called The Good Chook, the chief is going to be the figurehead, which he is into. You know, it's like he orchestrated the whole thing.'

I nod, unsure.

'Wait . . . what's this about your audition?' Suddenly she looks worried for me.

'Doesn't matter. I didn't die, that's the main thing.' Gigi doesn't need to hear about my audition fail. And her tale of pregnancy and chickens has been a good distraction.

'Do you think it's a boy or a girl? Oh god, Zoe, I have to tell Tea Tim!'

And just like that Gigi Maiers goes from devastation to cat-with-the-cream elation, and begins patting her growing fetus with a rhythmic tune.

We finish up and she walks me home.

'You know,' she says, 'I feel like I know you in a way I didn't before.'

'Because you didn't really know me before.'

'You're a great friend, you know that, Zoe Wylde child?'

'You're not bad yourself, Gigi mother-to-be,' I reply.

We embrace and promise to see each other again back in Bondi. I'm smiling as I watch her walk up the street singing to her child. Seriously, the kid is probably going to be the next Dalai Lama.

I'm toppled by a small football team of cousins who have decided to ambush me as a way of showing their affection. We cook and eat together, laughing and chatting about which bands are brilliant, which ones are overrated and why mid-week math tests are such a drag.

Sabrina, Daniel and I finish the dishes and sit with a bottle of wine. A peppery shiraz. Sam would approve.

'Tell us you're coming back?' Sabrina fills my glass.

'I don't think it went that well.'

'No? Well, fuck 'em off then,' Daniel encourages, which makes Sabrina and me peal into laughter. *Oh damn* is the closest I've ever heard Daniel come to swearing.

I am so grateful to them, and I'd love to spend more time with them, but I also know it's time to gather my own life, decide on my destination, draw the bow and shoot it forward.

The next morning is filled with the joys of waiting at the airport, as the first flight to Singapore is overweight.

I check my phone. No messages from Ross. I wonder how long it will be before I stop checking.

Tom is on his way to the airport too, getting a lift with a friend so his responses to my questions are monosyllabic.

'Are you okay?' I ask.

'Yeah.'

'Did you shag Abi?'

'Nup.'

'Did you have a fight with Dad?'

'Nup.'

'Is Dreadful Tina still being evil?'

'Yep.'

'Okay, well, you and the girls are picking me up, so I'll see you on the other side.'

'Yep.'

Something's up, and he's not happy. Lexie and Vivianne have gone quiet too, though I imagine their silence is more due to orgasmic ecstasy. Vivianne assures me they will be there to pick me up when I confirm I've made the second flight.

Sam sends a picture of Harry at the Gap asking how the audition went and telling me there are no Balinese wines he can recommend . . . because there are no Balinese wines. *When in Bali stick to vodka*, is his advice.

FORTY-ONE

THE TWELVE-HOUR FLIGHT IS THREE STOPS BEYOND ETERNAL, a far cry from the highs of business class with Ross. That feels like a lifetime ago and I feel the dual pull of repulsion and longing. I'm seated between an elderly man with a flatulence issue and a middle-aged businesswoman who elbows me every time he blows.

I try to focus on the new release thrillers that have been programmed. I don't want to go near anything romantic or sad, but of course my mind spins and spins back to the audition, then forward to the move out ahead and all the questions.

Why can't they give me an inkling? Like, say, *You didn't get it but you didn't totally suck* . . . or *you did totally suck but at least we didn't have to send you to hospital on a stretcher.* Anything really.

Finally, we descend and I make my way to my next flight to Bali. A tiny plane and a flight of turbulence. I arrive in Denpasar exhausted, in need of a shower and a swim.

•

Checking out of Denpasar airport, which has had a major revamp since my last visit to Bali, I'm swiped with the humidity and an extensive interview and thorough screening of my harp. Even though we're not on speaking terms right now, the thought of being separated from her for too long throws me into a spin. I wind up playing a piece for the customs officers to show I'm bona fide; they reluctantly stamp my visa but inform me the gamelan is a superior instrument. I beg to differ but keep my trap shut, knowing this is neither the time nor the place.

I walk through, harp and luggage intact, and Tom and Lexie are waiting for me, though neither is looking anything close to holiday happy.

'Hey babes.' I'm hugged and enveloped the way we all long to be at airports.

'Where's Vivianne?' I ask.

'Oh.' Lex looks away. 'She's just having a lie-down, she doesn't love the heat.'

This makes Tom laugh. 'Lex is in the dog house,' he announces.

'Lex, you did prepare her for the, um, wilderness of your villa, didn't you?'

'What? Hello producer, yes, course. It's just that the air-con we bought for her packed it in this morning, which I don't think is a big deal. Ratut is looking at it now.'

'And there's no running water,' Tom adds, smiling sweetly, enjoying his eternal desire to pull Lexie's plaits.

'It's fixed now,' Lexie retorts.

'Poor Vivianne. Is the air-con definitely getting fixed, Lex? It's just . . . my harp . . .'

Lexie loses it as we approach the ancient minivan she's hired. 'Oh will everyone chill the fuck out, we're in Bali. Hello, Bali time, anyone?'

She flings the sliding door open and lights a Balinese cigarette.

'Oh, Lex, gross.'

The trip up the hill is filled with the clove-infused smell of Lex's Bali cigarettes, Balinese radio and hot air blowing in. Lex only smokes when she's here; I think she sees it as a spiritual concern she adheres to when in Bali mode. I've always thought I was open to it but after two days in airports and transit all I want is air-con, a shower and nice sheets. I don't dare mention this out loud of course.

Lexie's villas, well villa plus shacks, are a half-kilometre walk from where anything other than feet, a mountain lion or a scooter can venture. So we have to walk through the jungle paths. Lex loves it, of course. While I, laden with my harp, do not feel as affectionate about the villa's remoteness.

We finally arrive. Lexie has owned the villas for over a decade, but she only comes once or twice a year. Her ex-partner has a lease on the land but Lexie paid for the construction and the sporadic upkeep of the villas. They are simple Balinese constructions which hold their own charm; rustic is an understatement.

Vivianne sits beside a packed suitcase.

'I'm sorry, everyone, Lex, I'm a redhead, I cannot do this heat. And this . . . this place, it's very beautiful but . . .'

She stops as a large green lizard scampers across the tiled floor and over her feet. There's a bird's nest in the top corner of the room. Mosquitos fly freely around the thatched ceiling. Tom sets to opening a bottle of gin. It feels like we've taken our place in a Joseph Conrad novel.

Vivianne is certainly experiencing her own heart of darkness chapter. The villas have met with major deterioration since Lex's last trip. The garden is overgrown and fast returning to vines, monkeys swing freely as do other as yet unclassified creatures passing through.

Lex attempts to calm Vivianne, she sits beside her cross-legged and rubs her back. 'It's like the Balinese say – a house needs human feet to keep the wildness at bay,' she coos.

Vivianne attempts to smile bravely; she's being quite stoic really.

Tom hands us our warm gin in plastic cups.

'It's very green, lush,' is all I can offer, slapping a mosquito off me and attempting to get as close as possible to the one sad coil that wafts smoky signs of defeat.

'Yes,' Lex forges on. 'In a few days it will be amazing, just watch.'

We all look out and up as the bird in its nest changes position.

The sound of the generator starts up for a moment before stopping again with an abrupt fart.

The air is as thick as custard. I can feel my harp recoiling in horror; any moment the strings will go.

Ratut, the 'groundskeeper', swears in Indonesian and calls out to Lex. Lex rushes out, and they stand, speaking in Indonesian, the main action seeming to be the lighting of another cigarette.

It's smoked in silence as Tom, Vivianne and I stare into the depths of our plastic cups and Tom silently refills them. It's too hot for anyone's mouth to be able to form words.

We take turns at readjusting our clothing, which sticks to our respective skin as perspiration permeates. Even sarongs feel heavy in this heat.

Lex re-enters. Sits on the bed. Finishes her drink.

'The power won't be back on till after sunset. Ratut is calling his cousin but they have to go to Denpasar for the piece, and there's a ceremony they need to stop in on first. Niece's tooth filing. It might be nice if we—' She wipes a trickle of sweat from her brow. 'Let's get the fuck out of here.'

With that we pretty much spring back into the minivan and make our way into Ubud. Tom hires a scooter. Vivianne and I try to check into a hotel but they're all booked till after the weekend. They do, however, agree to take my harp. Uma, a beautiful hotel off the main road, has an amazing pool and incredible food and air-con. We pay to use the pool and spa facilities, then, feeling slightly better, we reassemble poolside, with cocktails. I remember Sam's advice and order a lychee martini, though I'm still feeling somewhat flushed.

Lex and Vivianne are canoodling in the water, Tom watches as he chomps on peanuts and downs a Bali beer.

'What happened with Abi?' I venture, attempting to ignore the growing feeling of nausea creeping up my digestive tract. Jet lag.

'Nothing, she's cool, really cool.'

'So, why wouldn't you want to be flatmates?'

'She really gets me, and it's scaring the shit out of me,' he answers.

'Oh.' I take another sip, hoping the vodka will have an anti-septic effect on whatever bug I have brought with me from the plane. I pull up the sleeves on the cotton kaftan Vivianne has lent me. I only packed a few pieces for warm weather in case I got stuck in Singapore for a few days.

Tom picks at his beer label.

'She's not like anyone else and it's spinning me out. I don't know whether she's like my new best mate, but then she's hot, but I don't want to wreck things so I back off. She doesn't react. Just does her own thing. Driving me fucking nuts.'

'What do you want her to do, Tom? Make a move so you can freak out and reject her?'

Tom casts a look that says both *Yes* and *Shut up*. 'I just really like being around her,' he replies.

'And she likes being around you?'

He nods.

'Well she's obviously batshit crazy then.' Sometimes being a little sister means it's too hard not to tease. Tom retaliates by tossing me in the pool.

Just like I knew he would.

The day continues to improve with air-con, water and vodka. Lex and Vivianne are back on their own reinterpretation of hot lesbians in love in a pool.

Taking a moment from each other while Vivianne goes to 'freshen up', Lex sits next to Tom and slaps his thigh. 'You still up for it?'

Tom inhales quickly.

'What?' I ask.

'Turkey baster.' Lexie grins.

'I think you're rushing it,' replies Tom to my surprise; I'd always thought he would jump at an opportunity to have his bodily fluids close to Lex.

'Vivianne's thirty-eight and she's ovulating, today.'

'But, Lex, you two were breaking up a fortnight ago and it's only been a month, surely a few more cycles are okay?' I say, hoping to appeal to her world-wise producer side rather than her cuckoo, in love side.

Lex, obviously disagreeing, lights another clove cigarette, which brings audible groans from Tom and me.

'You're trying to seal the deal with Vivianne by pimping Tom as the sperm donor.' I'm still jet-lagged enough to say this.

'I agree,' comes Vivianne's voice as she sits beside Lexie, taking her hands in her own. 'I'm mad for you, Lex, but we should probably wait just a bit longer.'

'If I could make you pregnant I would right now,' Lex murmurs, which makes Tom and me moan again.

'We can practise,' whispers Vivianne, which makes my eyes roll and has Tom looking hungrily at them both again.

They begin kissing – I drag Tom off for another swim.

FORTY-TWO

MY TUMMY SETTLES AND ON THE WAY BACK TO THE VILLAS WE grab dinner at Indus – Balinese paella with fresh seafood, more martinis, more laughter.

The night is a long one and my villa is shared with a cacophony of wildlife of which I am terrified – birds, frogs, lizards and the occasional rat – making their way through the offerings to Ganesh on the porch. I hope Vivianne is faring better than I am. I am almost asleep when the generator re-ignites. I smell cloves and figure Lex cannot sleep either, so I get up and spot the light of the cigarette looking in through the glass-walled villa. I wave, but I can't make out Lex. I switch on the outside light and grab my robe. It's only then I see the cigarette isn't being smoked by Lex but by an Indonesian man, whom I have never laid eyes on. I gasp and attempt to scream . . . nothing. I lower my voice into a growl I know Gigi would be proud of, and call: 'Lex, Lex ... there's a man ... LEX! TOM!'

From the villa below I see a light go on and I hear Lex calling, 'Zoe, a bird?'

'A man, a man, a man, A MAN!' I am roaring now.

The man stands statue still in front of me, the thin glass all that's separating us. I am sure this is it, this will be my departure. Where the hell is Lex?

Lex appears holding a broom and wearing her look of ferocity, which tells me she's scared too; Vivianne with a snow-white face of terror is behind her. Lex asks in Indonesian who the man is.

The man remains mute. I am sure a huge number of them are about to descend and rape and pillage us while Tom, my darling brother, sleeps through the whole thing in his hut further down the hill where Lex is putting in a pool ... one day in the next fifty years.

I can see Lex is growing concerned and, though she speaks with conviction, her Balinese is pretty lousy. She begins to name all the Balinese people she knows, and finally he speaks.

'Gin.'

'Sorry?'

'Ratut says you drink gin.'

I can see now that the man is as scared as we are and obviously deeply intoxicated.

Lexie looks relieved. 'You want gin?'

'Quick get the mini bottles we have left,' Lex yells and Vivianne rushes to grab them.

Then Lexie's producer side rises to the fore. 'It's too late for gin. Bar's shut, you scared my friend. Go home and sleep. Now.'

She says a few words in Balinese and Indonesian harshly.

The fellow – exhausted and drunk – takes his hat off, rubs his head and moves off slowly, obviously disappointed with the lack of party atmosphere.

'Here!' Vivianne appears outside her villa and fills his hands with half-a-dozen bar fridge–size liqueur bottles of Tia Maria, Baileys and Frangelico.

He looks confused as she thrusts them into his hands. I am beginning to feel sorry for him. Lexie holds the broom up to show she means business. It's one of those mini brooms Ratut uses to clear the leaves; I'm not sure it's capable of doing anything other than sweeping the man.

He heads into the darkness. We stare at each other at a loss.

'Come and sleep with us, make sure you're safe,' Vivianne offers. I consider it but see by Lexie's face it's not the type of slumber party she's wanting, so I head back to my furry friends in my villa. How did Lexie talk us into this?

The next morning, before the bite of heat begins its feast, we sit out with Balinese coffees on the porch looking over the green. It is pretty in a wild, wild way.

Ratut has appeared and when we explain the horrors of the previous evening he shakes his head in dismay. Apparently, it was his drunk friend Noh, a wood carver by trade but quite a good sparky; Ratut had told him that if he was successful Lex would give him a bottle of gin for his efforts. Noh had been partying and figured now was as good a time as any to fix the air-con, and clearly he had no idea he would be accosted by the witches of Eastwick.

The incident causes great commotion in the village. Ratut's wife's parents, the village elders, come and perform a clearing ceremony and many of the villagers come to make offerings in the hope our space won't harbour bad spirits. Perhaps I should get them to perform one on me to ensure I've exorcised Ross.

In Bali there is pretty much a ceremony for everything. The 'clearing' takes up most of the day until once again the heat gets too much and we make our pilgrimage back into town in search of relief.

Tom and I FaceTime Dad, who seems pretty stable, but he switches gears when we ask about the settlement period for the house. 'Let's wait and see,' is his response, which translates to 'Please don't ask me.' And of course Dreadful Tina helps him out in the background: 'The sooner they're out the better, they've had plenty of time.'

We wind up the conversation and head back to the pool. I'm itching to check on the harp and, I have to admit, to play. It's such a part of my daily routine that more than a few days without it has me like a needy lover seeking a fix.

Thanks to Vivianne's interpersonal skills, the hotel is kind enough to let me use an empty conference room to practise. Lex and Vivianne arrive during my session and I play them the piece I've written for Clem and June. I avoid thoughts of the audition and focus on the notes instead.

Vivianne seems to genuinely enjoy it but Lex, as usual, has

her nose in her iPhone enjoying the free wi-fi access and checking emails for her latest gig.

As is often the case in Bali, the time softens, the next night is without incident and we take the van to Seminyak for a day on the beach. We arrive back in Ubud in time to have our usual one-hour discussion about which restaurant to try next as we shower and dress for dinner.

I opt for the one nice summer outfit I packed: a pale blue cotton toga jumpsuit of Clara's, which is so eighties but perfect for Bali – backless, sleek but comfortable. We head to Sari restaurant, slap-bang in the middle of the rice paddies, and try exotic-sounding juices and fresh salads.

It is so hot that being back in the van even for the fifteen-minute drive up the hill is in no way inviting, so I grab a double with Tom who scootered down. Just as Tom's fetching the bike my FaceTime sounds. It's Reg.

'G'day, dolly – where are you now?' he chirps.

'Bali, Ubud, and then home.'

'I've got a few kids in Bali, I think,' Reg quips, though of course there's no telling if he's kidding or speculating.

'Listen, doll face. Don't panic but . . .'

My stomach, already tender, makes a loud groan and my throat tightens.

'Who?'

'June, she's not doing so well, which I know is relative because she's here to cark it. No use panicking, but I thought you'd want to know.'

'Is she still conscious?' I ask, panic rising in my chest.

'Yeah, but they're calling her family in. She told me she's just bone tired.'

'But she has to wait.'

'I think she's trying but she's not winning.'

Fevered tears gather in my eyes. 'I'll get the next flight home,' I say.

'No, you enjoy your holiday. You staying some place fancy?'

'Not quite,' I manage as Tom pulls up ready for me to board the back of the bike.

'I'll get there as soon as I can, Reg. Tell her, will you?'

'Will do, Flossy.'

'And tell her Clem was in Western Australia and I am still trying to find him so, please, she mustn't go yet.'

'Okay, kid. Get on your bike. Who's the fella?'

'Just my brother.' I try to sound strong but the thought of June leaving . . . Not June.

'Thought you were getting a bit of jiggy-jiggy. Never mind, toots.'

Reg can still make me smile though he's sad too, he's said goodbye to as many friends at the hospice as I have.

'All right?' Tom asks as we motor up the hill. Actually, I am bilious, my tummy gurgles in a threatening manner and my full focus is on breathing so I don't throw up. My mind whirls with flights I need to list myself for. Not June. The air feels like fire even though it's cooled down, and I'm soaking wet and shivering.

'Pull over, I have to—'

I lean over the bike and upchuck.

Tom stops. 'Are you all right? Jesus, you're drenched.'

'I can't stop shivering.'

'Should I take you to a doctor?'

'No, I'm just overtired or it's food poisoning. Just get me home.'

We start again. I clutch him with all my might. *Just breathe, Zoe.* I swallow hard.

We near the Four Seasons Hotel and are stopped while a procession takes place – hundreds of spectators and locals on scooters and in cars are stopped and Balinese people in traditional dress pass, small children laughing and passing out flowers, more gamelan—

And then I spot them, a united aura of golden tanned incandescence. Ross and Jeanie . . . but it's not the Jeanie I've seen on my few permitted google stalks; it's Jeanie with a shiny new ring, Jeanie who seems to have grown five inches, all in the leg, increased two bra sizes, and . . . well, she looks exactly like the girl from Roxette. Short bleached spiky hair worn with confidence. Mini dress, phenomenal legs and heels that look resort glam rather than nightclub slutty. Earrings, Jeanie wears dangly earrings. Ross stands beside her in a white linen shirt with freshly trimmed hair and a band of shiny platinum. They're getting their photo taken, each is presented with a lei of frangipanis. Ross looks towards the bike as we pass.

I try to disappear into Tom's back as the retching recommences. Tom scoots on a bit before the next projectile pineapple juice lands as I call out, 'Ross!'

Everything blurs and whirls past. I hear Tom telling me to hold on. 'I saw Ross, Ross is here on his honeymoon,' I manage as I purge every fluid my body has ever held precious. The rest of the journey is my head on his back. Him gripping me with one arm as he rides with the other. I hear the scooter stop and feel him lift me and carry me up to the villa.

Next there's a fan on my face and Lex and Vivianne and Tom standing over me. Then Ratut is there as his mother scatters rice in the background and Lex presses a cold flannel against my head.

I vomit some more and when I open my eyes it's the dark of night, Lex is beside me. The net is over the bed, and when I look up I spot a bat staring down at me with huge saucepan eyes. It's inside the net and it spreads its wings and I scream.

I open my eyes and – Ross? Ross is standing over me talking on a phone. I try to tell him about the bat and ask why he's here, but I'm too tired and too hot and my eyelids shut.

FORTY-THREE

I'M IN A HUGE ROOM, IT'S CLARA'S LIVING ROOM, BUT MUCH
longer. The panel from the audition sit at one end.

I am at the other end with my harp. Beside me is Mum with
a double bass.

'I don't think it's going so well,' I tell her as the panel members
whisper among themselves and we continue playing.

Mum shrugs and laughs and plays on. Then she stops. 'Your
turn, Zo-blow . . . make it sing, baby.'

She is wearing Clara's opera dress and stands and bows as
the panel applauds her.

'Don't go. I won't know what to play, they're so fussy,' I call
to her.

Mum laughs as she packs her double bass away and flicks her
smooth black hair from her angel face.

'Play the song of us. That's my favourite.'

'Oh,' I say in recognition. 'Yes . . . I just have to remember the notes.'

She hands me a transcription that's in my handwriting but it's as thick as an atlas. She kisses me on the forehead, and then she bows again to the panel members, who provide her with a standing ovation.

'Now it's your turn,' she says as she blows me a kiss and leaves the room.

'Don't go! Mum!'

The relief of black, but in the dark I can't read the score, how am I going to play? How am I going to convince them in the audition? Why did she go? I should try to find her but now there's no doorway from where she left. I will feel my way to her, I think, I will find her again through the notes . . . she's in there somewhere . . .

FORTY-FOUR

WHITE. NO HALL. NO PANEL. NO MUM.

I'm in a hospital bed, which is funny because I'm usually the one beside them, so something is up.

My vision clears. Yes, I'm in a hospital room. I can hear hospital sounds of trolleys and quiet talks, I can smell hospital food. I'm not in Indonesia, I know that. Two men stand over me.

They're in the room. It's Tom and Ross.

'What happened?' I ask. Well, I think I ask.

'Dengue fever.' Tom looks pale. 'You nearly died.'

I endeavour to sit up. 'Serious?'

'No, ning-nong, I'm just kidding. Yes, I'm serious. Ross got you on a plane to Perth. He saved your life.'

'Oh.' I have no recollection of flying back.

'Was I conscious?'

'You had dengue shock syndrome, it's a complication of dengue fever, your body goes into acute shock,' Ross tells me gravely.

It's surreal watching Ross in medical mode with me. 'But how did you . . . You were on your honeymoon.'

Both men shift uncomfortably, and then Tom speaks. 'You said you saw Ross when we were still on the scooter. After you passed out I called him, I knew he was a doctor and I figured he owed you.'

Nothing makes sense.

'Thanks,' I say to Ross. 'What's going on?'

They both start to talk and I don't understand either of them.

'So, we're all in Perth right now?' I am trying to comprehend if I am actually awake or still dreaming . . . or worse.

'Closer than Sydney,' Ross soothes.

'How much time has passed?'

'A couple of days. You were exhausted.' Ross really is a doctor. Weird.

'Lexie's villa wasn't very conducive to sleep. How's your honeymoon?' I ask.

'I might go and get us some tea,' Tom offers. 'And call Dad and Lex.'

I remember Lex and Vivianne standing over me and fret. 'Where are Lex and Vivianne? Have they got it too?'

'Nope, you're the winner of the lucky door prize.'

Panic darts though me. 'What about June? What about my harp?'

'Your harp is with Lexie and they're back in Sydney,' Tom informs me, doing his *chill, Zoe* voice.

'I'll check about June,' Ross says then comes and sits on the bed.

Tom, sensing emotional radioactivity, hightails it down the hall.

Unfortunately, it's hard to read someone the riot act when they have recently saved your life.

'Thank you,' I manage. Ross grabs my hands. He looks stressed but still with a honeymoon tanned glow about him. I want to hug him and slap him all at once but right now I don't have the energy for either.

'I'm so, so sorry,' Ross purges.

'Pretty bad luck for you, me crashing your honeymoon and getting dengue fever. Or karma. I didn't know you and Jeanie were going to Bali, you never said.'

'I know . . . Zoe, I love you.' He looks at me intently.

I head for a wry laugh but all that escapes is a dry whimper.

'I don't want to live without you and you don't seem to be going so well at living without me.'

'Ha,' I manage.

He kisses my lips lightly.

'Ross, what did you tell Jeanie? Did you tell her who I am? Why you had to fly with me?'

'Don't worry about that,' he soothes.

And I get it. Yes, we are sitting in a hospital room in Perth and I am in a bed and on a drip but, really, nothing has changed.

'You should go now,' I tell him.

'I'm going to tell her, everything. I want to be with you. I love you,' he persists.

I think of Gigi and what I said to her.

'Yeah ... The thing is, Ross, if you really loved me, I don't think you would have married Jeanie. You're not a woman in reduced circumstances in the eighteenth century ... you made a choice. It wasn't me. I am grateful you came to my rescue – it's pretty much a version of the fantasy I've been having about you since we met, except, in the fantasy, you have balls and you're single and you don't fuck two women over, repeatedly.'

Tom, who has reappeared and is about to re-enter, hears this and U-turns back out.

'I stuffed up, I want to be with you.' Ross's voice is strained.

'Really, Ross? I think you haven't got a clue what you want and so you're opting for what's more convenient. And that doesn't bode well for any of us.'

'I want you,' he says quietly under his breath. 'I'm just fucked up.'

'Well go and un-fuck yourself then. Or go back on your honeymoon. But whatever you do, don't do it near me.'

He looks slapped, this couldn't have been the gratitude speech he was expecting.

'I love you, Ross, I've never loved anyone like I love you. I'll probably always be in love with you, which is not actually that fun. Still, I love you. But I don't respect you. I'm done, and please don't tell me to wait so you can detangle yourself from whatever web of spin you're currently in. I'm really, truly and utterly done.'

My eyes are closing against my will.

'I need to find June,' I whisper.

Ross kisses my lips again.

I hear voices. I feel Tom's hand around mine. I open my eyes for nurses to check my pupils and top up my medicine and brush my hair. And then I sleep.

•

The light of a sweltering Perth day offers a little curtsey via the window on the far wall when I open my eyes again. The bed next to me is empty. I'm alone in the room. A neat, clean light white hospital room.

Well, I'm still here, I think. And then I recall what I said to Ross. I feel a quiet sadness and a deep well of relief.

A desire for a hot cup of tea strikes, and maybe some toast with honey. I press the buzzer, and while I'm waiting I look around. It's a freshly painted room, I'm guessing it was designed in the sixties. There's the standard two visitors' chairs, one more cushioned chair and one painting on the wall. A ballerina, she's bending over to do up her ballet laces. It's sweet.

My breath stops as the nurse walks in.

'Who's the artist?' I gasp.

The nurse throws me a *You called me in here to ask me that?* look but she politely complies and reads it out.

'C Lang. Is he famous?' she asks in jest.

'Yes, to me he is,' I reply.

FORTY-FIVE

THEN IT'S ACTION STATIONS. I AM SHOWERED AND CHANGED and sent back to bed. I eat breakfast. I check my phone. I feel wobbly but pretty much myself otherwise.

There's a ton of messages from Lexie – video, pics and texts.

Ross has written a long goodbye and adds that June is still with us, her family are actually annoyed they got called in as she's stabilised again.

I call Tom and provide him with a shopping list.

I'm examined by doctors who tell me if everything remains stable and in good working order I should be allowed out in the next day or so.

'You gave us a scare,' is my father's typical understated reply when I call him. Then he adds, 'Don't do that again.' I agree.

I'm eating lunch and annoying nurses with my questions about the painting – which I am sure is of June. They think it was donated, it's been in the room for at least thirty years.

I have no shortage of surprise when Sam enters the room with a bunch of golden tulips. I do a double take, but it's him, sporting a lightweight grey linen suit with a t-shirt beneath. He looks sharp.

'How did you get here?' I exclaim, wiping bland chicken soup off my chin.

'I got your text. It sounded eventful and I'm here checking on the vineyard for a few days, so I reckoned I'd better come and check out the excitement.'

As always his appearance adds oxygen to the room and I yawn in relief.

'I can see this is having a huge impact,' he jokes.

I explain the painting and June and Clem. I imagine I sound slightly touched as I'm describing my attempts to find Clem and my meeting with his sister, Dorothy, getting increasingly emotional as I go. But he seems unperturbed.

'Am I mad?' I ask.

'You just want to help your friend, nothing wrong with that.' How is it his take on life and his presence in mine is always accompanied with a sense of relaxation and acceptance?

'Want to let me be your super sleuth?' he offers.

'Sure, but I've exhausted every avenue. I'm afraid he must be dead, that's why his phone's been disconnected, but at least I can take some pics of this.' I look back to the June painting. How can that be just a coincidence?

'Hold your horses,' Sam says. 'I have some insider trading I can use. I'll be right back.'

He disappears down the hall and returns five minutes later with an old-fashioned hard copy of the *White Pages*.

He sits and begins searching through. 'Lang ... hmm ... C ... Catherine, Claire and Michael, Clemency ... here.'

'Serious? What year is the *White Pages*?'

'Not too old – 2015.'

I hold my breath as he reads out the number.

'Bugger, it's the same one I had.'

'Only one thing for it.'

'What?'

'I'll drive by on my way south. Do a doorknock.'

My eyes widen, my heart leaps and I spill tea over my hand. Who is this man?

'Really? Would you mind?'

'I expect to be invited to their wedding.' He smiles wryly.

'Well of course, mentioned in the speech I reckon.'

We laugh and my mobile vibrates with a call with a UK area code. I know it's Julian.

I inhale and answer.

'You're in,' is the first thing he says.

Speechless, I swallow.

'Zoe?'

'But ... but I thought you all hated it.'

'Hated it? My dear, you were electric. Your time away has endowed you with a depth and a passion we'd be privileged to have.'

Sam watches me as my face explodes into a full-scale euphoric grin and my lip quivers and I begin crying. Sam sighs and hands over his handkerchief silently. Julian begins talking details, which I half absorb. Oblivious to my current residency in hospital he leaves me to celebrate.

'Guessing that was a positive call?' Sam offers gently and in response I squeal so loudly two nurses appear.

FORTY-SIX

I DON'T RECALL SAM LEAVING. I REMEMBER CHATTING AND MY eyes feeling itchy then another night of checks. I am completely fine, just tired.

Soon after breakfast a very dapper man in his nineties, though he looks a decade younger, appears. He wears a suit and tie and a hat. He takes it off to nod at me.

'Hello,' I say, curious.

'Good morning, young lady. How are you feeling?' He watches me closely.

I nod. 'I'm fine. How are you?'

'Beautiful morning,' he says by way of reply. Then he stands before the painting and my heart applauds.

'Clem? Mr Lang?' I say, but his back is to me and he doesn't reply. I call out again. Nothing. I wonder what's happening.

He stands there until Sam walks in with a fresh bunch of hydrangeas.

'These are from Clem's garden,' Sam says as though this were an everyday occurrence.

'Clem ... it really is Clem?' Tears are welling, though I try to hold them back. 'How did you ...'

Sam nods in understanding. 'Very complex. It involved driving to his house and ringing the doorbell. There was no answer, so I walked around the back and found him in his garden.'

'Really, just like that?' I'm gobsmacked. Sam grabs an empty vase, still calm.

'Just like that.'

'But, but what about the phone calls?'

'He's as deaf as a post. Had the phone disconnected because he never heard it ring. Can't stand hearing aids but he's quite a good lip-reader. Says he enjoys the peace of it.'

'Clem!' I cry out loudly as Clem turns to me grinning.

'Lovely to meet you, my name's Clem, Clemency Lang.' He comes over now and shakes my hand.

'I have to tell June!' My mind is flying to find the best way to do this. Sam seems to pick up my thought thread.

'Clem and I have hatched a plan. I thought he might like to accompany me to Sydney.'

'Clem, you're going to see June!'

Clem watches me closely. His eyes are just as June described, filled with kindness and decency with an absolute sparkle. His skin is quite subtle, freshly shaved and he smells like Yardley's English Blazer for men, his hair is slicked back neatly, he is of another age, yet ageless. Strangely he looks like June's twin. 'I knew she was still here . . . somewhere.' He speaks quietly.

'Are you well enough to travel?' I ask.

'I'm not the one in a hospital bed!' he jests. 'I'm as fit as a fiddle and now I know where she is wild horses wouldn't keep me away.'

'I want to be there too!' I exclaim, sounding like a teenager terrified of missing her first sleepover.

'Well, we're not going without you,' Sam announces. 'I fly back tomorrow. You're being discharged today according to your nurse.'

'Weeee!' is my incredibly mature response.

Clem sits by me and takes my hand. He speaks with a Bostonian lilt.

'I believe you have moved heaven and earth to try to find me for June. What a good friend you are. Thank you, Zoe.'

He is a gentleman in the true sense of the word. I just know he'd carry ironed handkerchiefs. We continue chatting. He, like June, never forgot. And he did write; his letters, like hers, were either lost or returned. He relocated to Australia after his only child, a son, died in combat in Vietnam. That nearly killed him, and it was a tragedy his wife was unable to survive. She gassed herself in their garage.

Clem looks to the painting as he speaks. After his retirement, he felt enough time had passed that it wouldn't be disrespectful to his wife to paint his memories of June. And he did for ten years straight.

'It was the only way I could think of to find her. I never spoke of her, not to a living soul. I did mention her to Dorothy, of course, but she's so forgetful now. Painting June helped me feel close to her. Beautiful June.'

'Clem, you do know June is in hospital?' I ask gently.

He studies my lips and then nods. 'A hospice. I understand. I bet she's still beautiful.'

'Yes, she really is.'

'Well then, we'd best get cracking,' he says, rising. 'At my age, and even at yours, Zoe, there isn't a moment to lose. It's later than you think.'

'That's what June says too.' And I think how true it is.

•

Tom collects me after I'm given the all clear and read the riot act about taking it easy. We head straight to the airport; Sam will accompany Clem on another flight. Fortunately, the red-eye is quite open and we score a row to ourselves. I sleep. Tom watches movies, and films me snoring, as big brothers do.

It's more than a small surprise that it's not Lex who picks us up from Sydney when we arrive in the early fog of a steamy Sydney Saturday, it's Dad. I look to Tom who throws me a *It was his idea* look.

Dad seems frailer, even though it's been just three weeks since I last saw him. He's definitely lost weight. My father has never picked us up from the airport, not once, never, ever, ever . . . even when he was working there. It was never his thing.

'What's wrong?' follows my greeting as I hug him hello.

'Just something I wanted to strike off my bucket list.' He laughs.

We bundle into his old Saab and head home. He drives so much slower than he used to, talkback radio is on quietly in the background. When did Dad get old?

Tom unloads the car. I'm happy but feel the heavy stab of reality with the 'sold' sign plastered over the front of the house. Luckily Lex and Vivianne provide ample distraction. I am fussed over and hugged and sent off to shower. I reappear. New linen, thanks to Vivianne, is on my bed.

I hop in and Dad brings me a cup of tea. Well made. Another first. He sits on the end of the bed.

'You scared me,' he says quietly.

'I'm sorry.'

'You've had a rough trot, no thanks to me.'

'It's okay, Dad.' I don't want to upset him and I don't think either of us has the energy for a tumultuous scene.

'You know, none of it was your fault, your mum . . . me.'

I don't know what to say. I sip my tea. I nod and try to smile. But it hurts, finally hearing him say what I've needed to hear since I was five hurts.

'I've told Tina we need to have a few more weeks till settlement. You need to have a rest before you traipse back to England. I know what I did with the house wasn't right. You and Tom are getting one hundred thousand each, I'm sorry it's not more but you know what she's like. I hope it helps you. I'm proud of you, Zo.'

I put the tea down and hug him, aware of how bony he is. In just a few weeks, a few months, it will be him in the bed in the hospice and it will be me sitting at the end of it bringing cups of tea. I don't want to miss out on being there for him.

'You need to have a sleep,' he says, disguising his own emotion with collecting teacups.

'Dad, can you play me something?' I ask.

We both know this is the best way for us to 'talk'. When I was very little, before Mum died, on occasion if one of us was sick, he would come and play a tune on the harmonica or the guitar, a nursery rhyme or just a melody. I realise that Dad is the original bedside musician.

'I think we can manage that,' he replies.

'The others can come in.' I can hear them rustling about outside.

So a little impromptu bedside concert takes place. Dad plays Van Morrison's 'Astral Weeks' on guitar, Tom accompanies him and Lex sings . . . and I fall asleep so happy to be home.

FORTY-SEVEN

I HAVE FIRST-DATE NERVES. REG IS AMPED UP TOO, HE HAS BURIED what hair he has left under a mountain of Brylcreem.

'What if she has a heart attack from the shock of it?' I whisper. We haven't told June about her visitor this morning. She is dozing in her light pink silk gown, looking luminous in her otherworldly way.

'Well, she's in the right place for it,' Reg observes. 'Calm down, doll face, you're making me nervous.'

I've played for June, we've chatted about my trip and the audition. Reg has whistled a few tunes that neither June nor I recognise and he has tried to teach us poker.

'I am tired, my darlings,' June says gently. She must be wondering why the hell we're hanging around. Where is Sam? Where is Clem? They were fine this morning, eating breakfast at Sam's house. They're planning a fishing day . . . depending on how things go with June.

A horrible vision strikes – Clem having a heart attack from all the excitement; Sam is probably with him performing resuscitation. Or Clem got run over because he's too deaf to hear passing cars. I feel clammy.

'You look tired too, Zoe darling. All this excitement, you must rest,' June says.

Reg points to his watch and rolls his eyes. I look to my phone. Nothing, not like Sam.

'So I will see you both later.' June tries again to get us to leave.

'Sure.' I fiddle with my harp. What a disaster.

Footsteps, slow and rhythmic. Reg pops his head out the door and, shining like the sun, provides me with a thumbs up.

'June, there's one more thing.'

June keeps her eyes closed and smiles.

'Your friend Clem. I found him.'

June's beautiful eyes open. Her face lights up, incandescent, her body straightens. 'Oh?'

My heart leaps, Sam waves as Clem, holding a huge bouquet of baby pink roses, enters and tips his hat.

'Good morning, dear June.'

June turns her head to see Clem, looking incredibly dapper again in a suit and shirt and tie. He lifts his hat and stands in front of her.

Sam and I exchange proud parent eyebrow raises.

Clem turns to us. 'Will you just look at her, she's even more beautiful than I remember.'

'Clem? Clemency Lang?' she asks gently, silent tears falling down her cheeks.

Clem walks to the bed and holds her hand. Their eyes lock and the rest of time and space dissolve as they enter the universe of each other. Neither speaks; they just squeeze each other's hands and look in wonderment.

Sam, Reg and I look to each other, chuffed with our efforts.

'Nice one, toots. Now if you could just get my Titianna to come and do that for me . . .' Reg chirps.

Sam gets Clem a seat next to June so they can continue to gaze at each other in comfort. Clem's deafness doesn't seem to worry June, they are mostly just saying each other's names and patting each other's hands.

June looks up for a moment and smiles radiantly.

'Oh, Zoe. You did it, you did it.'

'I had a lot of help.'

June considers Sam, I introduce them.

'Ah yes,' June says. 'Finally I meet Zoe's beau. Exactly as I pictured. Wonderful.' Sam smiles graciously knowing full well she's confusing him with Ross. I squirm slightly but don't want to ruin the romance of the moment by saying, *No, that was the no-good philanderer who saved my life, this lovely man is Sam my friend.*

'Such a pair,' June continues. We both smile. I blush.

'We should leave you and Clem to catch up,' I say.

'I always knew I'd find you again, always,' Clem says gently.

'I was afraid to think what might have happened. I kept writing to you though, even though my letters were sent back. And then I had nowhere to send them, but I still wrote them.' She indicates her top drawer, which Clem opens.

'In the blue jewellery box.' June urges him on.

Clem takes out the box, he looks to June.

'Yes, open it.'

Clem pulls out a neatly stacked group of letters tied together with a faded pink ribbon.

'That's the ribbon from my errant slipper, from the night we met,' June says coyly and they share a secret smile.

'These are all to me?' Clem asks, marvelling at the pile.

'Yes, all for you. Keeping them close made me feel closer to you.'

They stare in wonder at each other and the rest of us become invisible again. It's time to give them their space.

Sam arranges to pick Clem up in a few hours, we organise for a special morning tea and we leave them to it. I watch the two lovers as I leave; my heart feels like it could explode, seeing such joy in the union of two souls is a rare privilege.

There's a feeling you have when things work out, not the blast of huge whopping cymbals but the quiet of a solo clarinet, that inner smile that tells you you're on the right track. It has a resonance that vibrates deep into your being. Hanging out with Sam feels a bit like that, and watching June and Clem feels a lot like it. I think back to what Kip said: those little moments of life are the most cherished.

FORTY-EIGHT

MY DAY TAKES A TURN FROM THE LITTLE MOMENT OF CHERISHED quiet when Tom insists I travel with him to work things out with Abi. Apparently Tom screwed up big time and partied all night with the Bondi crowd forgetting he'd arranged to take Abigail out for dinner.

'Why do I have to be here?' I ask.

'She won't hit me if you're here.'

'I doubt Abi would hit you anyway.'

'She's pretty mad. I really fucked up. It's the second time I've done it.'

Abi greets us outside her room at the vet surgery. She was obviously not expecting us.

'I've got a sensitive situation going on. What do you want?'

Tom shuffles and mumbles. 'Can we come in?'

Abi twists her mouth. 'You may not like what you're about to witness.'

'Is someone being put down?' I ask.

'No, I have an IVF in action.'

Tom looks dumbfounded. 'Yours?'

Abi's mouth twists into an amused smile despite her clear desire to be mad with Tom. 'No, idiot. Sassy the labradoodle. She and Morrissey need a little help breeding.'

How is it nothing is simple in relationships even in the dog world?

'Are you coming in or not?'

We enter.

Morrissey, a black mass of reluctance, cowers before the golden, glamorous Sassy, who growls at him.

'It looks like she's just not that into him.' Tom tries to joke to break the ice.

'Maybe she likes playing hard to get,' I add.

'Well, they've had ample time and it hasn't happened so we are going to help them,' Abi announces with an unnerving efficiency.

Tom and I take a step back.

'Tom, you hold Morrissey. Zoe, just hang back with Sassy.'

We do as we're told. Sassy eyes me warily.

'So what's up?' Abi asks as she snaps on a pair of latex gloves. 'Hold him like that so I can access his privates.'

'Oh dear,' pops out of my mouth.

'Tom?' Abi waits for his reply.

'I'm really sorry about last night.'

Abi pumps two squirts of a clear-looking lubricant and smears it over her gloves. 'That's the second time. I don't have time or interest in that shit. Save it for your twenty-somethings.'

'I don't want to be with a twenty-something.'

Abi sets to work rubbing Morrissey's privates. Morrissey begins to pant happily.

Tom and I exchange a look of horror. Sassy growls.

'What *do* you want?' she asks as she continues the rhythmic rub.

'Oh you're really . . .' Tom fades out as he observes her at work.

'Tom?' Abi prompts.

Tom finally shifts his gaze from Morrissey's procedure to look at Abi.

'I want to be with you,' he says, terrified.

Morrissey's tongue hangs out; he begins to look heavenward in canine ecstasy. I turn away.

'As a flatmate?' Abi increases the pace.

'No, not as a flatmate. I mean, yes as a flatmate but not just as a . . .'

The pace increases again. Morrissey performs a happy howl. Sassy choruses.

'I'm into you, Abi,' Tom stammers.

Abi grabs a sample container. 'Here hold this,' she instructs. 'Now.'

A major howl. And Morrissey is released. He gives himself a shake and wags his tail.

'Is this actually legal?' Tom asks.

Abi rolls her eyes and puts Morrissey's outpourings into a syringe.

'Hold onto Sassy, Zoe.' I can see she is quite enjoying putting Tom through this; and it will make for an interesting anecdote in one of those 'the two of us' columns.

Tom hovers as Abi deftly injects Sassy with the sample. Sassy provides a martyred look of forbearance, has a little growl and shrugs her fur.

'And we're done. Good job, guys.'

She gives Sassy a pat and Sassy, unperturbed, licks her paws.

'If you're into me, that's great. I'm into you. But I'm not to be mucked around,' Abi states.

I think that's pretty evident from what we've just witnessed.

Abi continues as she cleans up, disposing of the syringe and gloves. Washing her hands. Putting the dogs back on their leads and delivering them both a doggie treat.

'You're welcome to be my flatmate and use the shed for your surfboards, but fuck me around again and you're out.'

Tom nods solemnly. I can see he's actually thrilled. Romance really does come in all shapes and forms. I think of what Ross said while we were in the Napa about the onset of romantic love in the eighteenth century. It's something the canines don't need to worry about, but us humans do. Whether it was to keep the peasants under control or some other reason, we evolved to this idea of romantic love and, though it's fraught, I don't see the desire to marry sex with love becoming extinct any time soon. In fact, I don't want it to. I want to have sex with someone I love, and love the person I'm having sex with. It feels good to know that.

Tom's obviously experiencing his own series of personal epiphanies as we head home.

'Thanks for being my wingman.'

'Thanks for flying to Perth with me and looking after me.'

He nods. I watch him, he still looks worried.

'Tom, we didn't kill Mum.'

'Yeah, I know that.' He attempts to dismiss me with his tone.

'Really, it wasn't our fault.'

He looks my way and nods.

'I've always thought it was . . . just a bit. But it was an embolism, our fight didn't loosen it, it just happened.'

He stays silent.

'I think we both need to forgive ourselves, maybe that's the way to stop you bonking women you're not into and stuffing up with women you are?'

'Maybe,' he agrees.

I think about how that also applies to me. How it so totally applies to me. How forgiving myself may stop me choosing men who don't choose me.

'I'll miss you when you move in with Abi.'

'You're the one heading to rainy London.'

'You're really into her, aren't you?'

He shrugs in a way that means totally and then eyes the waves.

My eyes are drawn to the water too, the place I return to time and time again for solace and inspiration. Now I just have to find someplace to stay before my contract with the London Symphony starts. But something's niggling at me.

FORTY-NINE

CLEM AND JUNE SPEND TWO DAYS TOGETHER. MOST OF THE time they simply hold hands and look adoringly at each other. Sometimes I spy them chatting quietly. Clem nods at her, not wanting to miss a moment even though June's soft voice would barely permeate his ears.

'So beautiful,' is the main thing he says, and with him there I can see she feels like a queen.

I'm playing the piece I composed for them as June slips away quietly. Possibly the most peaceful death I've ever witnessed. She's been extra perky all morning, which I thought was from having Clem beside her; they'd laughed about what they'd do on a day out together, the adventures they'd have.

'But in the end, I would just as soon be here like this,' she says to him.

And then she closes her eyes to rest and, so gently, with one sweet sigh, she leaves.

Family is called and Clem takes his leave. I hold his hand as we exit.

'I'm sorry,' I tell him.

'What an honour. We missed too much of each other's moments. I am so happy to have been here for her final one.' He holds the pile of letters in his hand.

'And she is still with me,' he adds.

FIFTY

Sydney, September 29th, 1997

My Dearest Clem,

I'm not sure why I persist writing letters you will never read but somehow they help me to feel close to you. Even after all these years the thought of your voice and your humour soothes me.

I caught sight of myself in the window reflection outside the newsagent's this morning and got quite a fright. Who is this little old lady?

I was slightly appalled but mostly intrigued. I decided to take a closer look in the looking glass when I got home. Usually I just put on moisturiser and lipstick and don't think about it. But today I stopped there, naked I might add, and took in the full view.

Being a widow and having all the children and grand-children off on their own adventures allows for these indulgences. Quite a few of my friends have already died – the number of funerals I attend far outstrips birthday parties and, heaven forbid, weddings.

I stood there, Clem, and I will confess what I felt was proud. I have earned every one of my wrinkles. Scars from childbirths, bumps from chickenpox, grey hairs from worry and loves. I may resemble a linen napkin that was left in the dryer too long, but my body and my face are a map of my life and I cherish it.

Everyone I've loved is on there. You are on there.

I have imagined seeing you at so many crossroads in my life. Once at a bus stop, once at Claire's school fete when she was twelve, once even in New York on vacation sightseeing; at the strangest times and places some semblance of you appears and for a moment I am struck by the nearness of you and what might have been.

I have often wondered what it would have been like to share this life with you, to have travelled with you, to have had children with you. It obviously wasn't our fate, more's the pity. But, Clem, perhaps I wouldn't have become the me I am if I had been with you. And I like who I am. So there can be no regrets.

I hope you feel the same. I pray your life has been filled with good health and love, babies and joy.

I hope next time around, if such a thing as reincar-
nation exists, we get to spend more of our lives in each
other's company.

So many people miss out on feeling love. I have been
blessed in loving many, not least of them is you. You
will be with me always.

Yours,

June

FIFTY-ONE

CLEM STAYS FOR THE FUNERAL AND MEETS THE CHILDREN AND grandchildren as 'just an old friend of June's from ballet days'.

Their story is complete.

Lex and Vivianne come to Sam's house with me after the funeral and make a huge fuss of Clem. He has lived through so much; he is at peace and busies himself with details of the following day's fishing outing with Sam.

Clem requests I play the Clem and June piece again. I don't know how much Clem hears but he's enraptured by it.

'Bravo!' he claps. 'That needs to be in a concert.'

'It's going to be in a film,' Lex announces.

We all laugh. 'Yes, that would be great,' I say.

'I'm not joking,' she answers.

'What? You don't even like my stuff, you're usually on your phone when I play,' I splutter.

'Because I'm recording you, you Wally. Have been for the past year. Every one of your compositions. I gave a sample of your work to a friend of mine who's a music producer. I thought we could get your stuff on a telly show at least, but it's gone way past that now.'

I feel giddy and I'm not sure I'm hearing correctly. 'What are you talking about?'

'You have a skype date with a major Hollywood agent tomorrow. Oliver Stone wants to use a few of your pieces, including Clem and June's, in his new movie.'

'Huh?' is all I can say.

'Tell her what the film is!' Vivianne bubbles. Sam grins at me from ear to ear.

'It's a time-travelling Romeo and Juliet thing. Leo and Kate Winslet are in it.'

'Huh?' Again I look around, trying to stay present while I digest this information. I wriggle my fingers, my toes.

I make Lexie explain it to me twice more before I begin whooping and Sam brings out a bottle of champagne.

The afternoon turns into an evening as Sam whips up a risotto and Tom joins us and we play on.

'Zoe Wylde, a living legend,' Sam says as he hugs me farewell.

'Thanks for being my partner in crime,' I say.

Sam winks at me and hugs me again.

I head home with a whirling mind.

•

I wake up early and skype with the mega agent. I have the film and the offer of writing more pieces for the soundtrack. A whole new world has opened for me by the time the call concludes.

I swim and as lap after lap melds with the sound of Mozart in my mind, I realise I am making plans. Ones I want to make happen. Ones I want to live.

I'm met by the ever-buoyant Gigi as I head out of the waves. She's waving to me, a torrent of excitement.

'Zoe, Zoe Wylde child.' My dripping wet body is no impediment to her squeezing me. Actually, she lifts me into the air and jiggles me about with her exuberance.

'You got the gig!'

'Yes!'

'Well, are you excited?'

I consider that.

'And has Jules called you? He wants to use your Clara piece in the program for next year. Wants you to give it a full orchestration. Is that wild or what?'

'Wild,' I repeat, as pieces click into place silently.

She places my hands on her perfectly tanned still perfectly flat belly.

'We're going so well,' she whispers. 'Tea Tim is beside himself. We've connected at an even deeper level, and the sex . . .'

I listen to Gigi's latest tantric sexual revelation, noting the positions she tries; who knows, perhaps I'll get to give them a whirl one day. She goes on to describe the prenatal percussion album she's about to record . . . and her thoughts on Julian.

'You know, he really is an old, old man.'

'Uh huh.'

I take my leave and head home, grab an untouched notebook and head to the Gap.

The full morning sun hits, it's a day that makes you whistle even if you don't know how.

I am full of the intention of writing down my 'goals' but of course I get waylaid by a little tune I hear in my head. I don't notice Sam and Harry till a warm head holding a ball arrives in my lap, pushing my notepad to the side.

I'm handed a hot cup of tea by Sam, who holds one for himself.

'I'm writing a to-do list,' I announce.

'Like Clara,' Sam muses.

It is of course Clara who has inspired so much.

'How was fishing?'

'Excellent, we're going again today. Want to come? Just at Camp Cove?'

'Yes, it's on my list,' I reply. He smiles but keeps looking ahead.

I decide to confide my list to Sam. I trust him.

'I'm not going to London.' It feels like a relief saying this, it's been on the edges of my awareness since I got home.

'No?' Sam doesn't sound surprised nor displeased.

'I'm going to stay here with Dad and the hospice and compose. That's what I want to do. And I'm going to play here. I'm meeting up with the Artistic Director of the Sydney Symph.'

Sam absorbs all of this with a slow low whistle. 'Zoe Wylde living life her way.'

'Wait, there's more.'

'More?'

'With the film and the sale of some of my compositions, and what Dad's given me, I will have enough money for a deposit. I'm going to buy my own place, with a fridge. My own fridge. Do you think it's worth asking Phil about Clara's?'

'Always worth asking, no one's living there, they haven't put it on the market yet.'

'Then we'd be neighbours.'

We continue looking out at the water.

'Harry would like that.'

I pat Harry, feeling thrilled, taking it all in.

'So, is this a plan or a mission?' Sam asks after a long pause.

I consider. 'Just a life really.'

'Pretty good one.'

'I like it . . . and, Sam?'

'Hmm.'

'I'd like to go to the opera with you.'

He grins now and takes another sip of tea. He says nothing but places his hand over mine, sending me into a stratosphere of tingles and hope.

A little moment. A moment I will cherish in my own symphony as the sonorous song of us, of all that has been, of everyone we've loved, of all that is and all that will be, rises.

ACKNOWLEDGEMENTS

FIRST AND FOREMOST, THANK YOU TO MY SUPERB PUBLISHER
Vanessa Radnidge for your faith, grace and steadfastness.

Thank you to Jaki Arthur for continuing to champion me
with such verve and heart.

Thank you to my wonderful editors Karen Ward and Deonie
Fiford for your excellent insights and making me work harder
to serve the story.

Thank you to my brilliant team at Hachette, for your support,
enthusiasm and being so fantastic at what you do.

Thank you to my super agent Dayne Kelly and the team
at RGM.

Writing and editing this novel I have been spurred on by
the love, support, inspiration and generosity of the following:
Antonia Murphy (because really you are an angel), Sarah Smith
Supernova, Maestro Heath Felton, Kim Lewis, Jacqueline Hughes
(Mum), Emma Jobson, Grania Holtsbaum, Ellenor Cox, Joanna

Briant, Mel Rogan, Edwina Hayes, Marie Burrows, Jonathan Wood, Jaison, Molly, Coco & Bodhi Morgan, Tim Pietranski, Chris Mitchell, Andrew Knight, Dr Janice Herbert and Rod Adams, Neal Kingston, Dr Robert Hampshire, Caroline Teague, Jen Vinton, Ian, Carmel, Jack and Jacinta Barrett, Christopher Barrett (Dad), Trudy Johnston, Eileen Hall, Mark & Stacy Rivett, Kym Wilson & Shaun O'Byrne, Ascham Speech and Drama staff and students, the fabulous writing team on Love Child 4 and of course Beau. Thank you.